The C

LONDON BOROUGH OF BARNET

30131 04398851 5

Helena Close lives in County Clare, Ireland with her husband and four children. She has been writing full-time since 2000, and has co-published four novels with her best friend Trisha Rainsford, under the name Sarah O'Brien. Her own first novel, the critically acclaimed *Pinhead Duffy*, was published in 2005. Helena is an avid sports fan and a huge Munster and Liverpool supporter. When she's not writing she likes to run, swim, work out in the gym and drink good coffee.

The Cut of Love is her second novel.

HELENA CLOSE

The Cut of Love

HACHETTE
BOOKS
IRELAND

First published in 2009 by Hachette Books Ireland
First published in paperback in 2010 by Hachette Books Ireland
A division of Hachette UK Ltd.

1

Copyright © 2009 Helena Close

The right of Helena Close to be identified as the Author of the Work
has been asserted by her in accordance with the Copyright, Designs
and Patents Act 1988.

All rights reserved. No part of this publication may be reproduced,
stored in a retrieval system, or transmitted, in any form or by any
means without the prior written permission of the publisher, nor be
otherwise circulated in any form of binding or cover other than that in
which it is published and without a similar condition being imposed
on the subsequent purchaser.

All characters in this publication are fictitious and any resemblance to
real persons, living or dead, is purely coincidental.

A CIP catalogue record for this title is available from the
British Library.

ISBN 978 0340 92018 3

Typeset in Sabon by Hachette Books Ireland
Printed and bound in Great Britain by CPI Mackays, Chatham ME5 8TD

Hachette Books Ireland policy is to use papers that are natural,
renewable and recyclable products and made from wood grown in
sustainable forests. The logging and manufacturing processes are
expected to conform to the environmental regulations of the country
of origin.

Hachette Books Ireland
8 Castlecourt Centre, Castleknock
Dublin 15, Ireland
A division of Hachette UK Ltd.
338 Euston Road, London NW1 3BH
www.hachette.ie

For Mike and the crew
Tara, Emmet, Niamh, Sadhbh and, of course,
Carra and Eoin.

One

Jane

Slut, slag, bitch, cunt, shitbag.

That's the word I hate the most: shitbag. And Daddy always says it after all the others. And then Mammy screams back at him. *Madman, weakling, piece of shit. Selfish, self-centred, waste of space.*

But at least in here I can't hear the words. I can hear their voices still, shouting at each other, but not the words, and I squeeze my eyes shut tight and wish I could do the same with my ears. Squeeze them closed when I don't want to hear stuff. Now the voices are louder, in the hallway and the words come. I look in the bathroom mirror. I'm not crying and I'm glad about that. And then I look at the blade, shiny new silver in my damp hand. I pull up the sleeve of my shirt, it's my favourite, red-check American Eagle, and I slice into my arm slowly, watching the first drops of blood on white skin.

Their voices are really loud now and I slice again, right under the first cut and then the pain comes, fast and silver like the blade and it makes me weak and happy and my ears pound

7

with it. Pound so hard that now I can't hear anything. Nothing except me breathing. I watch the blood as it slides down my arm. It looks pretty and this makes me smile. Makes me giddy. And I know now they'll let me stay at Leah's. If you ever want anything, wait until the fight is over to ask. But you need to wait a while, until they've calmed down and stuff. I smile at myself in the mirror.

The front door bangs. Daddy's gone. I wipe my arm with toilet paper and hold it tight against me until the blood stops. I sit on the loo and hold my arm up like a junkie I saw once in a movie after injecting himself. I roll down my shirtsleeve, but I can still feel my arm throbbing where I cut it. Throbbing like a lovely little secret, covered up now. My secret.

I close my eyes as another lovely wave of pain comes and I'm glad now that I didn't tell Leah in school yesterday about the cuts on my arm. We're in the loo after PE and I forget, stupid me, and take off my sweatshirt and she's like, ohmygod, Jane what are those criss-crossy marks on your arm? and I'm, oh those – my nana's mad cat did that, and Leah narrows her eyes and I nearly tell her and then Shona Henderson comes in . . .

I hear footsteps on the stairs. The knob on the bathroom door turns and then there's a soft knock.

'Jane? Janie, are you in there?'

There's a spider above the door. A big black guy with a fat hairy body. His web looks broken. Some of it is hanging down.

'Jane, open the door, honey.'

She's crying. I can hear her sniffling.

'Look, I'm sorry you had to . . . I didn't mean to argue, it just . . .'

I watch the spider and try to remember what I was thinking

about before she came. The pain comes again and I hold my arm tighter against my chest. Leah and secrets. That's it.

Leah wouldn't drop the arm thing so when we're walking home from school out of the blue she says best friends shouldn't have secrets. They should tell each other everything. No holds barred. This is what she says to me and I don't answer but in my head I'm thinking everybody has secrets. She definitely has because she never talks about Jack, never mentions his name at all. It's like he never existed. So I ask her straight out does she miss him and can she still remember his face – I mean it's months ago now. She looks at me as if I slapped her and she gets like really quiet and stuff . . .

'Please open the door, Jane. Let's talk.'

Mammy is still crying. I can hear her soft sobs, exactly like Ben's. She cries like a little boy. I wish I could shut my ears again and I won't listen to her talking to me. Telling me how sorry she is, how it's Daddy's fault, how upset she is. I won't listen to any of it so I tune out her words so it all sounds like a drone, like a really boring teacher. I think instead about Leah and how she saw a shrink, all of them did, the whole family. She didn't tell me about that either, and goes all silent every time I hint at it. I mean I'd love to see a shrink and lie on a couch and tell him secrets all day. I'd make up some really good ones so he'd think I was the maddest person in the world. That'd be so cool.

'Are you hungry? I'll order in pizza, how's that? Ben says he'd love some. How about you?'

The spider above the door is dead. Or else he's hibernating, but I don't think spiders hibernate. The toilet paper around my arm is pink with blood. It's throbbing now but I don't feel pain, just kind of numb.

'I'm just going to sit here until you answer me.'

I don't tell Leah my secrets either. Sometimes I really want to, they gnaw inside me and swell up until I feel like my head is going to burst and I want to tell her so badly but I swallow them back down and tell her little things instead. Like Daddy's house and how I so hate going there. I hate it, hate it, hate it and still I have to go. It's not fair because I'm nearly a teenager and I've got rights and stuff and it's so not fair to make me go, but Mammy won't listen about hating his house. She'll listen to the other things I say about Daddy but not about going to his house. That's like a rule that can't be broken. I tell Leah how my stupid brother Ben doesn't complain about going either. I mean if he complained as well then we might have some chance but I think he's only saying he likes it to stay well in with the two of them. I tell Leah that but not other stuff, not the black stuff in my head that you can't find the words to tell, even if you wanted to.

Mammy gives up and goes downstairs and my arm is grand now, the toilet paper's still white, with just a tiny piece of pink in it, and I wink as I'm passing the mirror and I'm glad they had a fight because this weekend is Daddy's and I'm like all psyched up for a shit time and now if I play it right I won't have to go.

I start to pack my bag before I even ask. I just know I'll be allowed now and I can't wait. I haven't slept in Leah's since the thing with Jack, and her dad says we can get pizza and he's going to take us swimming on Sunday and it'll be so cool. As I hunt for my new pink top I decide to ring Daddy myself. I won't ask her to do it because he'll scream at her again and rant and rave about his rights. And how he only sees us every fourteen days and how the time is so 'precious' to him and that it's his absolute right to see his children. Sometimes I want to say to him, Daddy, what about my rights, do I have any? Every second weekend my life has to stop so that our dad can see us. I have to stay in his small cold flat and share a room with Ben. I mean how gross is that?

I sit on my bed facing the brand-new poster of Zac Efron looking straight at me and I then I see it, as clear as day. They shouldn't have split up. They should have stayed together and they could still have their fights and not these really huge ones that build up and up until they burst out and make you think anything can happen. The everyday fighting is something you get used to and you can nearly tell when it is going to be bad and stuff. Daddy'd come from work and Mammy would be in the kitchen and they'd start in low tight voices and bang things and stuff and you just knew it was going to start and get bad and then be over. I mean it's easy. Go up to your room and play CDs really loud and then it's over. Except ages ago, when we were still all living together, they did it in front of Leah. In front of my best friend. I was so mortified over that.

We're like sitting at the kitchen table doing our homework when Daddy comes in. Mammy has lovely new boots on. I remember that because Leah says how cool they are. I don't look up when he comes in, I just say hi and keep writing Irish verbs.

Mammy's making pasta at the cooker and Daddy stands beside her and asks her what time she came home the night before, in a voice just louder than a whisper. I pick up a silver gel pen and ask Leah does she want a loan of it but she's looking at Mammy's back. Daddy's voice gets louder and he shouts slut, slag, slut, and bangs the kitchen table with his fist and my Irish verbs shake and the writing blurs because tears drip down before I can stop them.

And then he says shitbag and the tears really come and Leah's staring at me and Mammy puts her arm around me and

I try to push her away and she says it's fine Janie, Daddy's just tired that's all, why don't you and Leah play in your room and finish your homework later? Leah pretends nothing has happened and this makes me feel worse and I'm like raging because I have to stuff all the fighting into a tiny part of my head and now I have to put part of Leah there too and I shouldn't because she's separate and my best friend. And there isn't enough room.

The fighting back then was like my nana's radio. It was always there, sometimes loud, sometimes soft, sometimes barely there at all. But always there and just like the radio, I got used to it and I didn't mind much. Except for the time of the rope, but that mightn't really have happened because I was crying and my leg was bleeding. Ben says it didn't happen and I made it all up and when I try to tell him what I think I saw he scrunches his eyes shut and blocks his ears with his hands and says shutupshutupshutup. But the picture of that day is always fuzzy in my head, like part of a movie you're trying to remember and you can see blurry outlines but not faces or voices or stuff. Sometimes I think it happened and other times I think I dreamt it or saw it on telly or something. Like a secret that you forgot. Maybe I'm wrong about them living together after all. How could I have forgotten the rope thing?

Ben walks into my room, doesn't even knock on the door.

'Get out,' I shout, glaring at him.

'Are we going to Daddy's?' he asks.

'How should I know? And by the way, knock before you come into my room,' I say, throwing a pink, heart-shaped cushion at him.

The minute he's gone I feel bad. Poor Ben. I'll make him popcorn later. I jump off my bed and start to tidy my room, folding all the clothes and laying them in the wardrobe and I'm thinking all the time, weighing in my head which is better – Daddy here or Daddy gone?

Daddy here, definitely. I mean at least fighting is a kind of talking. Now they don't talk at all. He collects us on a Friday by beeping the horn outside our house and he drops us back home the same way. They never even say hello how are you, which is hard to believe because they must have been in love once. I can't imagine being in love and then not talking at all and I swear when I get married I'll never be like that. Sometimes Daddy sends Mammy texts and I know they're from him because of her face. Her mouth goes into a dead straight line and she punches out an answer on the phone really hard.

The texting is like silent fighting and sometimes I want to say that to Mammy. I mean it's so not mature to be doing that stuff and I can't understand why they don't just sit down and talk it out. We learnt all about that in Religion – how you can solve things by talking and listening.

So I wait a couple of hours and then I send him a text and just ask straight out. I've nothing to lose and he can't be mad with me in a text. And I can't see his mouth going into a hard line, and his eyes full of hurt, like Ben's. But straight away he answers and says yes! It works every time. I text Leah then to tell her and she rings me back and says ohmygod, we're going to have the best time, and she has *High School Musical* taped and it's been like months since we had a sleepover.

Ben has a big sulky head on him the next morning.

'Why aren't you going to Daddy's?' he says, his eyes big and round and always so sad-looking. When he looks at me like that I want to thump him, I want to shake him and thump him and tell him it's not my fault. None of it.

'Cos you're a douche,' I say, smiling.

'Jane! Don't speak to Ben like that,' says Mammy, but she's talking and giggling on the phone and doesn't really mean it.

Ben drops his head so low I think he's going to end up in his bowl of Cheerios. He gives me the puppy look again and I smile my best smile. Then there's a honk outside and we both know what it means.

'Bye Ben, have fun,' I call out as he leaves the kitchen. He turns back and glares at me.

Mammy drives me to Leah's and I'm so excited I can't stop talking. I tell her all about Leah's dad and how he's a mad laugh and how Leah is the best friend I've ever had.

Mammy laughs as we pull up outside Leah's house. 'You like it so much there I'm afraid you'll want to stay for ever,' she says, looking at me.

'Don't be silly, Mammy. That's just stupid.'

She smiles at me, a glad smile, as if she's asked me a question, and I've given the right answer. I touch my arm, feel the raw, sore lines under my T-shirt and smile back, but I'm thinking how not stupid it is at all, how I wouldn't have to share a room with my horrible whingy little brother and I won't have to listen to Daddy or answer his questions about Mammy. Or answer her questions about him.

Leah comes flying down the path and I jump out of the car and we kiss and hug and scream as if we haven't seen each other for years and our mams talk and smile at us.

But I see Mam looking at Mrs Collins, at her long thin body in black loose trousers and cream jumper. I bet Mrs Collins was really pretty when she was young. She has brown hair like Leah's and dark brown eyes, the exact same colour as Ashton Kutcher's, and she's so skinny. I know Mam is shocked when she sees her. I see Mam examining her with questions in her eyes but she doesn't say anything to her. Just touches her on the arm and calls goodbye to us and drives away.

In the kitchen we make hot chocolate and talk about Darren Tierney – a boy at school that Leah likes. Then Mrs Collins comes in and of course I change the subject. She stands at the worktop smiling at us but saying nothing. I smile back but I wish she'd go away. She always makes me feel like I've done something wrong. Even before Jack died she made me feel like that. But it's worse now. She doesn't like me and I know it and she knows I know.

'Jane, how are you?' she says eventually.

I smile at her. My nana says I have a great smile. That the whole room lights up when I smile. 'I'm fine, thank you, Mrs Collins.'

She keeps looking at me and makes me feel like I'm lying. I sprinkle chocolate flakes into my drink and my hand shakes for no reason.

'Hurry, Janie, *Lizzie McGuire* is starting in like two minutes,' Leah says and we head towards the living room with our hot drinks.

I love Leah's house. It's like one of those houses for sale in the *Irish Times*, all cream and beige and stainless steel. I always read the property part of the paper and look at the pictures of mansions in Dublin. I imagine living there and going to Grafton Street every Saturday with my friends. Leah's house could be in the paper. It's always tidy, everything, I mean absolutely everything, has a place. In my Mam's house we dump stuff everywhere, Ben and me. She tries to make us clean up and sometimes we do but only if she makes us. And Dad's – his flat is just the pits. Gross. I'd never bring Leah there. But there's something different about Leah's tonight. There are newspapers thrown on the couch – I have to move some to find a place to sit down – and the wooden floor is sticky like somebody spilt juice on it.

We meet Daddy the next day in the swimming pool. We're having a ball – Leah's dad is so funny and he throws us across the pool and then swims under our legs and puts us on his shoulders and tosses us away. Mrs Collins sits in the viewing gallery with a newspaper on her lap. But she doesn't read it, she just watches our every move and I watch her back and she sees me looking.

And then Dad arrives with Ben and ruins it all. I feel colour flood my face and I sink underwater to try to cool down and the two dads talk, knee deep in water, arms folded across their chests. I keep ducking my head under the surface but I can hear my dad talking louder and louder. I can see the glint of his earring and that annoys me more than his voice. I mean for God's sake, he's old – only gay men do things like that. Wear earrings and listen to the Scissor Sisters and talk about themselves all the time. Mam's friend Anna says that about him.

Leah is racing Ben and her little brother Pete and I follow them and pretend I don't hear Dad calling me. I bet he wants to bring me home with them. He wants me to sit in his dirty flat and watch the portable telly flicker and crackle. Then he'll say let's turn off the TV and play a board game. And he'll smile, his teeth and earring glinting, and he'll make me feel bad because I don't want to play stupid board games. I don't want to be there at all.

But Mr Collins insists on bringing me back to their house for dinner, he tells Dad that dinner is ready and Jane's overnight bag is still at home and that the arrangement with Mam is that he'd drop me home. Ben has his head down as they talk and he glances up at me, straight into my eyes, and I get that urge to thump him again, it's like he's blaming me for something and I don't know what it is, and then when he looks down at the ground I want to put my arms around him and hug and tell him I'll see him later. But I don't say anything, just watch him and Daddy leave – they're going to McDonalds for their dinner. It's raining and I watch them climb into the car and I think for the first time that Ben has no friends. I mean he never goes to anybody's house to play, he quit rugby and wants to quit karate, and karate's just the coolest thing. Everybody loves karate and Leah and I are going for our Brown Belts in a few weeks.

The Travellers have set up camp up the road from Leah's house and after dinner we walk past them, just for a nose. There's a boy of about fourteen and he's kind of good-looking – for a Traveller I mean. No freckles or dirty-coloured hair. This boy is dark and he holds a tiny kitten in his arms outside a small caravan. Leah giggles as we pass and I smile at him. A dazzler of a smile.

'Can I rub your kitten?' I ask. Leah laughs.

He looks at us suspiciously and then gives a tiny nod and returns my smile. I look at him, into his eyes, and then I know. He's not normal, not the full shilling, as Nana says. His eyes are flat, they have no questions in them.

I stroke the little kitten's small warm head. I can see into the caravan. It looks brand new, there's plastic still on the seats. And loads of children and the smell of something cooking, stew I think. There are about six caravans and a horse and a kind of trap thing that you fix to the horse. Some of Leah's neighbours are out at their gates, huddled in knots watching the Travellers. We walk on and I think they've picked the best spot to camp. There's a wood beside them that leads right down to the riverbank and they're facing the big green with all the lovely shrubs that a landscape gardener from Dublin planted. I tell this to Leah.

She shakes her head. 'All of the neighbours are going mad – they don't want them here.'

'Why?' I ask. We're going into the wood and I can smell the pine trees and feel the soft carpet of needles under my feet. I like the woods. It's dark but cosy – like a comfy room with the lights turned off.

She looks at me, her brown eyes smiling. Her hair is tied up in a ponytail and swings as she walks. It looks lovely.

'Come on, Janie. Would you like them beside you? They're dirty for one thing and they're robbers and you'll never sell your house if you have them on your doorstep.'

I think about this and the property pages of the *Irish Times* and I laugh out loud. The caravans would never be in the pictures.

'Why? Are you selling your house?' I ask. We stop near a big oak tree. We always stop here and sit on the lowest branch and try to make it move.

Leah climbs up beside me. The branch creaks. 'No, of course not. Which one of us has put on weight? It didn't ever creak before.'

'Yeah, that was last year, when we were like way younger. So what does it matter then?' I pick at my nails and remind myself to ask Mam to paint them.

'I don't want to be a fat lump.' We both laugh.

'You know what I mean. If you're not selling your house then it doesn't matter about them. It doesn't matter one bit.'

She shrugs. 'Hey, did I tell you? Dad might be taking us skiing at Christmas.' Her eyes are round with excitement. A knot of jealousy burns in my throat.

'Cool. You and Pete?'

She nods eagerly. 'I don't know if Mam will go. She's . . . she doesn't want to leave the country at Christmas, the crowds . . . I don't know. Anyway I can't wait to buy cool skiing gear. You'll have to help me.'

I nod and pick a perfect oak leaf from the branch and inspect it closely.

'Hey, Janie, I have like the best idea – why don't you come with us?'

I laugh. 'I'd never be allowed. Dad has us for a full week and he'd never allow it.'

'He might, you never know until you try. I'll say it to my lot and you do the same. Come on, Janie, think of all the cute little French boys just waiting to meet us.'

I grin. 'Cuter than Darren Tierney?'

She narrows her eyes and smiles back at me. 'Maybe.' She shakes her head. 'Never.' We laugh and the branch creaks and we laugh more and I push her and we tumble on to the soft, piney earth.

'He's joining karate. Him and a couple of the other boys.'

'No way – how did you hear that?' I sit up and dust needles from my jeans.

She tips her nose and smiles slyly. 'I have my ways.'

The boy calls us on our way back.

'I'm sellin' dem,' he says and points to a wooden crate at his feet. A small girl in a halter top and shorts sits cross-legged next to the crate. She strokes a tangle of kittens, all soft fur and pink noses and cute miaows.

'Selling them? How much?' I say. Leah giggles again and it's annoying.

The small girl smiles up at me. Her hair is a mass of tiny brown springy curls and she's really pretty. She wears tiny gold studs in her ears. 'I'm Charlotte and it's my birthday,' she says and smiles a smile that Nana would love. I smile back.

'Five euro. Five euro.' The boy bends down and picks up a gorgeous one the colour of yellow sand. Suddenly I want him more than anything in the world. More than ski trips or ski clothes or HMV vouchers or a new picture phone.

'I'll buy him – can you keep him for a week and I'll come back next Sunday? Please?' I smile at him.

'How many days is Sunday?' he holds up both hands to me and I take a step backwards. He hasn't a clue what I'm saying. The little girl stands in front of him and, holding his hand, she counts out seven fingers.

He nods. 'Five euro.' He holds out the kitten and I take him and he licks my face with a tiny pink tongue. Leah pulls at my arm. My sore arm and I almost groan out loud.

'They won't let you. Remember you asked last year?' she whispers but I shake my head.

'They'll let me. I want the sandy one and that's what I'll call him – Sandy.'

Mrs Collins drives me home to Mam's. It's raining now and the wipers swish the windscreen clean. A tiny bobble-head dog nods at me from the dashboard.

I hope she doesn't talk to me but I know in my heart she will.

'How's school?' she asks after a while.

'Fine, Mrs Collins,' I say, staring straight ahead. I try to guess the next question. Something about karate or Leah. Always the same.

'It's great that you and Leah are such good friends.'

I smile at her as she drives.

'Does she ever talk to you?'

This is a new question. A question I don't like.

I smile again. 'All the time. We talk about everything.'

She pulls up at traffic lights behind a bright yellow mini. She looks at me, her brows knitted together like she's puzzled or something. I smile at her again and look away.

'Does she ever talk about . . . about Jack . . . about what happened?'

Her eyes are boring into me and I want to cry. 'No,' I say in a quiet voice, 'she doesn't.'

Mrs Collins keeps looking at me as if I'd just told a huge whopper of a lie. I pinch the inside of my arm, the sore part, through my Nike top. I think about the pain and it stops the tears.

'It must be hard for you, Jane.' The traffic lights go green and we move and I say nothing. 'When people break up it's always hard.'

I nod my head at the bobble dog. I imagine my mam and dad actually breaking up – you know – like somebody smashes them against a wall and they shatter and fall to the ground. Like eggshells. Smashed-up broken eggshells. This makes me smile – breaking up is such a dumb thing to say.

'If you ever want to talk to me about anything . . . anything at all . . .'

I bite my lip and look out the window.

'Can I ask you something?' she says then, completely out of the blue.

'Sure.'

'It's just . . . well . . . last night, do you remember anything about last night?'

'Yeah. We had pizza and we watched *The X Factor* and then . . .'

'No, Jane. After that. After you went to bed? Did you wake up at all during the night?'

'No,' I say. I have no idea what she is talking about but I feel I've done something wrong anyway.

'It's just that . . . it's nothing really. Anyway, you're always welcome at our house, you know that don't you?'

I nod again and am delighted when I see our road ahead. Dad's car is parked in the drive. Mam's car is gone.

We pull up outside and I thank Mrs Collins and I jump out of the car and hope she doesn't get out too. But she's over straight away. Dad rolls down the window to talk to her and I climb into the front seat.

'Hi, sorry I'm a bit late. The traffic is chaotic even though it's Sunday.'

Daddy smiles up at her. 'Not to worry. There's no sign of their mother yet,' he says and laughs. My stomach is in a knot because I don't know what he'll say next. I hear Ben in the back seat playing his Game Boy.

'She's always like this, you know. And if I'm late I'm the worst in the world.' He laughs again, a high laugh like a girl's.

Mrs Collins smiles at me. 'She'll be along soon. I bet she's caught in traffic too. Take care Jane, see you Ben,' she calls and goes back to her car.

Daddy turns up the CD he's playing and doesn't speak to me. Doesn't even look at me. He drums his fingers against the steering wheel in time to the music. After a few minutes he checks his watch.

'Bitch,' he says, his fingers drumming hard. I look out the window at our house, at the rain dripping down the glass on the porch. At the plant in the big blue pot that Nana gave us in the summer. I look up at my room. The window is slightly open and the blind moves in the wind. I wonder if it's wet.

'Fucking bitch – that's all she is,' Daddy says.

I hold my breath for a second, then let it out slowly.

'A shitbag.' He checks in the rear-view mirror. Then I feel his eyes on me so I look at him.

'Jane – I have you every second weekend. That's all. Two days out of fourteen. I'd appreciate it if you didn't go off on sleepovers. It really isn't fair.' His voice is cold and strange.

'You said it was all right and Leah asked me and . . .'

'I wasn't in the mood for your sulking this weekend. In future I don't care if the Queen of Sheba asks you, have the sleepovers on your mother's time.'

Just then I hear Mammy's car pulling up beside us. The knot in my stomach relaxes. Ben turns off his Game Boy.

'I told you she doesn't care about you. She couldn't give a damn,' he says, loud enough for Mam to hear.

She glares at him. 'Come on, kids, we'll miss the start of *ER*,' she says and walks to the front door. Her boots make a crunching noise on the drive and her handbag swings on her shoulder. Daddy beeps goodbye, doesn't even say it. Just beeps it instead.

Mam's friend Anna calls later, just as *ER* is over. Mam's been crying because someone died in the episode – she always does that and Ben and I laugh – so does Anna now when she sees her wiping away tears with the back of her hand. They open wine and smoke out the patio doors and talk and talk. They remind me of Leah and myself, talking about clothes and shoes and make-up. And boys. It's weird listening to Mammy talking about boys but she does it with Anna and they giggle and whisper and say ohmygod-ohmygod. Just like us. I kiss Mam goodnight and go upstairs to bed. Then I remember that I didn't put my swimming gear into my schoolbag and I know I'll forget it in the morning. I go back downstairs. I can hear their voices and I know that they're not talking about shoes or boys. They're talking about Daddy.

I listen outside the door and a tiny part of my brain is telling me I shouldn't.

'I think he has a girl,' Mam says.

'No way. He must be paying her,' says Anna and they both laugh.

'What makes you think he has?' says Anna.

'Well, remember the huge fight we had a few months ago when he decided he wasn't taking the lads every weekend? That he wanted some weekends to himself?'

'Yeah,' says Anna.

'Well, it's that and there's other little things too. He wants to swap weekends on the twenty-fourth, and he has – I don't know – a kind of smirk on his face – I know him well – it's a kind of "I've one up on you" smirk . . .'

'Do you care?'

Mam laughs. 'You must be joking. I care about the way he messes the kids around though – you know – fits them in with his plans – drops them when it suits him – like the whole world revolves around him.'

'How fucking selfish can you get?' says Anna.

'Tell me something I don't know. I can't even look at him now, Anna, never mind talk to him. He makes me physically sick, just the sight of him alone.'

'You're well rid of him.'

Mam laughs again. 'The thing is I'll never be rid of him. He's their father so I'll never be rid of him. Will I open another bottle?'

'Absolutely. Fuck him – mad bastard,' says Anna.

'Fuck him is right – do you know something, though? It's only since he left that I realise how bad things were – how tense I was all the time and how difficult he was to live with. Jesus – he does my head in.'

'He's a bit of a psycho all right – I was scared to call to the house sometimes.'

Mam laughs. 'It didn't stop you though – he knew if I was going out on the town with you I might actually enjoy myself.'

I shut my eyes tight and try to block out their voices. Then I pinch my arm hard – the inside white part that's really sore now – I pinch until the pain fills my ears and I can't hear words anymore. I pinch so hard that blood comes again. I go back to bed and shut my eyes tight. I want to go downstairs and tell them they're wrong. Tell them that he's just Daddy, not mad and psycho and all the stuff they're saying about him because Mam doesn't love him anymore. And most of all I want to tell them that they're right, Daddy has a girl and it's me. My arm throbs and I rub it where it's cut. I rub it hard.

The next day Leah flies over to me as soon as the bell rings for first break. Everybody in our class swarms out to the yard, the whole place a live, talking sea of navy-blue uniforms.

'Guess what?' she says, 'I asked Mam and Dad about the ski trip, about you coming with us.'

'Did you?' I say as I bite into an apple. It has just rained and water swirls on the tarmac. Some of it has rainbow colours in it.

She looks at me. 'Dad is going to say something to your mother.'

I take another bite of my apple and stick my toe in the rivulets of water.

'So? What do you think?' she says. She opens a bottle of juice and takes a long drink and smiles at me with Ashton Kutcher eyes.

I shrug. I don't know what to think. I don't know who or how to ask for things anymore. Not when I have to do it twice. And not when I have to decide who to ask first.

'You do want to go?' she says.

'Of course.'

'Because if you don't want to then that's fine.' Leah turns her head away and takes another drink.

I know it's not fine. I know Leah and her moods and I know it's not fine at all. The bell goes then.

My aunt Sarah takes me shopping after school on Thursday. Just her and me, girls only, and we go to the Crescent. I like Sarah, she's fun and sometimes she acts really childish even though she's like an accountant or something and I have to tell her to grow up and cop on. She buys me a cool pair of jeans in Penneys and a lovely pair of Ugg boots.

We're just coming out of Topshop and I really need to go to the loo. She says she'll meet me in Awear and I run through the crowded shopping centre. I see Mrs Collins just as I come out of the loo. I'm about to stop and say hello but there's something about her that's . . . wrong. Something really weird. It's like she's following somebody, stopping and starting and ducking behind a pillar. So without thinking about it I follow her.

She's wearing a wine fitted jacket and black pants and I struggle to keep up with her, with all the darting and stopping, but then I get the hang of it. It's fun and I'm bursting with curiosity. What is she doing? She slips into a shop doorway, and scans the crowd in front of her. My eyes follow hers and rest on a tall man holding a little girl's hand. I know instantly that he's the one she's following. He walks away and Mrs Collins follows and so do I.

I feel like those private detectives on telly or one of the Spy Kids, looking for clues and unravelling mysteries.

The man stops outside a toy shop and the little girl pleads with him to go in. She pulls his arm and he laughs down at her.

He has a nice face. Mrs Collins is in front of me, I see the side of her face, her dark hair, poker-straight. She so looks like Leah I can't believe it. Again I wonder what she's doing following a man around the Crescent and I think maybe she's having an affair with him. That'd be lousy on Mr Collins. I mean he's such a laugh but it's kind of romantic too. Maybe that's why she doesn't want to go skiing, maybe she has other plans. The little girl finally gets her way and she drags the man into the toy shop.

Then I hear my name over the intercom.

'Could Jane Harris please come to Customer Services at Tesco, Jane Harris please,' a tinny woman's voice says. I look over at Mrs Collins. Straight into her eyes.

Two

Alison

'I miss you, Jack.'

He smiles at me. There's a crop of pimples on his forehead and his eyes are dark and brown and crinkled at the corners.

'I'm here now, aren't I?'

'Are you?'

He laughs and the familiar sound of it makes me laugh too.

'Don't go away again, Jack.'

'I will if you get all weird on me, Mam.'

We're sitting on the beach in Lahinch but it's not summer. It's autumn – I know by the smell. The beach is deserted except for a group of surfers having lessons on dry land. The tide is so far out it seems miles away.

'How's Dad?' Jack runs his hand through his hair. There's a smudge of sand on his cheek.

'He's fine.'

'That's all you ever say about him. He's fine, is he? Doesn't miss me at all – doesn't care?'

'That's not what I meant.'

'Isn't it? Same fucking answer every time, Mam. He's fine. Fuck's sake.'

'Watch your language, Jack.'

'Or what? You'll ground me? Stop my allowance? You won't get me credit for my phone?'

'Please stop.'

The pain in my chest tightens like an elastic band and the air is almost gone. I reach out to touch him but he inches away from me. I can feel his anger and I want to quell it, to placate him.

'I'm going. Fucking hell.' He stands up and brushes sand from his jeans and begins to walk away down the beach. He has no shoes on.

'Jack, please, just stay for another few minutes, five minutes,' I call after him. But Jack is a tiny stick person by now, miles away and I shut my eyes and open them again and scream . . .

I sit bolt upright and look straight into her face. I don't know where I am but I can feel tears running down my cheeks and I have an unbearable pain in my chest.

'What are you doing? What's wrong?' I whisper, but Jane just stares at me. She stands at the edge of my bed in pink pyjamas exactly like Leah's and stares at me. The street light outside throws a circle of light into the room and it makes her look orange. Then she stretches out a hand and touches my shoulder and then turns and walks away. I watch and the pain eases and Brian's voice next to me makes me jump.

'I'll get her, Ali, she's sleepwalking.' He swings out of the bed and switches on a reading lamp. I watch as he pads out of the room. He takes a long time to return but I'm happy lying in bed, savouring Jack and the sound of his voice again and his smile and his dark chocolately eyes. Open. Seeing.

'Are you OK?' Brian says, as he climbs into bed. He reaches out a hand and lets it lie lightly across my body. I turn on my side, my back to him, and he pulls his arm back.

'I'm fine. Is Jane all right?'

Brian takes a while to answer. 'I guided her back into bed, her mother told me what to do if it happened so . . .'

'When?'

'When what?'

'When did she tell you?'

Brian yawns. 'She rang while you were out walking. We had a long chat.'

'Oh. She said nothing to me when she dropped Jane off. Nothing at all about sleepwalking.'

'Poor Jane.'

'Mmmn,' I answer as I push my body to the edge of the bed and close my eyes. I know I'll sleep now because Jack came. It was so good to hear his voice. So good I'm almost happy.

'Ali?'

I don't answer.

Jesus Christ! Jane's father is actually really handsome. He has those classical good looks – regular features, all in proportion, strong jawline, thick luxurious hair. He smiles up at me from his car and I can barely hear what he's saying I'm so taken with his face. Why hadn't I ever noticed that before? He's saying something about his wife, or ex-wife, and how she's late and I can hear a Game Boy but I am transfixed by his mouth. I struggle to remember his name. Something with a D, and I almost put a hand out to trace his mouth with my fingers, but stop myself just in time and play with my locket instead. A tiny, cheap Argos one that Jack bought me for Christmas one year. I fiddle with its little heart shape, empty of photos since the day I put it around my neck. I smile at Jane's dad, again, smile at his mouth and decide I have to get away before I do something stupid.

'I have to run, goodbye. Bye kids,' I say hurriedly at the first opportunity.

My hands shake as I sit into my car and reverse out of the drive. Fuck it, I'm losing the plot, I'm seriously losing it I think as I drive away, barely able to see the road. But excitement or adrenalin or both course through my body and then I laugh and almost miss a red light. I'm still laughing as I pull up at the woods near our house. I can just make out the glint of river and I can't resist and run the few hundred metres towards it. I'm not frightened. I spend so much of my time here that it feels like home and home is never a scary place.

Blood pounds in my ears as I stop at the riverbank. The water is still and a huge cartoon moon throws a path of light in front of me. I hug myself tight and start laughing all over again and then something strikes me. This is how I feel when I follow him. This exact feeling. So if I stop following him and just gaze instead at Jane's dad's mouth everything will be fine. I burst out laughing again and then I remember his name. Dermot. Dermot Harris. Architect, ex-addict of some description – alcohol, I think – and ex-husband. And did I hear some rumour that he is an ex-architect too? I know very little about him, I've always dealt with Evelyn, Jane's mam. I know that his family were wealthy once. That they lived in Scotland for a while. That his marriage split up last year. That he didn't want to but that she forced him out. That was his story according to her and her story was that the marriage was over

31

due to mutual lack of interest. That she merely did the decent thing and put it out of its misery.

She told me this last year on a cold November night when we were sitting in my car outside the Mechanic's Institute. The girls were at karate and it was running late. I barely listened to Evelyn as she spoke. My head was full of Christmas and a holiday home we were thinking of buying in Spain and a new children's book I'd just started work on that morning. Things were pretty good way back then.

I hug myself again in the cold, damp night air. I can hear dogs barking and the low hum of generators. The Travellers, I think, and suddenly I'm consumed with laughter again and I imagine what would have happened if I'd just bent down and kissed him, right in the middle of his speech about his late wife. Late wife. I laugh out loud at this. I'm standing beside a huge old oak tree and I can smell rotting conkers and pine and a slight wind rustles the leaves. I could stay here all night and I think of the guy I read about in London who decided to live in a ditch for six months. A City man who was used to shiny, waterfront pads and Savile Row suits. He wanted to test himself. To see how little you really needed to live. To de-clutter in the extreme. And the problem was that once he'd done it, he didn't want to go back. Couldn't face the layers and layers of material things that cover you like quicksand. I think this now and picture waking up here every morning and watching the river and all its comings and goings. Its animals and birds and fishermen. Its runners and walkers. The constant stream of guests it entertains every day.

My teeth begin to chatter and I find that I'm shivering. I'm not wearing a coat, just a thin cardigan I'd thrown on as I left the house with Jane. Poor Jane. What's going on in her little head? I see her in my kitchen last night, stirring her hot chocolate, giggling with Leah, but it always seems like she's pretending. Like in the movie *Freaky Friday* – a grown-up in a child's body. Or maybe I'm just going mad, thinking these thoughts about my daughter's friend.

A noise from behind me makes me jump. I don't panic, it's probably just a night animal. I scan the dark wood but see nothing. The moon is half-covered now with thick black clouds and a few drops of rain begin to fall. I shiver again and turn to walk back to my car. I walk through the wood, conscious of every sound, my lungs taking in air, my feet crunching on the soft earth, my heart beating in my chest. Again I hear a noise, on my right side this time. I stop dead still, and look into the blackness. And then I see him. A boy's face, half-hidden behind a tree. Standing not ten feet from me. At first I think it's Jack and I smile.

'Jack, it's me, it's Mam,' I say.

I notice that the boy has hair as black as night and his likeness to Jack is uncanny. But the minute I speak he disappears, a small dog running beside him. I hear his footsteps running away. I walk slowly towards the road and sit into my car. As I put the key in the ignition and music fills the small space I wonder why I'm never scared anymore. Never scared of anything.

Richard arrives right on cue.

'Ali, Ali,' he calls through the letter box. 'It's Dick.'

It's Monday morning and I'm sitting at my computer in the study, pretending to work. Exactly like Jack in *The Shining*. I always laugh when I think of that.

'Coming,' I say to myself and walk to the door to let my brother in. I always say about him that any grown man that allows himself to be called Dick has serious issues going on.

He's standing in the porch with his usual bunch of garage flowers and bottle of matching garage wine. He's tall, over six feet, with a shock of grey hair that he says gives him character. And he needs all the help he can get in that department.

'Come in,' I say and he follows me to the kitchen. The room is a tip. Soggy cornflakes are scattered across the island, some are stuck to the black shiny marble. Somebody spilt milk and it has formed a pool under two cereal boxes.

'Sit down,' I say, nodding to a metal and leather high stool. It's strewn with Leah's dressing gown and Pete's pyjamas. I put on the kettle and decide to give Richard instant coffee. Just to annoy him.

He drops the flowers on a clean inch of worktop and moves the clothes to sit down. He looks around for somewhere to put them but just leaves them on his lap. I find clean cups and wait for the usual concerned brother on a Monday morning conversation. I know all the lines in this little family play.

'So, Ali, how are you?'

I keep my back to him, heaping Nescafé Gold Blend into two cups.

'I only have instant. Brian did the shopping – he doesn't drink coffee so he never remembers to get any.'

I bring the cups to the table and stir sugar into mine. There are lumps of congealed sugar mixed with tea in the bowl and I have to dig out two spoons. I laugh and show the bowl to Richard. 'I'll have to get a wife – look at the state of that.'

'Brian emailed me – you're all off skiing after Christmas – I think that's a great idea, Ali. Just what you need.'

I put my cup on the table and look at him. His eyes, full of confidence and assurance. His florid, meaty, eager face, wanting something from me. Something I can't give him.

'What *do* I need, Richard?' My voice is low and I look straight at him. He looks away and begins to fidget with Leah's dressing gown. 'Come on, tell me. I'm all ears. What do I need?'

He takes a sip of coffee and grimaces slightly. 'All I meant was the break would do you good. The whole family. It'll help you to . . .'

He stops and shrugs and looks at his hands.

'Please continue. Would help me to what? . . . Let's see. I know – would help me to forget! That magic state of mind that everybody feels I should be striving for.'

'That's not what I meant, that's not what I meant at all.' He looks petulant as he says this, like Pete having a little tantrum.

'Nice touch, Dick, quoting T.S. Eliot while dispensing concern and advice.'

'There's no need to be like that, Ali.'

'"The Love Song of J. Alfred Prufrock" – my favourite. Pretty thoughtful of you, Dick.' I never call him Dick and am enjoying it.

He sighs and shakes his head and won't meet my eyes. 'I didn't mean that. You know I didn't.'

'I don't want to fucking forget,' I say and he grimaces again at the swearing.

I begin to clean the work surface. I pull the cereal boxes from the worktop, where they seem to be welded to the marble, and I dump them into a press. Then I find a dishcloth and begin to scrub vigorously at the dried-on cardboard remains. At the milk and sticky sugar and the debris that was breakfast.

'Ali, Ali – stop and sit down. Talk to me.'

I scrub away, harder and harder. The silence stretches out in front of us until it forces one of us to blink.

'Remember last year, Ali? The summer we went to Inisheer?'

His voice is quiet, lacking the usual Richard zest for life.

I attack the cooker with my dishcloth, wiping and wiping at the burnt-on stains.

'And Leah got stung by a jellyfish on the beach and . . .' he chuckles, almost to himself, 'Jack wanted to pee on her because he saw it on *Friends* – he told us that the cure for a jellyfish sting was fresh pee and there was uproar . . .' he starts laughing.

'You were shouting at Jack, telling him how he really picked his comedy moments and Leah was crying and yelling for Jack not to pee on her and Brian was trying to think of a solution and . . .' he stops and laughs again and I stand still now, the dishcloth tight and balled in my hand. I want to tell him to get out, that I don't want his little reminisences, his little anecdotes and stories.

'And then one of the muinteoirs from the Irish college came over and put some salve on Leah's sting and he told us that the best cure was in fact fresh pee . . .' His voice trails off.

'Why are you telling me this?' my voice is icy calm.

'Ali, I didn't mean . . . I . . .'

I look directly at him. A tear has escaped from his eye and slides down his cheek.

'I noticed something about him that day.'

I turn back to the cooker, clenching my fists.

'He never gloated. I would have if I was him but he never said a word. Never said told you so, I was right. Just went off about his business, kicking ball with Peter,' Richard's voice cracks a little. The silence between us starts all over again.

'I'd better be going,' he says eventually.

I turn to face him again. He's still holding the pink dressing gown and the Spiderman pyjamas. 'See you.'

He nods and then heads for the door. I don't follow him. He

turns at the door and takes a few steps towards me again. I lean away from him and he gets the message: no hugs.

'Ali, look. I'm leaving you this card. It's a therapist friend of mine. She's wonderful, I've gone to her myself . . . and . . . well . . . here it is. I'll just leave it on the windowsill.' He puts the card on the windowsill, next to a small china dog that holds up a sign saying *Best Mam in the World*.

He smiles at me and leaves, and tears well up in my eyes and anger constricts my chest. I follow him to the door and call after him as he walks down the path. 'Can she bring children back from the dead?'

He turns to look at me. The morning is still and damp and clean-looking. Richard's shiny BMW is parked in the driveway. Somebody whistles in a nearby garden and a car starts up in the distance.

'No, Ali. She can't. But she can help those left behind to accept it.'

'That's the problem, Richard. I do accept it.' I say this as he gets into his car. I watch him wave at me as he reverses out the drive and I know I've been horrible to him but sometimes I get so tired of his sanctimonious offerings on life. And today I resent him bringing up Jack. Making me remember Jack's face, me shouting at him, blaming him in some weird way for the jellyfish sting.

I go back inside and switch on the radio in the kitchen and make real coffee and then I decide. I'll follow him today and introduce myself. See if the penny drops. See if there's a flicker of recognition when he hears my name. Will I be hurt if there isn't and if I am hurt then is that completely irrational? Suddenly my morning is full of purpose and I run upstairs to get ready, bringing my coffee with me.

I know his routine now as well as my husband's. I know that on a Monday, if I want to catch up with him, he'll be having lunch in the Clarion. I know that he'll sit on one of the couches facing the river, usually the one furthest away from the main entrance. I know that he'll have the soup and a wrap, more than likely chicken tikka, and that he'll have a strong double espresso to finish. Then he'll read the paper for a little while before making his way back to the library.

He's the city librarian and I really don't know why that surprises me so much. He's youngish for that kind of job – late thirties – but then why do I think that librarians should be old and doddery?

He has a family. A boy and a girl and a wife who drives a red Peugeot and has blonde highlights which she has retouched every fortnight in Bellisimo.

Today I arrive just as he's having the coffee. I sit a good bit away from him. Other times, if I'm feeling confident, I'll sit within ten feet of him. Once, about three months ago, I sat right opposite him but I didn't have the nerve to make eye contact. It was enough to be so close and I was intoxicated by the sheer power of it. Adrenalin beat in my veins like an addictive drug and I was sure he could hear my heart thumping. I was so close I could smell his aftershave. I could see where the crisp white collar of his shirt sat stiff and unwielding against his neck. Where his trousers creased as he folded his legs and leant back into the deep, red couch to read his paper – the *Irish Times* of course – and sip his almost black coffee. He never glanced at me once but I think he was just being polite.

Now I can see the rise and dip of his head as he reads and drinks. I order a coffee just so that I don't look suspicious and then he stands up and folds his paper and walks past me like he doesn't have a care in the world. For a second I consider shouting at him – bursting his bubble in some way – but I know that if I wait and watch then in the long run that'll be way more satisfying.

I follow him out and as usual he follows the length of the Shannon back to the library. He pauses at Poor Man's Kilkee and walks to the edge of the river. I duck behind a parked car, hoping he hasn't seen me. He peers into the river like he's searching for something specific and then he walks away, picking up speed. I hurry after him, aware that my heels on the pavement make a loud clacking sound. I follow him discreetly through the glass doors of the library. It's a lovely building – it used to be a granary and I admire it now as I climb the stairs to the first floor where the actual library is situated.

There are so many places here to hide. So many nooks and crannies and aisles and columns. I go straight to the children's section and check out the titles under C and note that my books are not included on the shelves. I check this every time I come here and always feel insulted. I decide that this is how I'll introduce myself to him. This is the perfect way to let him hear my name.

I scan the library floor and see him talking to an African man over by the computers. He's so at home and relaxed and I can tell by his face that this is his little empire. Suddenly my phone rings and I pounce on it to stop the noise.

'Hello?' I whisper, ducking behind an aisle of books on post modernism.

'Ali? What happened to you? I've been waiting for over half an hour.'

It's my sister, Rachel, pregnant for the first time. I'm supposed to meet her for lunch.

'Rachel, I'm sorry. I had an appointment in Leah's school and it ran late. I'm so sorry.'

'No problem. Did Richard call?'

'At ten thirty. On the button. Flowers and wine.'

Rachel laughs. 'That's a surprise. Are you OK?'

A little bit of my earlier anger with Richard threatens to spill over again. 'I'm fine.'

'Glad you survived him. I'll call you later and we'll rearrange lunch.'

'Great,' I whisper.

'Listen, are you going to see Mammy later? Because . . .'

Somebody touches me on the shoulder and I almost scream. I turn around and look straight into his eyes. I hear my sister's tinny voice calling me on my phone, 'Ali, Ali are you there' and I hear a small child counting to ten at a table near us.

'You can't use your phone in here,' he says, looking directly at me with the clearest blue eyes. I'm transfixed by the eyes and can't seem to break away from them and Jack's voice is in my head and he's hungry, he's telling me he's hungry, 'Mam, Mam, is there anything at all to eat, did you do the shopping yet, is there any Nutella?'

'I'm sorry, but you can't use your phone in the library. Could you please switch it off?' He repeats his order, his voice kind but firm.

I nod and see vague recognition in his eyes. But before he can put a name to the face I turn and hurry through the exit doors, almost getting caught in the barriers. I take the stairs two at a time and as soon as I reach the pavement I gulp in damp autumn air but my lungs won't expand properly. I can't get enough air in. I start to walk, still gulping air, and remember my sister and hold the phone to my ear but the line is dead.

The wonderful rush of adrenalin kicks in as I walk back through town. It fills my head and my heart and makes my body feel light and pain-free and perfect. I'm glad then that the introductions have been postponed. I'm glad and I'm almost happy and I run into the supermarket to buy some shopping. Food. We need food. The lads will be hungry and Brian never buys enough. He doesn't realise how much food children eat. I start at fruit and vegetables and immediately see a row of Halloween pumpkins lined up, grinning at me.

And then Jack is here, age four, sitting on a supermarket ride, a spaceship. He's wearing a Batman suit with a cowboy hat and it's Halloween. I can see the fat, orange pumpkins, the mounds of monkey nuts and bananas and shiny, red apples.

'Mam, it won't go, make it go, Mam, please, please.'

His voice is tiny, a baby's voice. His eyes are huge, brown, sad. His eyes are always sad, even when he is laughing. I don't like brown eyes and wish his were blue, like his father's.

'It's broken, honey, I can't make it go. I know what we'll do, we'll go on Postman Pat. How's that?' I say.

He looks straight at me. 'This one.'

'It's broken, honey, it won't work. We've already put coins in and it just won't work. Come on, we'll try Postman Pat.' I take him by the arm. He pushes my hand away.

'THIS ONE.'

'Now Jack, keep it up and we'll go straight home.'

'I want the spaceship or none.'

'Oh Jack, stop.'

He climbs down from the spaceship, the cowboy hat tilted at an angle on his small head. He looks at me once, and then walks ahead towards the exit doors.

I drop my empty basket on the floor and look around for

the long-gone spaceship. For the baby that was Jack, already determined in the world. For a sign of his stubborn little backside waddling off in a huff. I pick up the basket and wander through the aisles until I find the Nutella.

Leah arrives home with a kitten on Wednesday evening. A marmalade-coloured one she calls Sandy.

'Where did you get him?' I ask. I hate cats and she knows it.

'I'm keeping him,' she says, her chest out defiantly, an implacable look on her face. Brian peels spuds at the sink. Pete is sitting on a stool, eating Koka noodles and watching us.

I laugh. 'No way, my dear. You can take him right back to wherever you found him.'

Her eyes fill with tears and I soften immediately.

'I found him on the road, he was crying and was so scared and he's only a baby.' She lifts the kitten and buries her face in his fur.

'Somebody around must own him,' I say.

'I've asked and nobody knows where he came from. Can we keep him, Mam, please?'

I shake my head. 'I'm allergic to cats, Leah.'

Tears spill down her face and she narrows her eyes at me. 'No you're not. You just hate animals. You wouldn't even let Jack get a dog.'

I don't hear this – I feel it instead like a punch in the gut.

'Leah,' says Brian.

I walk out and go into the study and swallow tears. I switch on the computer hoping work will offer a refuge. There in front of me is my so-called new children's book. The first chapter. Static for months, stuck on the third page. Word count 334. I stare at the words on the screen in front of me but they don't make sense. And then before I know I'm even doing it I go on to Bebo and find Jack's page. The Bebo page that was to be deleted months ago and I almost did, almost wiped out pieces of Jack that I never knew existed until he was gone.

Mothers shouldn't see their sons' Bebo pages. Shouldn't read the smutty comments, the personal ones, the sexy quizzes. Shouldn't understand the teenage jargon about music and girls and sport. I know it backwards now. I know every face in every photo in his picture gallery. I know that in his celebrity lookalike photo fit he's most like Gael Garcia Bernal (82%) followed by Mia Farrow (64%). He's least like Brad Pitt (4%).

I know that he has friends on Bebo called Colinator and Rory's Demons. Seanie M and Perfect Patrick. Girls called Gorgeous Niamh and Smelly Mel. And Hugsy. I know Hugsy the best. She likes to write. She likes to draw pictures of hearts and flowers on Jack's whiteboard. She likes Kings of Leon and Fionn Regan and of course the Chilis.

And she likes to leave comments for Jack – even though he's gone and won't ever be answering them. There's a new one today.

Been thinking about you all day and the way you love nutella and jam sandwiches. Disgusting!!! Love ya loads and miss ya sooo much. Sleep tight.xxxxxxxxxx

There's a bright red heart at the top of the comment box. I've never met her, Hugsy. But I love her already for not forgetting.

Later in bed I will him to come. In any shape or form, in any condition. Cut and bruised, the back of his head split open. Angry and hormonal, shouting and banging doors. Loud with a gang of his pals, their voices rising and falling in that lovely half-boy, half-man sing-song way. Or fresh from the longest shower in the world, with total disregard for his carbon footprint, his hair damp and glossy wet, the smell of Lynx overpowering and cloying. But he doesn't come. I can't make him.

Three

Jane

'Hi, Mrs Collins,' I say, as brazen as you like. I smile at her. She looks all guilty and confused and I want to ask her straight out are you having an affair and what's it like?

'Hi, Jane, fancy meeting you here. Is your mam here too? I just dropped in to change a pair of pants in Vero Moda . . .'

I smile again and then look at her hands. She doesn't have a bag. She knows I know. We stand there in silence.

'I heard your name on the tannoy. Your mam will be looking for you.'

I nod.

'So, you better hurry. See you soon,' she says.

I nod and begin to walk away.

'Oh Jane,' she calls. I turn back and see the man and the little girl coming out of the toy shop. Mrs Collins has her back to them now so she doesn't see them disappearing into the crowds of shoppers.

'Yes?' I say and I smile at her.

'Leah got a new kitten.'

'Did she?' I say, my voice shaky. I keep smiling at her though. She nods. 'A gorgeous little guy – she's called him Sandy.'

'Lovely,' I say. 'That's a lovely name.'

'Anyway, see you soon. Are you going to karate tomorrow night? The Brown Belt is close now, isn't it?'

'The end of the month.'

My name is announced over the intercom again and as I wave at Mrs Collins and run towards Tesco I swear that I'll kill my aunt for mortifying me like that. Why couldn't she just ring me? I check my phone and it's dead.

On the way home in the car I hear Sarah's voice, chattering away non-stop. The chart show is on the radio but it's turned down low. I pinch the inside of my arm so hard that it makes me gasp out loud but Sarah doesn't hear. She just keeps talking about the outfit she's wearing at the weekend and how her new boots are to die for. I pinch again and this time it's the hardest I've ever done and tears come to my eyes and I blink them away. Fucking bastard Leah, I say in my head over and over again.

Dad picks us up for karate on Friday because Mam has to go to a meeting. Ben is being a right little shit and I tell him he has to go to karate because Mam said and he cries like a big baby. Daddy is on the phone so he doesn't hear us. He's laughing and joking and calling somebody Hon. Ben wipes his eyes and sits as far away from me as possible and looks out the window. And then I feel sorry for him, I mean he hates karate and he has no friends and stuff and he doesn't understand stuff the way I do. Dad's voice is all giggly now, like a girl's. *You're the best, Hon, you're my Doris Day. Kiss kiss* into the phone. I want to puke.

Leah is waiting for me in the hall. She told me all about the kitten yesterday as if last Sunday never happened so I let on I didn't care and nodded and smiled at the kitten stories and our teacher, Mrs Doran, made a big fuss and then she asked if I was going to get one too because I'd said I was on Monday. I shrugged and said probably.

'Guess who's inside?' she says, grabbing my arm, and pulling me into the loo.

'Zac Efron,' I say and she gives me a withering look.

'Darren! Darren is here and two other boys from Racefield. I'm going to be mortified doing karate in front of them,' she says, jumping around the loo.

'Have you got deodorant?' I ask, remembering that Mam's had run out earlier on me.

'Brilliant thinking, Jane Harris,' she says and roots in her hold all. We spray ourselves and the small room mists up with spray and the smell is really strong.

When we go into the hall I want to turn right back out again. Daddy is at the top of the room where the mirrors are, talking to John, our karate teacher. I pretend I don't see him and go and sit on the radiator, dragging Leah with me. The boys are in another corner, their brand-new karate suits Daz-white and setting them apart from the rest of us.

'What's your dad doing?' Leah asks, looking over at him.

He's doing moves now with John and my face goes a bright hot red. I search the room for Ben and he's at the very back, with the rest of his group. Their teacher chats away to them. Ben stares up at me. Big baby eyes always ready to cry. Why can't he just toughen up? Be a boy and just get tough?

I will Daddy to leave and finally he does, giving me a big maniac's wave on his way out.

When we come out of karate, there's no sign of Daddy. The car is still there, parked in exactly the same spot, but it's empty. Leah is still inside, practising a move she already knows inside out – I mean she's the best in the class and the teacher's pet and I think she's just showing off. Ben shuffles beside me and it's foggy, so when we breathe out we look like smokers.

'There's Daddy,' Ben says, pointing across the street.

Daddy is sitting beside Mrs Collins in her car and their heads are close together. They're talking and they don't even notice that karate is over. Then Leah comes out all smiles. Darren and his friends are with her.

'See you, guys,' she calls as they run to a big, silver people carrier.

Ben stamps his feet beside me. Leah haws and her breath comes out in a white magic puff.

'There's my mam,' she says. 'Oh look, that's your dad in with her.'

Daddy sees us then and waves and climbs out of the car as Leah crosses the road.

'So, how are the karate kids?' Daddy says as he starts the engine.

'Fine,' I say, staring out the window.

'It's a fantastic martial art,' he continues.

The car is cold and I shiver. Ben switches on his Game Boy, the tinny music from his game fills the car.

'I've always wanted to do it, you know. Just take the time to learn a disciplined sport like that.'

I barely hear him. I'm thinking about the kitten again and how mean Leah is sometimes. She has no right to be so mean. I plait a thin rib of my hair and wonder why she did it.

'Your instructor, that John guy, he's brilliant, really talented,' he says, and turns to smile back at both of us. We're pulled up at traffic lights and his grin looks eerie and too young for a dad. He looks like a boy.

'Anyway, we're all going to dinner next Wednesday at the

Collinses. How's that?' He winks at me and turns back to drive.

My head bursts with curses and swear words. Fucking bastard. Cunt. Fucking bollocks. Shitbag. I keep my mouth shut tight so none escape. But I really want to say them out loud. I want to scream them. Leah is my friend, not his.

'That'll be fun, won't it Ben? You can play with their son, what's his name?' says Daddy.

'Peter,' says Ben. 'His name is Peter and I don't like him.'

'Of course you do. It'll be fun. Alison is so kind to ask us all.'

Alison. He's calling her Alison. Why can't he stay out of my life?

'And I have another surprise. I'm joining your karate class.'

I tell Mammy about the karate. It's Tuesday and tomorrow we're going to stay at Dad's for a few days because it's mid-term. I don't want to go. Ben is upstairs playing another stupid fucking computer game. Mam is doing my nails in the kitchen. A French manicure just like hers. Pale pink with snow white tips, like you'd dipped them in frost.

'Daddy is joining karate,' I say, watching her file my thumbnail.

'Keep your hand straight, Janie, there, that's better,' she says. 'What did you say about Daddy?'

'He's joining karate.'

'And? What's the problem? I do aerobics, Uncle Sean does kick-boxing.'

I look at Mammy and she stops filing and smiles at me. Her hair is long and blonde, just like mine, and her eyes are green with gold and brown flecks. I want to look like her when I grow up but everybody says I look like the Harrises. Like Daddy. I hate when people say that.

'He's joining our class, Mam. Our actual karate class,' I say. 'He'll be the only dad there. The only adult besides our teacher.'

Her hand stops filing. 'Are you serious?'

I nod. I can feel her anger building up like something you can see or touch.

'I don't bloody believe him sometimes, do you know that?'

I say nothing. My hand shakes from holding it out so straight. She begins filing again, furiously, like she's in a mad rush to be done and I'm sorry I told her. I know now that there's no way I can talk to her about Daddy and going to his house or wanting a kitten or Leah being mean. It just makes it all worse.

'I'll sort him out on this one, Janie, don't worry about it,' she says, smiling tightly at me. 'Which colour pink? Ice-cream Soda or Candy?'

Later in bed I hear her talking to him on the phone. I hear her voice rising and rising until she's shouting at him and telling him to *just fuck off, you're insane, that's what you are, just plain mad.* And then I hear her crying. Soft and quiet but definitely crying.

Leah's kitten is gorgeous. We're in the sitting room, all the children, and there are lovely smells coming from the kitchen. I can hear Mrs Collins laughing and Daddy talking to her and I'm kind of proud of him, he can make Mrs Collins laugh and maybe this dinner will be grand after all. But Sandy's so cute. I don't want to like her, I want her to be horrible, like the cat Nana has who scratches and hisses and never lets you pet her. And she really likes me and falls asleep in my arms, purring quietly. Leah smiles at me.

'She's gorgeous, isn't she?' she says, taking her out of my arms and hugging her. The kitten miaows softly.

I know Leah is being a bitch but I know too that if I say anything she'll just deny it.

'Don't hold her so close to your face, she probably has worms,' I say.

Leah hates stuff like that. She puts the kitten down on the couch and rubs her hands on her jeans.

Daddy talks the whole way through dinner. Talks and talks like it's going out of fashion and Mrs Collins hangs on to his every word and says go away and are you serious and laughs at all his jokes and I smile at him and he reminds me of Daddy a long time ago, maybe even before Ben was born and I used to sit on the step and wait for him to come home every night. He'd open his arms and say where's my girl, my best girl, and I'd run to him, bury my head in his smell and then he'd hold me up, right up to the sky but I knew he'd never let me fall.

Mr Collins arrives home from work during dessert – apple tart and ice cream – and sits at the table. He winks at us and shakes Daddy's and Ben's hands.

'Do you want dinner?' Mrs Collins asks, but she doesn't get up or anything.

He shakes his head. 'No thanks, I had my dinner. Four Mars Bars and three litres of Coke.' He smiles at us and we laugh.

'So, how are things? What have you lads been up to today?' he asks and Peter and Leah talk over each other, telling him about their day. Daddy and Mrs Collins begin talking again.

'And what about you, Ben?' Mr Collins says.

Ben shrugs and fiddles with his fork. I realise that he's turning into a real dork brother.

'I know those old days – so boring you can't even remember what happened,' says Mr Collins, smiling at Ben.

He helps himself to the last slice of apple tart and pours coffee from a silver pot in the centre of the table. Then he smiles at Mrs Collins and Daddy.

'So, Ali, did you ask Dermot about the skiing trip?' he says.

Leah and I look at each other and she reaches out and holds my hand under the table.

Daddy looks at Mr Collins. 'Evelyn mentioned something all right. It's the week after Christmas, isn't it?'

Mr Collins nods. 'That's right. It includes the New Year so it should be gorgeous there.'

'I have the children for New Year,' says Daddy. He picks up his cup and sips his coffee.

'So?' says Mr Collins, and Mrs Collins glares at him. Everybody is quiet now, even Peter, who's always fidgety. For no reason I feel my face burning. Glowing like the fire in Nana's grate. Hot, bright red. I pull my hand away from Leah's.

'So, I value my time with my children,' Daddy says, his voice quiet.

I look down at my plate, at the crumbs and melted ice cream.

'It's a while off yet, we'll see what happens,' says Mr Collins. 'Now, is there any more apple tart or did those two girleens eat it all?'

Leah and I laugh but Daddy just keeps looking straight at Mr Collins.

'I only get to see them for two days out of every fourteen. Have you any idea what that's like? How hard that is for me?' Daddy says in that quiet voice.

Mrs Collins is very cross now. I can see it in her eyes. She's giving Mr Collins filthy looks.

'At least you get to see them,' Mr Collins says.

'Brian, stop it right now. Off you guys go and watch TV for a while,' Mrs Collins says, but nobody moves.

'I'll come with you guys,' says Mr Collins and follows us out into the sitting room.

We watch *The Simpsons* and Mr Collins laughs out loud, roars laughing and everything is grand again. Then we watch *Cheaper by the Dozen* even though we've seen it forty times but I'm in love with Ashton Kutcher and Leah loves him even more than me. Peter is upstairs and Ben doesn't care what he watches so we get our way. Mr Collins laughs his way through that movie too.

It's late when we leave and Ben is nearly falling asleep and Mr Collins is asleep, snoring on the couch. Ben and I climb into the car and I watch as Daddy and Mrs Collins are still talking at the front door. Then they shake hands and he walks away. She calls him back and kisses him. But only on the cheek, I think.

Daddy has a surprise on Saturday. I'm sitting there in his horrible flat, watching the flickering Bogger telly, a choice between RTE 1 and RTE 2 and he comes into the tiny living room. I'm in my dressing gown, curled up on the couch. He sits at the edge of the couch and looks at me and smiles. I keep watching the telly and it goes from colour to black and white to colour for no reason.

'Jane?'

'Yeah?' I turn up the sound a little.

He takes the remote from me and turns it way down. 'Did you sleep OK?'

I shrug. 'Fine.'

'You were up during the night, I heard you. You woke me.'

I shrug again. 'You must have been dreaming.'

'No I wasn't. You were in here, walking around. I couldn't get back to sleep.'

'Maybe it was Ben.'

'No. Ben came in and slept at the bottom of my bed.'

I shrug again. Maybe we've a ghost. It is Halloween.'

'It's no big deal, Jane. Sleepwalking. Did I ever tell you I used to do it too?'

He smiles proudly at me like he's told me something good – something that I'd like to get from him, besides blue eyes.

He claps his hands together then. 'I have a surprise for you both today. I want you to meet someone.'

The picture on the telly is in colour now but is rolling up and down the screen. It's such a crap telly. I shouldn't even bother watching it.

'Someone very special. We'll go to the cinema, how's that?'

I shrug again. I know it's the girl, it's 'Hon', I know it in my heart and soul. I say nothing.

He pats me on the leg and goes to the kitchen. Ben arrives all bleary-eyed and rubs sleep from his eyes.

'Baby,' I say and laugh.

'Shut up, you,' he says and plonks down on the deck chair opposite me.

Daddy has only one proper couch and Mammy says why doesn't he buy furniture and make the place nice and comfy for us, but she says this to me, not Daddy.

'Sleeping with Daddy. Big baby.'

'Fuck off, Jane.'

'Naughty, naughty, Ben. I'll tell,' I say and he glares at me.

And then I see this look in his eyes and I can't describe it but it makes me think of when he was small, a little toddler, and he'd follow me everywhere and say Janie, I lug you.

'Do you want toast?' I ask.

He nods and the look is gone from his face. I go to the tiny kitchen. Daddy has some of his music blasting on a small stereo on top of the fridge. It's loud and I'm glad. I make the toast and two cups of milky tea, while Daddy reads the paper, sitting on a stool near the window.

He brings us to the cinema. Ben is all excited because it's the new Batman movie and Daddy gets him a huge carton of popcorn and a giant coke. I don't want any. I scan the crowd in the lobby of the cinema to see if I can pick her out. I examine girls' faces, tall ones, fat ones, old ones, but I can't picture Daddy with any of them, except maybe Mammy.

Then I see her and I know it's her even though she's still a bit far away. I know by the way Daddy is smiling at her and the way she smiles back. I know this is 'Hon'. She smiles at him first and then at us, and Ben is there beaming at her and I want to thump him in the head. I don't smile. I pinch my arm really hard through my pink shirt with the tiny flowers. I think I hate her as she stands now in front of us and kisses Daddy. Right on the mouth. She's wearing cool Rock & Republic jeans even though she must be like ancient, at least as old as Daddy. Lovely blue jeans that have the crown symbol on the back of the pockets and a pale cream angora sweater and a tiny fitted jacket. She has round eyes and a pretend smile and a loud mock voice like somebody in a play.

'I'm delighted to meet you. I've been waiting for Dermot to introduce us, haven't I, Der?'

'This is Fiona. Fiona, Jane and Ben,' says Daddy, like she doesn't know our names already. Ben says hi and I just nod at her.

She links arms with Daddy and looks up into his eyes and he smiles down at her and now I know I hate her.

We go into the cinema and I sit in the dark and listen to her whispering her way through the film. Whispering into Daddy's ear. Every time I try to concentrate on the movie my eyes blur so I go to the toilet and roll up my sleeve and pinch the hardest ever and say fucking bastard at the same time over and over, and then all the curses I can think of, but I don't cry and the pain in my arm makes me not want to.

I know he doesn't want me to tell Mammy about Fiona. He doesn't say it out loud but I know afterwards, when she's gone and we're in McDonalds and he says isn't Fiona really nice but it's a question. Stupid Ben nods at Daddy, his mouth full of Big Mac. I look out the window on to the rainy street and wonder what Leah is doing right this minute.

'Can I have a kitten, Daddy?' I ask.

He stops eating chips and looks at me. 'Why don't you ask your mam?'

I shake my head. 'She said no last year, remember? We can keep it in your flat and then we can see it all the time and . . .'

'Don't be ridiculous, Jane. I'm at work all day. How can I look after a kitten?'

'It's not that hard, Daddy.' I take a bite out of my cheese-burger but I'm not hungry and the smell makes me feel sick.

'What do you know about looking after animals? It's like having another child. And anyway Nana has a cat. You can play with him any time you like,' he says.

'That's Nana's cat and he's horrible,' I say.

'No way, end of. Now, who wants to go for a walk in Cratloe Woods?'

'I do, I do,' says dopey Ben.

So I tell on him even though I know I'm not supposed to. It's a week later. Tuesday night and Mammy's really tired and Ben's even dumber than usual. He has a problem with maths and it takes him like for ever to understand something simple and Mammy's helping him at the kitchen table. I'm watching a re-run of *Buffy* and it's fun trying to remember all the things that happen in the episode. But I can hear Mammy shouting at Ben in the kitchen. I turn up the volume but I can still hear her and she's really mad with him and I know he takes years to do his homework but the shouting only ever makes it worse and Mammy should know that by now.

I get up and go into the kitchen. Ben is hunched over his copybook, his eyes glued to the page, and Mammy is banging things around.

'You're not concentrating, Ben. You're well able to concentrate when you're playing your Game Boy.'

Her voice is tight and angry. She picks up a pot and starts to scrub it really hard, bashing it against the side of the sink. Ben sits there all hunched up, rolling his pencil around in his fingers.

'Are you listening to me, Ben? Try to work out the sum yourself.'

She turns around and folds her arms, watching him. He doesn't move.

'I said, try to work out the sum yourself.' She grabs the copybook, looks at it and then pushes it back down in front of him. 'Now,' she shouts, 'do it now.' She turns back to the sink.

'We met Daddy's girl last week,' I say. She stands really still, even her hands in the dishwater.

'What did you say?'

'We met Daddy's girl last week.' I walk out and go back to *Buffy*. She follows me and walks over and switches off the TV.

'Jane, tell me what happened,' she says and sits down beside me. She smells lovely, Chanel. I know the name because it's on her dressing table and sometimes I take a squirt. Her nails are Black Cherry tonight, every one of them perfect and unchipped.

'Nothing,' I say.

'Come on, Jane. You said you met Daddy's girl. Where? When?'

I shrug.

'Jane. Answer me.'

'Last week. Last Saturday. He said he wanted us to meet someone special and he brought us to the cinema and . . .'

'And?'

'And we met her, that's all.' I'm sorry now that I said anything.

'What was she like?' Mammy's looking straight into my eyes. 'It's OK, Janie, you can tell me. You know that.'

My eyes fill up with tears and Mammy reaches out and holds my hand tight. 'You can tell, Jane. It's fine.'

So I tell. All of it, I tell all of it. What we did. What she said to us. What she wore. The way her voice sounded mock like she was acting in a play. The way Daddy called her Hon and the way she smiled up at him and whispered in his ear through the whole film and the way they kissed on the mouth. I'm crying now, tears pour down my face and I tell Mammy that I hate his girl. She wipes my tears away with her hand and kisses me on the forehead.

'This should have been cleared with me first, Jane,' she says. 'He should have told me he was introducing her to you.'

I wipe tears from my eyes with my shirtsleeve.

'The cheek of him, prancing around all lovey dovey and he

hasn't even the decency to say it to me first. Fucking bastard. Selfish bastard.'

She should be saying this to Daddy, not me, but I say nothing, just try to stop crying.

'Come on, I'll make you and Ben some hot chocolate,' she says and catches my face in both her hands. 'Forget about him, Jane. I'll sort it out.'

So we go into the kitchen and Ben is still doing his maths but Mammy is kind to him and she makes hot chocolate and even finds marshmallows to put on top. But all the time her face is different. It's closed, like she's trying to hold something in. Something mad and angry and scary.

It's Friday night. Karate night and I can't miss it because of the Brown Belt and then we have to go to Daddy's for the weekend. But I know something is up when he calls to the front door for us. Mammy answers like she's been waiting for him and we stay in the kitchen. I open the door a little so that I can hear and Ben rolls his eyes and buries his head in his Game Boy.

'You should have told me,' Mammy says first. I peep out through the crack in the door. Daddy is there in the hallway, looking straight at her, kind of smiling at her.

He laughs. 'She's not a drug dealer or a psychopath or anything. She's actually a very nice lady,' he says. 'Now, can I have my children, please, or we'll be late?'

'No, you can't as a matter of fact. You can't have them. You're messing them around, Dermot, and I'm not wearing it any more.'

He laughs, a horrible, mean laugh and it echoes in my head, like I've heard it somewhere before – in a film maybe, and his eyes are weird and I'm really scared. I'm scared he'll do something, scream at Mammy or hit her even. I want to close the door and put my hands over my ears and pretend none of it is happening but it's fascinating, like a horror film. You just keep looking.

'I'm messing them around? What about you? The biggest fucking slut in Limerick, with your fucking bling social life? Please. I'm embarrassed that I ever lowered myself to marry you.'

'Get out.'

'No, I won't, slut. Give me my children.'

He smiles at Mammy and folds his arms and just stands there and I'm scared but she isn't.

'Get out or I'll call the Guards. I mean it.' Mammy's voice is shaky now.

'Go on then, shitbag. Here, use my phone if you like.'

Mammy takes his phone and throws it against the wall and it crashes against the mirror and the phone falls on the black and white tiles of the hall floor and then the glass from the mirror falls on it like rain. I look back into the kitchen and Ben's body is shaking. He's still playing his game but his hands shake.

Daddy grabs Mammy by the arm really tightly and he laughs that crazy laugh and I kind of remember the time of the rope, the look on his face and the doorway and my arm and the blood.

'Stop, Daddy,' I say.

Both of them look at me. Mammy is crying.

'Janie . . .' she says.

Daddy smiles at me but I think he's mad with me too, because I told Mam about Fiona. I look down at the smashed phone.

'Have it your way. I'll go off and have a terrific weekend with Fiona. Have it your way, darling,' he says to Mammy and then he bends down and picks up the pieces of his phone and walks out.

Mammy hugs me and then she goes into the kitchen and hugs Ben and says ye don't have to go to karate and Ben's delighted but I don't want to miss it because of my Brown Belt.

So I go and all the time I hope Daddy doesn't turn up and he doesn't. And John, the instructor, never even mentions him, which is great. I don't say anything to Leah and I think she even forgets I'm supposed to go to Daddy's because she says after karate, can you sleep in my house tomorrow night? and I say yes, straight away.

Sometimes I think there's like something in the air and it makes all parents fight or be happy or be sad all at the same time. Leah's mam and dad are not talking to each other. Every time Mr Collins comes into the room Mrs Collins walks out. And she always has her phone with her, texting and texting like she's a teenager. Mothers only text when they have to.

The atmosphere is awful and I can't bear it and I wish I'd stayed at home with Mam. Leah and Peter act like there's nothing wrong so I do the same. Then after we go to bed and Leah is snoring softly beside me I hear them fighting. I hear their voices starting off slowly in low murmurs and then louder and louder. Something about the Pope dying and Rome and camper vans. And then a door bangs and somebody is out in the back garden and then there's quiet. I pinch my arm in the dark, pinch it hard and squeeze the tears in my eyes back and I wonder are Leah's mam and dad breaking up too. The house is very messy – toys everywhere, the hoover just sitting right in the middle of the hall. A smell of cat pee from the couch in the living room. Clothes thrown on chairs. That's a sign of breaking up. That and the fighting. As I drift off to sleep I'm glad that the fight is not about sluts or shitbags. The Pope dying and camper vans is a much better fight.

The next morning I'm just sitting there having my Coco Pops and Mrs Collins starts the sleeping thing again.

'Jane, how did you sleep?'

Leah has gone to brush her teeth. We're alone in the kitchen, except for Sandy, who's asleep on the chair beside me. Mr Collins has taken Peter to rugby training.

First I think she's worried that I might have heard the fight.

'Great. I was like so tired. I fell asleep the minute my head hit the pillow.'

'It's just that . . . well . . . you sleepwalk – did you know that?'

I go bright red. 'I don't . . . I didn't know.'

'It's OK, Jane, lots of people sleepwalk. Your mam knows. She's said it to us already.'

I'm mortified now. It's like telling somebody that you wet the bed. And anyway it's not true.

'I don't sleepwalk.' I look her straight in the eye and I want to say something back to her. Like why do you follow men or I heard you fighting last night.

She puts out her hand and touches my arm. 'Jane, if there's anything troubling you please tell me. I know how hard it must be for you right now. I mean breaking up is . . . there just aren't any winners.'

She tilts her head sideways like she's asking me a question, but I don't know the answer.

'You see, sometimes it's a sign that you're upset – it just comes out like that in some people . . .'

'I'm not upset. Not at all.'

She looks at me and I hold her stare and then luckily Leah comes back into the kitchen and Mrs Collins finally shuts up.

Mr Collins and Peter don't come home. We're all sitting around the kitchen table having Sunday dinner and I know we've been waiting for them to come but then it just gets too late and we have dinner.

Leah is upset, I just know she is. She's like I was at the very start – like the time Mammy and Daddy fought in front of her. I want to say to her it'll all be fine, you'll live, but I think that'll only make her angry and even more upset. So we eat in silence and for the first time ever I don't want to be in Leah's house. Well, not ever, I didn't want to be here either when Jack died, I mean who would in their right minds – all that crying and stuff.

Then the doorbell rings and Mrs Collins goes to answer it. Daddy is standing in the doorway, a big smile on his face. Mrs Collins is standing behind him, and she's smiling too. He's got both hands behind his back.

'Hi, Janie,' he says.

'Hi,' I say but I'm wondering why he's here and if he's still angry with me. I hope he doesn't say anything in front of the Collins'.

Something miaows and I look around for Sandy. So does Leah.

And then he brings his hand around and there is the most beautiful kitten I ever saw.

'Ohmygodohmygodohmygod,' I say and run to Daddy and take the kitten in my arms. She's stripy, like a tiger, and her eyes are green. I love her.

'Is she mine? Really, is she?' I say and hold her up in front of me.

'She's yours, Janie. Do you like her?'

'I love her, Daddy, I absolutely love her,' I say and hug him with one arm. He hugs me tight to him and says oh Jane and I smell him and it reminds me of when I was little and how much I miss him. Miss that smell and the roughness of his cheek against mine and his strong arms around me. I notice then that

Mrs Collins is crying and Daddy sees too and he takes her by the arm and steers her down the hall.

'Let's introduce her to Sandy,' I say to Leah and we go looking for her. The kittens love each other straight away. Leah puts my guy down and Sandy starts licking her and playing with her.

'Look Jane – they're like best friends already – just like us.'

'Leah, please,' I say, looking down at the kittens mock-wrestling each other now.

'What?'

'We don't lick each other.'

Leah bursts out laughing. 'You're disgusting sometimes, Jane Harris.'

'I wonder if they really are girls – I mean wouldn't it be so cool if one was a boy and they had babies together and stuff?' I say as the kittens start the licking thing again.

'We could have a wedding – they do that in America – have weddings for dogs and cats . . .'

'No way.'

'I'm serious. They have invitations and wedding cake and guest lists. I swear Jane – I'll show you on the Internet.'

I laugh. 'I believe you. I'm so happy, Leah, my very own pet.'

So Daddy drives me home and Lucky – that's what I call her – Lucky sits on my lap all cosy and contented. And I talk and talk and tell Daddy lots of stuff about school and music and everything. He laughs.

He drops me outside our house and as I get out he catches my arm.

'Hey Janie.'

'What Dad?'

'Do you really want to go skiing?'

I grin at him. 'Yes. Why?'

'Well there's nothing definite yet but I said to Alison that if you really want to go then . . .'

'Ohmygod, Daddy you're like the best . . .' I lean over and kiss him and he hugs me.

'Mind Lucky, Daddy, and text me about how she is and stuff, won't you?'

'I will, I promise. And I'll email you as well with regular updates, how about that?'

'Brilliant.' I stroke Lucky, who's sound asleep on the front seat. 'I can't wait till next Friday, bye Dad.'

'Bye hon,' he says.

I run in to tell Ben all about Lucky and I think what a good name it is for a kitten.

By next Friday I can't wait to see Lucky. I don't want to ask Mammy straight out if she's allowing us to go to Daddy's for the weekend but then he texts me and says I'll pick you up for karate tonight and I think then that they've sorted something out. And then when I get home from school Mammy is all dressed up – I mean she looks fabulous, like really glam, and I smell her Chanel and her lovely red bag is in the hallway. She's going away for the weekend to some castle in Mayo with my auntie Sarah. That's all she says.

Ben has a big pussy face on him and I think it's the karate. After dinner Daddy beeps and we kiss Mammy goodbye and I fly out to the car but he's left Lucky at home.

He bought a karate suit, Daddy did, and it's mortifying. It's the longest class of my life and I hate him all over again, even if he did give me Lucky. Leah is smirking when Daddy and John are sparring and I catch her grinning at Darren Tierney and his friend Josh. I go ten shades of bright red and I add Leah to my hate list. Bitch, fucking bitch. Daddy is taking up the whole class and I can't bear it and I run in to the toilet. I sit in a cubicle, pinching my arm through my thick karate suit. I roll up the sleeve and scrape the skin on my arm until long streaks of blood appear. Then I pinch where I just scraped, holding my arm out so the blood doesn't get on my suit. It's hard to get blood out of a karate suit.

Leah knocks on the door and I jump.

'Jane, are you OK?'

'What do you care?'

'I'm just asking. If you want to be in a mood that's fine.'

'I want to be in a mood. Goodbye.'

'Suit yourself. I don't know why I'm friends with you, you're so moody.'

'So are you,' I say, but she just leaves. I sit there for a minute and then I wipe my arm with some toilet paper and I go back to class. I see Ben's face in the back of the room as I come in. He barely looks at me and then drops his eyes, even when the instructor is talking to his group. Daddy is sitting down on the floor, his back to the mirror, legs crossed. How gross is that? I manage to survive the rest of the class and I don't even say goodbye to Leah, don't even look at her as I leave.

I swear Lucky is bigger already! Ben loves her and the minute I see her I forget about the karate. And it's so funny because she'll only sleep in Daddy's shoe and we all laugh at this and it looks so cute. Her tiny little head curled into her body in Daddy's shoe.

On Saturday we go to the pet shop in Fox's Bow and we buy her a kitty basket and the cutest little pink collar with a tiny bell on it and worm tablets and a bright pink bowl. But Lucky doesn't like her basket, she wants Daddy's shoe so he lets her sleep in there.

On Sunday afternoon Mammy rings Daddy. I know it's her by the way his voice goes, and he takes the phone into the kitchen but the flat is so tiny we can hear everything. He's not mad though or anything. He keeps saying into the phone no problem, don't worry about it, and I stroke Lucky and I think maybe things are getting better since Lucky came. He comes back into the sitting room.

'Mam's been delayed, kids, so you're staying here another night,' he says, smiling at us.

'We can't – what about our uniforms? And I need my PE gear for tomorrow,' says Ben.

I'm hoping we don't have to go to school so that I can spend another whole day with Lucky.

'Mam says Jane has a key, so we'll drive over and get your clothes and stuff. And I'll make special lunches, anything you want.'

All of this is a first but we go and get our clothes and Daddy makes sausage sandwiches for lunch and two Actimels each and a bag of pistachios. Ben falls asleep on the couch and Daddy lifts him into his bed and I'm just going to bed when Daddy's phone rings. I think it's 'Hon', she always rings when she thinks we've gone to bed, but it's not.

'Hello? Ali, is that you? What on earth is the matter? Where are you?'

He pauses and looks over at me. 'I'll be right there, Janie will be fine on her own for a little while, right Jane?'

Four

Alison

'I planned the Pope's death, Ali. Planned it all. Arrive on Friday and sure enough he pops his clogs on Saturday and then hey presto I orchestrate the invasion of the two million mourning Catholics and I do it all to make it a crap weekend for us. Total logic.'

Brian is sitting on the edge of the couch, a bottle of Miller in his hand. I think he's slightly drunk. I see empty beer bottles on the coffee table. He's grinning at me, in a kind of half-pissed, sarcastic way.

'You've had too many beers, Brian. Go to bed,' I say, 'we'll talk in the morning.'

He laughs. 'Famous last words, Alison. We never talk. We never fucking talk, we never have sex, we never communicate on any level, do you know that?'

'There's no need to shout, you'll wake the children.'

'There's every fucking reason to shout, Ali. If I shout then there's some chance you might hear . . .'

'Oh, it's all my fault is it? The lack of communication? None of it is down to you?'

He takes a long swig of beer. 'At least I try.'

I borrow his sarcastic little laugh. 'Right. Heave the old boner into my back at night and if I respond then we're communicating? Lovely.'

He looks at me and pushes a hand through his hair. 'You need help.'

'Yeah. I could do with a cleaner.'

He bends his head and picks at the label on his beer, then he looks at me.

'Ali, please. Rome was . . . I thought it would help. A weekend on our own and you've always said you wanted to go . . .' he hangs his head exactly like Peter and I feel momentarily sorry for him.

'I can't believe we're having this argument again. It was months ago. But OK, let's have it out. Rome was hell, Brian. I'm sorry, but it was hell. And it wasn't just the crowds. You didn't listen to me when I told you I didn't want to go, I didn't want to leave the house. I told you that.'

I look at him now and all the hurt and resentment of that raw spring weekend comes back. My fear of leaving home, of travelling, of arriving. My fear of the strange city, the smells, the noise. And then the icing on the cake, crowds and crowds of people, panic attacks as I'm being moved by seas of people. The chanting and praying that you could hear from our hotel room. The prison that that room became. And Brian and his sad, lost face.

'I just thought . . .' he stops and his face registers my anger.

'You just thought you knew what was good for me. Like everybody else you knew. You talk about communicating, then why didn't you hear me when I said over and over I didn't want to go?'

He doesn't answer.

'I wanted to go to Rome before Jack was . . . before he . . .'

He looks up at me, tears in his eyes. 'Say it, Ali. For fuck's sake can't you just say it? Before Jack died. Before he died.'

A fist of black anger chokes me. 'Did you learn that in therapy, Brian? How to be . . . "honest" with yourself? How to say it out loud and clear for the whole world to hear? How can you buy into such bullshit?'

He looks at me like I hit him.

'I will say it, Brian. But it's not what you want to hear. There's before and after. And after is hell. And after changes everything.'

He shakes the last drops of beer in the bottle and doesn't look at me when he speaks.

'I lost him too, Ali.'

I blink back tears. 'And I don't want a camper van, either, Brian. I don't want to play happy families next summer, running around Europe. It'll be Rome all over again. Don't you understand that?'

'Did you hear me? I lost him too. You don't have a monopoly on hurt, Ali.'

I bite my lip hard. 'Did you hear me Brian? I don't want a fucking camper van.'

He shrugs. 'It's not for you. Leah and Peter will love it.'

I laugh. 'You don't know your children. You never did.'

I watch as this last dig finds home. It makes me feel stronger. More in control.

'Goodnight, Ali.' He lines up the bottle with the others on the table and walks out of the room.

I sit for a few minutes, watching the picture on the TV. The sound is turned down but I know the movie. *Eternal Sunshine of the Spotless Mind.* I watch the flickering pictures, the actors mouthing their lines, and I try to guess what they're saying. And then I wonder how that fight bloody started in the first place. The camper van. It started with the camper van and his cool announcement that he'd just bought one on eBay. Or maybe it started way before that. Before Rome. Before Jack even?

I wake up during the night. It's pitch dark. I'm on my own in our bed and my heart thumps in my chest. And then I hear a noise on the landing and I remember that Jane is sleepwalking and I jump out of bed.

She's standing looking over the banisters, down into the hall below. The bathroom door is half-open and a path of light spills on to the landing. I walk slowly towards her, afraid to startle her. Only when I'm beside her and holding her by the shoulders do I say her name.

'Jane,' I whisper.

She keeps peering down like she's looking for somebody. She leans over another fraction.

'Jane,' I say again and pull her back a little by the arm. She winces and lets out a groan, like she's hurt.

I turn her around and steer her towards Leah's room. Her eyes are unseeing and she seems so small and vulnerable as I gently push her by the shoulders. I get her as far as the bed. The room is lit by a small Simpsons table lamp. I ease her into bed, sitting her down first, then lifting her legs in and then her arms. She winces again when I touch her arm. I ease up the sleeve of her pyjamas.

'Oh Jane,' I whisper when I see the cuts, a row of red stripes on snow-white skin.

I try to talk to her the next morning but I know even as I'm trying that it's not going to work. I look at her as she smiles and eats her cereal and talks to Leah and I know she's in trouble. I don't know how or what or why. Just that she is.

Brian doesn't come home for dinner. His phone rings out and then I decide to hell with him. He gets communication – what he's presumably been looking for – and he can't handle it at all.

Leah, Jane and I sit down to eat. Chicken and roast potatoes but it tastes like shit. The doorbell rings just as we finish. I go to answer and Dermot Harris stands there with a kitten in his arms. He puts his fingers to his lips and winks at me and I usher him into the hall. I'm struck once again by how handsome he looks in a long, black overcoat and grey silk scarf. He looks like a film star, somebody who's just too good-looking to be from Limerick.

Jane's face is an absolute picture and I suddenly start crying when I see her delight. Dermot takes my arm and brings me into the living room. I sit on the couch, and he sits right beside me, opening his coat as he does so. Close up his face looks so smooth that I want to reach out and touch it. His features are unbelievably regular, in perfect proportion, nothing out of place.

'Ali, are you OK? What's up?' He looks into my eyes, his face full of concern.

I shake my head. 'Nothing. Everything.' I smile through my tears.

He reaches out and holds my hand and I know it's not meant to be sexual, not at all, but it sends waves of something that vaguely reminds me of sex through my body.

'Come on. Sometimes it helps to talk to a stranger, if you know what I mean.'

'We had a fight last night. Brian bought a camper van on eBay . . .'

'What?' says Dermot and I'm delighted with his horrified reaction.

'Yeah. Never even mentioned it before . . .'

'They're fifty grand at least!'

I shrug. 'Anyway it was just a silly fight and he never came home for dinner.'

'He's probably just taking some time out. Cooling off a little. It'll be fine,' he says and then he hugs me to him in a tight bear hug, a man hug, and my face brushes his for a second and I pull away. He smiles at me, white, perfect, even teeth.

'OK now?' he says.

I nod.

He stands up. 'Listen, Ali, we should exchange phone numbers, you know, with the children and stuff, you'd never know . . .'

'Of course. You're right. Hang on, I'll get my phone.' I go back into the kitchen and find my phone. He's standing in the hallway when I come back out. His coat is buttoned. I don't want him to go.

'I'm sorry about last week . . . the dinner . . . Brian . . .'

'Don't be, Ali. He had a point. I'm seriously considering letting Jane go skiing, that's if the invite's still good?'

'Of course. Em . . . Jane . . .'

I try to find the right words.

'What, Ali? It is OK isn't it? I thought it over and, well, all things considered I think it would be great for her.'

I look at him and smile tentatively. He steps back a little and fixes his scarf.

'No, that's fine. It's just, well . . . she sleepwalks . . . do you know that?'

His voice is quiet and steady as he answers. 'Of course I know. She's doing that for a while now. It's no big deal and we've been told not to make it into one.'

'There are marks on her arm . . .'

He looks at me intently. 'What do you mean?'

'There are cuts on her arm. I saw them last night when I put her back to bed. She was sleepwalking.'

He steps back a little and stands up straight. 'What exactly are you getting at?'

'It's just she has these cuts – scratches, on her arm . . . and, well . . .'

He stares at me now, waiting expectantly for me to finish.

'And I was wondering what happened?'

'Did you think to ask Jane?'

'No . . . I didn't . . . no.'

'Well, I'm sure there's a perfectly logical explanation.'

'I'm sure there is.'

'She probably did it while she was sleepwalking. It happens all the time with them. They hurt themselves and don't even realise it. That's the big danger really.'

I nod and smile at him. He smiles back.

'Anyway, here's my number, Ali,' he says then, 'I'll put it in for you.'

I hand him my phone.

'Thanks for last week. For being so understanding,' he says without taking his eyes from the phone.

'No problem.'

'You're terrific,' he says, holding out the phone to me. I take it and he bends down and quickly brushes his lips against mine.

'Jane,' he calls, still smiling at me. The even-toothed smile, white against the grey silk scarf. And then they're gone in a blur of man and girl and kitten and I stand in the hallway, my bum against the warm radiator, arms wrapped around my chest.

'When is Dad coming home?' Leah asks. She's standing in the kitchen doorway, eyes narrowed. I wonder for a second if she's seen the kiss and misinterpreted it. Then I think she couldn't have.

'I don't know,' I reply.

'Are you like fighting or something?'

I know I should answer her. I know that Brian had a point about not communicating last night and that the less you do of it the harder it becomes. I know that Leah is older now, that she's hurting too, that I should talk to her. I also know that I won't.

'No,' I say and smile at her.

She stares at me and runs up to her room, pounding the steps really hard as she moves. I shut my eyes in the hallway, waiting for the crash of her bedroom door.

'Jack, I know you're there. I can see you.'

No answer. There's a shape like Jack sitting on a low stone wall, right in front of me. A shape like him, and a feeling of him, but every time I reach out my hand the shape dissolves into tiny pixels. Into nothing.

'Jack, please, where are you? Jack, don't. Don't do that, don't go. I just want . . . I just want to see you, that's all. See your face.'

It's Monday morning and I've slept badly and it's wet and the house is a silent tomb. Everybody's gone to work or school. My day stretches out in front of me like a series of impossible tasks. Write a few hundred words. Entertain my brother if he decides to bestow a visit on me. Clean up. Make the tomb into a proper home. Go see Mammy with my pregnant, happy sister. Make dinner. Talk to my husband, my children. Ring my friends who've all but given up on me. I'm tired already just thinking about it all. I half-heartedly pick up a cloth and begin to wipe down the worktop and a tiny voice in my head starts up a little chant. Go on, do it, what harm are you doing? You're not hurting a soul. I scrub the sink with all my might, sweat breaking out on my forehead. Go on, it's Monday. The beginning of another long week. Follow her this time. Just follow her, you don't have to make your presence known. Go on, it helps doesn't it? Helps more than Richard? More than Brian?

I check the clock. If Richard is coming he'll be here in half an hour. That decides me.

She has her children in a crèche. She drops them off every morning at the same time: 10.15 a.m. rain, hail or shine. Sometimes they cry, they're just babies, blonde and chubby cheeked and designer labelled. She drives a red Peugeot. She parks the car near the crèche and walks to work – an auctioneer's office in the city centre. This morning I just miss seeing her with the children and I'm glad. There's something desolate about it all. About the way she hands them over like little blonde packages to be collected at a later time. The Fed-Ex Mom. There's something about the way she walks away even if the baby cries, even if the little girl calls her over and over. Mommy, Mommy I want to go home. Her feet seem lighter as she turns on her heel, and heads off down O'Connell Street. She's almost skipping by the time she goes into work. Today she wears a red suit, a bright scarlet suit with matching red shoes. It should look loud but it's lovely on her.

I sit outside a coffee shop across the road and wait. It's cold but I wear my long wool coat and a scarf pulled tightly around my neck. Bits of last night come back to me. Brian arriving home, sleeping in Peter's room, not even saying hello or goodnight. Leah and her silence, like I'd done something wrong. Peter, as happy as a sandboy, having spent the whole day with his dad, his innocent non-stop chatter a relief in the silent house. And a half-dream of Jack and the gnawing tormenting hunger to see his face.

I can see her outline through the office window, which faces directly on to the street, her red-suited body busy already, answering phones and giggling with another auctioneer, who leans lazily against her desk.

I order a coffee and sip the hot liquid, but I can't taste anything. I feel like I've been drinking all night and am suffering the mother of all hangovers. Maybe you can have other kinds of hangovers, emotional hangovers, Jack hangovers.

She stands up then and picks up a package and her handbag and comes out into the cold, wet street. I throw five euro on the metal table and follow her red-coated figure.

First she drops off a package to a solicitors' office in Glentworth Street and then we end up in Fenn Wright Manson.

I root through the clothes on a rack and she talks to a shop assistant about an upcoming wedding. She goes into the dressing room with an armful of clothes and while she's in there I have an idea. I leave the shop and run back up to her office. I glance quickly at the houses for sale and pick one at random, a semi near the maternity hospital. There's a glossy brochure with a colour picture of the house and I take this to the receptionist.

'I'd like to view this house, please,' I say and smile at the neat blonde girl.

'Of course. When would suit?'

'As soon as possible would be great. I'm in Limerick for the morning and don't have much time.'

'No problem. You could see it now if you like – Tom Rourke is free.'

I smile at her and my voice shakes a little as I speak. 'Look, I hope you don't mind but I'd really prefer to view it with a woman auctioneer – I had a bad experience years ago and I've never quite gotten over it.'

Immediately I see the flaw in my plan. There are probably more women auctioneers in the office than her. I am also shocked now at the brazenness of it all. At the cheek of it, pushing it further and further every week.

'I'll check the diary and try to sort something out,' she says.

I nod. 'That'd be great,' I say, trying to think of a way out.

'I think Laura Culhane is free. I'll just give her a quick ring on her mobile.'

My heart thumps at the sound of the name. At it's absolute ordinary everyday sound. Laura Culhane.

The receptionist is talking on the phone and I can picture Laura in the changing room in Fenn Wright Manson, in her bra and knickers, phone to her ear.

The girl hangs up and smiles at me. 'Twelve midday, how is that?'

'Perfect.'

'There's a map on the back of the brochure and I'll give you Laura's – that's the auctioneer's name – mobile just in case.' She scribbles something on a Post-it and I take it and smile and murmur thanks and am back out in the street gulping air like it's being rationed. She comes flying after me.

'Excuse me? Would you mind giving me your mobile too? Just in case there's any delays – you know what the traffic is like in town these days.'

'Of course,' I say, my face going bright red.

She hands me a biro and some headed paper. I look at the blank page and consider giving a wrong number but the antici-pation of her ringing me wins out. I lean the page against the wall and scribble down my number before I can change my mind.

I'm early so I wait in my car, with the radio tuned to some talk show that I can't follow. I've parked down the road, a little away from the house. My head feels strange and I feel faint. Her number is stuck on the dashboard, daring me to ring it. I close my eyes and consider just driving away and suddenly there she is, pulling up outside the house in a shiny red car. She climbs out of her car, surveying the house with its giant for sale sign in the front garden like as if she's gathering her thoughts before launching into auctioneer mode. Her hair is shoulder length, fair but expensively highlighted. She's not particularly pretty, but is very well presented.

Her phone rings and she roots in a lovely soft leather bag and holds the phone to her ear. I watch as she chats and laughs, her eyes scanning all the time, looking for her prospective purchaser. A tiny part of me wants to get out, brazen as you like, and just present myself. Her gaze, as she continues to speak on the phone, rests on my car. I turn sideways, fiddling with the dash and when I look up she's closed her phone and is checking her watch.

She turns and walks up the cobbled path to a green front door with stained-glass lights. I can hear keys jangling in her hands and then she disappears inside the house. My heart is pumping loud now and a thrill races through my body. Three minutes. Five minutes. Seven minutes. When my phone rings I jump and give out a tiny scream. I look at my bag on the floor like it has a time bomb in it. The ringtone gets louder and I lean down and root for it. I hold the vibrating phone in my hand, resisting the urge to answer it. Her number flashes on the dial. The ringing stops. Then starts all over again. I throw the phone on the passenger seat, afraid that I might answer it. It rings out. I check the house. She's still in there. Then the phone beeps a message. I laugh out loud and pick up the phone and read the message. *You have one new voice message in your mailbox.* I dial the service and her voice is in my ear. Light and happy and bubbly. *Hi. Laura Culhane here from Johnson Burke Auctioneers. We had an appointment at twelve to view a property in Farranshone. Em . . . I was wondering if you might ring me at 087 23121256? Thanks.*

I throw the phone back down on the passenger seat, my breathing ragged now from excitement. Then I see her coming out of the house, standing at the doorway, looking up and down the street. She checks her watch again. Checks her phone. Pulls the door behind her. Another glance at her watch. Another glance at her phone. She folds her arms and I can't see her legs but I imagine she's tapping her toe. I can see impatience in her face, her mouth drawn in a tight line. She puts the phone to her ear again and my phone rings. On the seat, moving around as it vibrates. I let it ring out. She marches down the path, phone still to her ear and mine starts the ringing all over again. It rings and rings as she climbs into her car. Then it stops as she pulls away. I duck down as she passes me.

Every part of my body is shaking now and I lift my head and see the yellow Post-it with her number on the dashboard, the nodding dog just above it, and for some unknown reason I laugh out loud. Laugh so hard that tears stream down my face. My phone rings intermittently the whole way home. Laura Culhane does not give up easily.

Brian's car is in the drive when I get home.

'Where were you?' he asks as I hang up my coat in the hallway.

'A guard wouldn't ask me that,' I say and walk past him into the kitchen.

'I've been trying to reach you on your mobile, so has Peter's school.'

A pain squeezes my heart. 'Why? What's wrong with Peter?' I ask, my voice a whisper.

'He's fine. He's up in bed. He feels pukey and the school couldn't get you on your phone.'

'I didn't hear it ring.'

'I left three messages, Ali.'

I take a deep breath. 'I'm going to check on Pete.'

I climb the stairs and go into Peter's darkened room. He's asleep and I sit by the bed and stroke his head. A bright yellow basin, known as the puking basin, is on the floor beside him. He opens his eyes and smiles weakly at me.

'Mam,' he says.

'Petey, how're you feeling, sweetheart?' I ask but he's asleep again. I hear the soft thud of the front door as Brian leaves to return to work. I feel Peter's forehead and then kiss him softly on the cheek. I pad out of the room and stand like somebody lost on the landing.

And then before I can even think about it I open the door to Jack's bedroom. It's been weeks, and I sit on his bed, holding a pillow to my face, burying myself in his smell. And with the smell come the tears, like Pavlov's dogs and I cry into the pillow. Silent crying, so Peter doesn't hear. I force myself to stop, wiping my eyes with the edge of the pillowcase. I look around his room, untouched since that day. The poster of Jessica Alba, which we fought over and of course Jack won, still on the wall. His rights were far more important than how his sister and brother would take images of half-naked women on his wall and what the hell would they be doing in his room anyway? I smile up at Jessica Alba. She's a familiar face to me now. Almost a friend.

On another wall the Red Hot Chili Peppers watch me like an intruder. I walk to his chest of drawers and finger the objects on it. I feel like the little servant girl in *Girl with a Pearl Earring* when she enters Vermeer's studio. Everything is exact and has an exact position and I am vigilant in the way I observe this. I pick up a photograph of Jack with his best friend Tommy Danaher. They were both about six or seven when it was taken. Front teeth missing, heads shaved like David Beckham, Tommy grinning, Jack almost smiling. I close my eyes tight as my heart squeezes again in that pain like no other. And there he is in front of me, a beautiful small boy.

His face is thinner than the Halloween of Batman and the cowboy hat. His eyes are browner though. He stands in the hallway in his underpants, skinny little legs on soft green carpet. The door of his room is open. The walls are painted a rich yellow, the colour of the sun, and they glow light into the windowless hall.

'I won't go, I hate him,' he says and crosses his arms on his bare, narrow chest.

'But it's his birthday and you like Tommy, you always play with him at school,' I say. Jack's sister is crying in another bedroom and Jack is making me really mad.

'Get dressed, you're going and that's final. You told him already that you'd go, so you must now.'

He stares at me with those big eyes. I think he's going to cry. I look down and see he's wetting himself. A stain appears on his underpants and urine is dribbling down his legs towards the carpet. It forms a little puddle on the floor before it soaks into the carpet, turning it black.

'Jack, it's all right, you don't have to go. I'll ring Tommy's Mom, how's that?' I say.

But I'm really mad at him too. I know he has beaten me. He has won and his brown eyes tell me that he knows too. He walks into his sunny bedroom and I stare at the stain on the carpet. Sometimes I don't like Jack, not one bit.

I open my eyes. I feel faint and realise that I'm hungry. I fix the pillows on his bed and stand in the middle of his room, eyes still watching from the walls, and breathe in the smell one last time. Then I look at his wardrobe and I just can't resist. I can't resist the smell of him, stronger in here, where his clothes are. Boy smell: socks, sweat, Lynx and hair gel. I stroke his clothes, hold them in my hands, feeling them gently like precious silks.

A newish tracksuit bought on a lovely, warm Saturday. A grey sweatshirt with his smell so strong that it makes me gasp and tears come to my eyes. I run my hands over his things and it's as if I'm rummaging though the rooms of his short life. His football jersey, his karate suit, a too-small pair of Simpsons pyjamas. Why hadn't I ever given those to Peter? I bang the wardrobe door with my fist and something slips out. His hurley. There's his name in indelible marker, *Jack Collins*, *Abbey Sarsfields*. I take it in my hands and rub the smooth wood of the boss. There are grass stains on it.

'Mam, I'm home.'

Leah's voice invades the house and I shove the hurley back in the wardrobe quickly and close the door.

'Jack's my favourite. Why don't you ever bring him to see me?' my mother says. She's sitting in a chair in the sunny nursing home sitting room. It's Thursday afternoon and outside the window peacocks roam up and down a gravel path.

My sister reaches out and takes my hand.

'Take no notice,' she whispers.

'I know,' I whisper back.

'There's always a favourite, do you know that?' my mother says, looking intently at me.

We nod in unison.

'Richard is special. Ever since he was a little boy. And Jack is so like him. Why did you only have one child?' she asks me.

I have a sudden urge to slap her across the face but I tell myself that she can't help it. That it's Alzheimer's and she doesn't really know what she's saying. But if that's true then how can she twist the knife so expertly? Better even than when she was of sound mind.

'My baby is due in a few weeks, Mam, remember I told you all about it?' says Rachel.

Mam looks blankly at her and laughs. 'Do Mama and Dada know?'

I roll my eyes but Rachel persists. 'I'm Rachel, Mammy, your youngest daughter. I'm married to Donal and we're going to have a baby.'

'I want to go home to Mama and Dada. Will you bring me?' she says.

We don't answer.

'Jack would bring me. If you let Jack come he'd bring me

home.' She looks straight at me as she speaks and at that moment I would bet my life that she knows exactly what she's doing. The only grandchild she ever talks about is Jack. I watch two peacocks in the garden, pecking at the ground, and I wonder how they ever ended up in a nursing home in Limerick. Rachel continues her pursuit of civilised normal conversation with a woman who frankly isn't around anymore.

'Leah is in sixth class now and Peter is in third, isn't that right, Ali?' Rachel says.

I nod and smile and my mother looks completely baffled.

'And Leah will be going into first year next September, time flies, doesn't it? She can't wait for her new cousin to be born, she loves babies,' Rachel persists.

I watch a woman in an armchair near us. She mumbles away to herself non-stop, and even laughs now and again and I think first how awful it is and then I think maybe it's a grand way to be. Oblivious. Ignorant. I feel suddenly claustrophobic and the air thins and I can't seem to get enough of it into my lungs. I calm myself and gulp air. Rachel's voice continues its one-sided conversation. 'I must bring you in your warm purple cardigan, it's getting quite cold now. Christmas is only around the corner.'

'Have you got a car with you?' Mam says, looking at me.

I shake my head.

'How did you get here so? Do you think I'm stupid?' She glares at me and turns away in a huff, throwing me filthy looks. Tears spring to my eyes and I feel like a small girl again, and the worst thing in the world is Mammy's disapproval. Rachel seems to know and reaches out her hand and squeezes mine and tears escape and run down my face.

Mam looks at me, eyes narrowed. 'You were always a little bitch,' she says, her voice venomous.

A hard knot of anger mixed with self-preservation begins to form in the pit of my stomach. 'Is that right?' I say.

'You never cared about anyone when we were growing up. Mama always said you were selfish.'

'Mama was right as usual . . .' I say but Rachel interrupts.

'Ali, leave it . . . she doesn't know what she's saying, she thinks now that you're her sister . . .'

'You're wrong, Rachel. She knows exactly what she's saying. All that stuff about Jack? She knows.'

'Ali, look at me, she hasn't a clue. You know that.'

Rachel's face is earnest and full of concern. My baby sister, who's having a baby and none of her family are remotely interested.

'I'm sorry,' I say.

'For what?'

Mam glares at both of us now and I glare back at her.

'For not being there.'

She grips my hand again. 'I'm sorry too, Ali. Because really, I haven't been there for you, when Jack . . .'

I turn away and look at the mumbling woman near us.

'Where are Mama and Dada?' Mam says, her voice rising. She has an expression on her face that makes her look like a complete stranger.

'Now, Mam, calm down,' says Rachel, stroking her arm.

She turns on Rachel and pushes her arm away, almost knocking her off the chair.

'Where are Mama and Dada? Why won't you two bitches tell me?'

'They're dead, how's that? Dead and gone a long time ago. Happy now?' I say.

The mumbling woman looks over at us and a nurse comes

out of nowhere. 'Would you like a cup of tea and a nice scone, Helen?' she says to Mam.

I get up and leave the room. I sit outside on a bench in the cold November evening. The peacocks look out of place, their exotic plumes garish and almost vulgar in the dull light.

'You're Helen's daughter, aren't you?'

I almost jump with fright as a nurse in a blue, quilted jacket sits down beside me.

'I was would be a better description,' I say.

She's my age, maybe a little older, with short no-nonsense hair and a lovely smile. She laughs and takes out a box of cigarettes. Marlboro Lights.

'Want one?' she asks, offering me the open box. I take one, even though I haven't smoked in years. We both light up, swirls of smoke rising in the still cold night.

'Jesus, I'd forgotten how good it feels,' I say, inhaling deeply. The smoke is like a drug, making me dizzy and almost giddy.

'I've tried a hundred times to stop but there's always a good reason not to,' she says.

'I know what you mean.'

'You're Jack's mam, aren't you?'

I look at her. 'How do you . . . how did you know Jack?'

She laughs softly. 'He used to drop in here the odd time, just call in out of the blue to see his nana. My God, she loved him, didn't she?'

'He . . . I didn't know that. I didn't know that he called like that.'

She pulls hard on her cigarette, the way only seasoned smokers can. 'He was lovely. The last time was last Christmas Eve. He came in the morning and spent ages here and all the nurses said it about him, the way he could spend so much time with her. And then we heard . . . we heard what happened.'

I flick my cigarette away and watch it glow before it dies altogether.

'He had the exact same brown eyes as his nana and the very same smile.'

'His memory was better though,' I say, wanting the conversation to be over.

She looks at me, not knowing how to react. 'It must be hard for you.'

I look at the peacock, strutting around, pecking at the hard winter ground. There's a tree in front of us, its branches gnarled and bare and dead looking. I can hear the rush of the river nearby.

'Will I leave you a cigarette or two for later?' she says as she stands up to leave.

'No, thanks. I'm fine.'

She pats me on the shoulder before she walks away.

My phone rings in my bag and I let it ring out and then have second thoughts and check to see if it's one of the children. Dermot Harris has left a message. How he'd been thinking about me today for some reason and how he'd rung just to make sure I'm OK. It makes me feel good, his concern, so I send him a text thanking him. He replies immediately and the contact somehow makes me smile.

Rachel finally comes out and finds me in the garden. She sits beside me, her coat buttoned up to her chin, an aqua-coloured scarf wrapped around her neck.

'Why do people sleepwalk?' I ask.

'It depends.'

'How about if a child starts to do it? To sleepwalk?'

She shrugs. 'It's probably symptomatic of some kind of major disturbance in her life.'

I nod and crunch the gravel with the heel of my boot.

'There are things you can do, Ali. Sleep clinics, psychologists, I can give you some numbers . . .'

I laugh. 'It's not for me or my kids.'

'Who, then?'

'A little girl. Leah's friend. And she has these cuts – marks – on her arms and . . .'

Rachel waits for me to continue.

I stand up and stamp my feet. They're beginning to numb in the cold. 'Let's go, it's freezing.'

'No. Tell me about Leah's friend – the marks – that could be self-harming – another sign that she's terribly upset . . .'

I look at Rachel and laugh. 'You think I'm talking about Leah, don't you?'

Rachel takes my icy hand in her gloved one. 'How about we go for a drink and a chat, Ali? God, we deserve a drink after putting up with Mam.'

'The last thing I or my children need is bullshit therapy – we've heard it all at this stage, so please, Rachel, spare me.'

I see her soft, hurt face and wish I hadn't said it. Poor Rachel.

I smile. 'I'm sorry, Rache, I know you're trying to help but . . . look I have to get home, Peter has soccer training tonight and . . .' I say but it's a lie.

She stands up, her bump neat and tidy under her wool coat.

'Maybe next week?' I say. 'Next week is fairly quiet and Brian will be around. We can have a chat and . . .'

Rachel nods but I see the questions in her eyes and I feel bad, like I'm doing something terrible to her. We walk in silence to our cars.

Brian arrives home on Sunday morning with the camper van. The kids are excited and I go and watch as they examine every inch of it. They open the cupboards in the miniature kitchen and ooh and aah and fight over the bunk bed that's only inches from the roof of the van. Brian is like a child at Christmas, beaming and summoning passing neighbours to come and have a look.

'Come on, Mam,' Peter says, climbing down the steps, 'sit up front, it's fabulous.'

I smile but make no attempt to move. He grabs my hand and pulls me towards the van door. I climb into the passenger seat, beside Brian.

'Let's go for a spin,' Brian says and the children scream from the back.

'Let's go, can we like sit back here?' says Leah.

'Sure, close the doors and off we go. Does Barcelona sound OK?' Brian says and the kids scream louder.

'Yippee! Barcelona!' shouts Peter.

I want to get out. A replica Eiffel Tower swings from the mirror and the dashboard is covered in stickers from different cities and countries: Paris, Milan, Belgium, Rome. Brian starts the engine and it shudders noisily and then the whole van vibrates to life. He reverses slowly down the wide gravel drive and out the wide gate and all the time I want to get out, and I think about just opening the door and jumping and my breathing starts to quicken and I'm back on the plane to Rome, my lungs about to burst from lack of air, my head pounding with blinding white pain.

'I want to . . . Jesus Christ, Brian, what was that?' I say as the van thuds against something on the road. 'Stop the fucking van, we've hit something,' I scream, searching for the handbrake.

Brian stops the van and jumps out and I follow. First I think maybe I imagined it, maybe it was just a bump on the road, a piece of debris but it had been a sickening thud of something alive, something with flesh and skin and bones. Leah sees it first and screams 'Daddy, look what we did.'

My heart is pounding and I don't want to look, I want to press a button and rewind. Just a few minutes of a rewind. The length of a song.

'Christ, where did he come from?' says Brian and I feel faint. Already I see him in my head, a chubby toddler out playing on a Sunday morning, his belly full of Coco Pops. He never sees the van coming out of the drive, he just keeps running past, his little world all safe and happy and good.

'Who owns him?' Peter says.

'I don't know, he doesn't have a collar on,' says Brian.

Collar. I hear the word collar and my dreamt-up toddler disintegrates in my head and I look and see the lifeless body of a small, brown dog. The street is Sunday morning quiet, the only noise is the humming of generators from the Travellers' encampment at the top of the road.

I bend down to look at the dog, and at the same time so does Brian. Our heads clash and I suddenly feel a burst of anger at this man with his fucking camper van and his trips to Rome and his midnight erections.

'Be careful, you've caused enough damage already.' I examine the lifeless little body under the back wheel of the van. His eyes are closed but a tiny pink tongue peeps out of his mouth. There's a small smear of blood on the tarmac beside him.

'Is it Butler's dog?' asks Peter.

'Oh fuck,' Brian says. 'Is he dead? He might just be stunned.'

Peter snorts with laughter. Leah is crying.

'Reverse the van,' I say and I stand up and brush dust from my trousers. 'Think you can manage that much?'

He doesn't answer, just gets in the van and pulls it back a bit so that the dog's small brown body is exposed.

'It's not Butler's anyway, at least that's something,' says Brian.

I glare at him and notice then a boy and a little girl approaching us from the caravans.

'Uh oh,' says Peter, 'worse than the Butlers, it's the knackers.'

I narrow my eyes at Peter. 'Travellers, Peter,' I say, 'that's what they like to be called.'

The street is still and empty except for the sound of their footsteps as they approach. And then the boy – the dark-haired one that I think I saw in the woods – starts howling. Just looks at the dog on the road and throws his head back and howls like an animal. Peter slinks behind me.

The little girl is really pretty. She doesn't look like one of them at all, not really. Her hair is a mass of tiny curls, hanging to her shoulders, which are bare and skinny in a small halter-neck summer top. She's about seven years old and has the most gorgeous pair of blue eyes.

'I'm sorry. Jesus, I didn't see him, I'm really sorry . . .' Brian stands there, explaining.

'Is Joe Mac dead?' the little girl says. The boy is still howling.

Brian nods. 'I'm so sorry. Is that his name?'

She looks at Brian, curls falling softly over an exquisite face. Her eyes are brimming with tears and some spill out and slip silently down her cheeks.

The howling boy kneels down and rubs the dead dog, and then lies on the tarmac beside him. 'Joe Mac, it's me, Frankie Ward. 'Mon Joey, let's go. Let's go, boy,' he pleads with the dog and I know the minute he speaks that he's mentally challenged.

He gets up suddenly and runs at Leah, who's nearest to him, and grabs her by the arm. She screams and Brian jumps at him and pushes him back to the ground.

'Don't!' I shout. 'Are you stupid? Can't you tell there's something wrong with him?'

Leah is crying and so is the boy.

'Come on Frankie, we'll bring Joe Mac home,' the small girl says.

Then she looks at Brian. 'Frankie's big but his head is small so Ma says I have to mind him. You can't push him like that.'

'I'm sorry . . . I didn't realise . . .'

'He wouldn't hurt a fly, Frankie wouldn't.'

'I'm sorry,' says Brian.

'Get the dog, Frankie.'

The boy gathers the limp body in his arms, tears and snot running freely down his face. He stands up and walks away, the little girl following.

'What a great morning's work,' I say to Brian, my voice tight. He looks at me and I realise he's crying.

'Ali, fuck yourself,' he says and walks away. Leah and Peter look at me. I go into the house and begin to clean up the kitchen, banging things as I do so.

Leah comes in and leans against the work top. 'Daddy's packing a suitcase.'

I don't answer, I just keep cleaning and banging. 'Did you hear me, Mam? Daddy's leaving.'

I ignore her and scrub and scrub and turn up the radio when I hear him talking to the kids in the hallway and then the slam of the front door and Leah's soft tears and then the slam of her bedroom door.

Dermot Harris sends me another text later on that night. The children are in bed and I'm sitting on the couch and the texting starts and I'm actually enjoying it. Funny, stupid stuff about what's on TV. Like a real-time running commentary. Eventually we text goodnight and I go upstairs to bed, checking on the children first. Peter is asleep, his duvet kicked off and his body flung across the bed. I cover him and kiss his soft hair. My baby. I go into Leah's room and see her bulk under her cream wool throw. She'd locked herself in her room for the day, refusing to talk to me after Brian left. I walk over to her bed and reach out to touch her head and realise that I'm touching something soft and pliable. A pillow. I pull down the throw and see pillows where Leah should be. Immediately my lungs constrict and I feel like my chest is going to explode.

I run out of the room and down the stairs and grab my phone. No reply from Brian. Bastard. I leave a message and then ring again immediately and repeat the process and then I wonder if should I ring the police. Or Richard. I dial a number and can't hear the phone ring my heart is thumping so hard and my breathing is erratic. He answers immediately.

'Dermot, Leah's gone,' I say and start to howl.

Five

Jane

I stay up when Daddy leaves and sit on the couch with Lucky, watching fuzzy telly. Ben is asleep but it's weird being on our own in the flat and I feel better with the noise of the telly. I wonder what's wrong with Mrs Collins and why she's ringing Daddy. I wonder this over and over as I watch the flickering screen and then I know it's pointless. It's like sometimes grown-ups do things and no matter how hard you try to work it out or find reasons there just aren't any. They do stuff and that's that.

Drunk people pass the window of the flat, singing and shouting and my heart thumps and Lucky wakes up on my lap. I turn up the telly a bit louder. I want to ring Daddy and tell him to come home. Instead I make toast and tea and wait for him to come back.

My phone rings suddenly and I say Jesus Christ and see Leah's name on the screen as I answer it.

'Leah?'

There's just crying on the other end.

'Leah, is that you?'

More sniffles.

'Jane? Where are you? I'm outside your house and all the lights are off and . . .'

'Outside the flat?'

'No. Outside your real house. Can I stay with you?'

'I'm in my dad's place. Leah, what's up?'

She's crying now.

'I left. I hate them, Jane, the two of them, so I left and I walked around for ages and then I kind of ended up here.'

'Your mam rang my dad and he's gone over to your house.'

'Why?'

'I don't know. To help look for you I suppose.'

'Can I come to the flat?'

'My dad won't have it. He'll tell.'

'I can hide in your room.'

'OK, but hurry – he'll be back soon.'

'Where's the flat?'

'Barrington Street, look . . . maybe you should just go home, Leah.'

Her breathing is raggy and I can hear tears in her voice. 'I know where Barrington Street is.'

'Leah . . .' I say but she's hung up.

The phone rings again and I answer straight away.

'Leah, please, it's too . . .'

'Jane, this is Alison Collins.'

'Oh. Hello, Mrs Collins.'

'Have you heard from Leah?'

'No.'

Silence.

'Are you sure?'

'Positive.'

'You said her name when you answered the phone. Look,

Jane, she's missing and it's important that you tell us where she is. Anything could happen her. It's late and . . .' She starts to cry.

I want to cry too but I bite the inside of my mouth hard. It tastes salty.

Then Daddy comes on the phone. 'Jane, tell me if you heard from Leah. The Guards are involved now, this isn't some little game, this is serious.'

'I haven't heard from her, Daddy.'

More silence. 'I'll be home in a little while, Jane.'

I wait and wait for Leah to come and I try to ring her but I've no credit left and then I think she's dead. Murdered by the drunk people or some psycho and is dead and covered in blood in a laneway near Barrington Street. It's cold in the flat but the night outside is quiet now. I can hear Daddy's alarm clock ticking and Lucky purring and I strain to hear the sound of Leah coming. I think every footstep is hers.

Then Ben is standing in the doorway and I scream in fright and he jumps and legs it into Daddy's room. I follow him and the smell of piss hits me straight away.

'You wet the bed, didn't you?' I say to his back. He's curled up in Daddy's bed, the duvet over his head. He doesn't answer. I go to the drawer in our room and pull out clean pyjama bottoms. The smell of piss is really strong in here. I pull off his bedclothes and dump them on the floor of the kitchen. Then I go into Daddy's room.

'Here. Put these on, Ben,' I say and leave them on the bed for him. 'It's OK,' I add as I leave the room.

I load the washing machine, still listening for Leah, and then I hear Daddy's key in the lock.

He comes into the kitchen and doesn't say hello or anything, just goes straight to the coffee pot and starts to fill it.

'Did you find Leah? Is she all right?' I ask. My bare feet are cold on the blue lino floor.

He bangs down the coffee pot and I jump a little.

Then he looks straight at me like he hates my guts. I want to pee.

'Do you care, Jane? Do you really care if we found her or not?'

'I . . . Leah is my best friend—'

'You lied on the phone. I'm not stupid. Ali told me that first you thought it was Leah.'

He looks at me and I hear the hiss of the coffee pot as it heats up. A siren sounds outside on the street. I drop my eyes and look at my bare feet on the lino and for some reason it reminds me of walking in the sea. Bare feet in ice-cold blue water.

'Jane, your mother is a liar. I'm trying hard to bring you up to be different to her. I'm obviously not succeeding. Ali knew you were lying on the phone. How dare you let me down like that.'

I start to cry and hate myself for it.

'Go to bed.'

'Is she . . . is Leah OK?

'I said go to bed.'

I leave the kitchen and go into my room. It still smells of piss. I climb into bed and it's freezing and my feet are numb. I check my phone to see if Leah has texted. Nothing. I burrow under the quilt, tears running down my face. I pinch my arms so hard that I let out a cry, so hard that the tears stop because the pain takes my breath away and fills my head and stops me from thinking about anything else except the pain.

He comes in later and I pretend to be asleep.

'She's at home. A squad car picked her up in William Street,' he says and closes the door as he leaves the room.

Mammy is cross. I come home from school on Thursday and Mammy is like pacing the floor and I ask what's wrong and she just says nothing, did you do your homework yet and I say in my head right here we go again.

Then Daddy rings me after tea.

'Hi Jane, how are things?'

'OK, Daddy.'

'Has Mam said anything to you?'

'About what?' I pick nail polish from my nails. Mulberry, that's the colour, but it chips easily.

'Well, I've had a few problems at work and well, I'm burnt out so I need to take some time, some me-time.'

I say nothing because I don't know what to say.

'Just a couple of weeks. You'll have to mind Lucky, Mam said it was OK.'

'Serious?'

Daddy laughs. 'Serious. I'll miss Ben's birthday, though. I'm very upset over that.'

I say nothing but all I can think about is Lucky coming here for a whole two weeks. I bet Mammy will love him.

'Anyway, is Ben around?'

'Yeah. I'll get him for you.'

'Thanks, Janie. And Hon?'

'Yeah?'

'I love you, you know that.'

'Yeah, hang on a sec.' I run into Ben's room and hand him the phone.

I go downstairs to make noodles and Mammy is in the kitchen, all dressed up. She looks fabulous, her hair is straightened and she's wearing a new beige suit. The skirt has a slit up the side and her boots are long and shiny and laced right up the whole way.

'You look nice, Mammy.'

She smiles and strokes my head. 'Thanks, Janie. Were you speaking to Daddy?'

I nod.

'He told you, so?'

I nod again.

'He's burnt out – needs some "me-time",' she smiles at me as she says this but it's like a sneer. 'Anyway. Sarah's in the living room, she's going to sit with you two. Bed by ten thirty, Janie, promise me?'

I smile at her and she hugs me. 'You're a good girl, Jane Harris,' she says into my hair. Then Ben comes into the kitchen and he's crying.

'What's wrong with you?' I say. He glares at me and goes to the fridge and opens the door and then bangs it closed. I hate him now, for being a little shit, especially when Mammy isn't mad anymore.

Mammy puts a hand on his shoulder. 'You'll see Daddy again in a couple of weeks.'

'It's the stupid fucking cat. Daddy's worn out from minding that stupid idiot.' He runs out of the room and I think he's gay. Always crying. Always.

In bed that night I wonder what burnt out looks like. Do your brains sizzle like sausages in a frying pan and if you don't do anything about it do you just turn into a pile of dust like on *Buffy*? And what makes you burnt out in the first place? Is it like one single thing or loads of things and will me-time fix it just like that? Like magic?

Mammy has another hot date on Friday night. She's had her hair cut and coloured and Sarah is coming to mind us for two nights because she's going to a party in Donegal. At karate

Leah begs me to sleep over – she's been out of school all week with a head cold and I haven't seen her since the running away thing. So I beg Mammy and it works but she makes me promise to come back early on Sunday for Ben's birthday.

We get a DVD and Mrs Collins orders pizza and lets us stay up really late and sleep on the couches in sleeping bags. Leah's had her hair cut too, all razored at the ends, really cool.

We cuddle up in our sleeping bags after the movie.

'I love your hair,' I say, as I pick at some pizza crust.

'That's like the tenth time you've said it, Jane.'

'I know. That'll tell you how much I like it.'

She looks at me, her brown eyes wide. 'Mam brought me as a treat.'

I laugh. 'I must try running away. I wouldn't mind a few treats.'

She narrows her eyes. 'It wasn't like that, Jane. I'm not some spoilt brat.'

She looks away in that huffy way she has and I know if I'm not careful she'll go into one of her moods.

'I'm sorry, Leah. I didn't mean it. Anyway it must have been horrible for you, out alone at that time of night.'

She looks at me. 'You don't know the half of it, Jane. A guy flashed me.'

'Fuck off.'

She laughs. 'I'm dead serious. I was like just coming around the corner from your mam's, minding my own business, and then I like see this guy coming towards me—'

'Nooo . . . no . . .' I shout.

'And he waits under the street lamp and I'm thinking will I try to cross the road and then I say no I'll just keep going—'

'Oh my God, stop.' I put my hands over my ears.

'And then he opens his coat and he has no trousers on and his thing is like . . .'

The two of us dissolve into hysterical laughter.

'I'm going to be sick,' I say, holding my stomach.

'You would have if you saw his thing, just hanging there, Janie, like a fat, white sausage . . .'

'Oh stop, Leah . . .' Tears are streaming down my face now.

'And I like stood there and looked. Like a fool.'

I laugh louder.

'And then he touches it and it wobbles and he says . . .'

'Noo . . . stop.'

'That's not what he says. He says, "Say hello to Dinkie."' She looks at me wide-eyed, her face straight and then we really crack up, rolling around the couch holding on to each other.

'And . . . what happened?' I say between the laughing.

'I ran as fast as I could.'

I snort and try to say something.

She laughs at me trying to talk. 'What? What are you trying to say?'

'Did you say goodbye to Dinkie?'

And off we go again, laughing and crying and hugging each other.

'Was it scary?'

'Not really. He wasn't a scary guy, just dumb.'

'No, not that. The whole thing, the running away?'

She shrugs and her face closes like Mammy's does sometimes.

'Why did you run away anyway? You never told me.'

She smiles. 'It was stupid. They had a fight, Mam and Dad, and he left and I was peeved and . . .'

'And he hasn't come back?'

She doesn't answer and a tiny part of me is glad about this. That makes Leah just like me. She'll have to live in two places and we'll be able to make jokes about it, and about them and the way they fight and pick at each other.

'I know what that's like, Leah.'

'What do you mean?'

I hear the narky moody thing in her voice again. 'Just that I know what it's like – you know – when they split up and there's loads of fighting and . . .'

She laughs. 'They're not split up. They're not splitting up.'

I pick up my glass of juice and take a sip. 'My dad is gone away for a while. He's burnt out.' I look at her.

'Burnt out?' she says.

I nod.

'From what?'

I think about this for a second. 'I've no idea.' We both laugh.

'My dad's in Brussels on business, that's all. He goes there like every other week.'

This is true about Mr Collins, he travels a lot with his job. But I know she's lying to me. Holding her secrets inside herself instead of just saying them out so we could have a good laugh about it all.

'Where do you go when you're burnt out?' I ask her.

She smiles. 'I haven't got a clue. Not somewhere hot anyway.'

'Antartica?'

'Ryanair don't fly there.' She looks at me dead serious and then we burst out laughing again.

I'm up first the next morning. Really early because it's barely light outside. I'm thirsty so I go into the kitchen and I nearly die. Mrs Collins is sitting at the table with a boy, the boy from the caravans that had the kittens. I'm glad I'd put on my dressing gown.

'Jane, good morning. This is Frankie.'

'Hi,' I say.

'Sit down, Jane, I'll get you a bowl and you can help yourself to breakfast.'

I sit down opposite the boy because I don't know what else to do. I wish Leah or Peter would come in. The boy looks at me, smiling a kind of stupid smile. I can smell him, a horrible smell of sweat and boy and dirty, damp clothes. Then Mrs Collins puts a mug of tea in front of him and he touches the locket swinging from her neck. He smiles at her and she strokes his cheek and then goes to open the big, silver fridge that beeps at you if you take too long to pick out what you want. I'm mortified sitting next to him and play with a teaspoon on the table.

'Joe Mac got kilt,' he says to me.

I nod.

'Kilt stone dead.'

He's smiling so I smile back.

And then tears pour down his face like you'd suddenly turned on a tap and he starts to howl, he howls like somebody is torturing him and it's the scariest sound and Mrs Collins comes over and puts her arms around him and shushes him. I sneak out of the kitchen and back into my sleeping-bag bed in the living room. I can still hear his howls and her voice whispering to him and my whole body shakes. Leah sleeps through the lot.

'He's a weirdo, watch him, Leah. He's been out there for hours.'

It's the next morning – Sunday – and the boy is standing outside the house, just staring at the drive. Weird.

Leah peeps through the slats of the wooden blind. 'Why is Mam bringing him into the house though?'

'She probably feels sorry for him – maybe he reminds her of Jack.' I say it without thinking and straight away she tenses and I feel the mood coming.

'Dad mashed his dog.'

'What?'

'Dad ran over the dog in the new camper van.'

'Where is it?'

'The dog? Dead. He took him away – you should have heard him crying, Jane. It was unnatural.'

'No, you fool. Where's the van gone?'

She shrugs. 'Dunno. Being serviced or something. Anyway the dog had this name, a stupid name . . .'

'Dinkie?'

She laughs at my weak joke. 'No. A person's name – like Joe Ryan or something. I never heard crying like that in my life.'

'Look, there's your mother out talking to him. Jesus, she's bringing him in again.'

Leah looks at me and holds her nose. 'No way am I sitting next to him if he's staying for lunch. You can have the honour, Jane.'

'You must be joking.'

But he doesn't stay for lunch. A little while later there's this massive rap on the door. Mrs Collins goes to answer it and we peep out of the living room to see what the commotion is.

A huge man stands in the doorway, thick, wiry, grey hair springing from his head, a dark-green stained sweatshirt stretching over his chest and belly.

'Frankie, Ma'am.'

'Come in. He's in the kitchen, having hot chocolate.'

The man doesn't move from the doorstep.

'We're so sorry about his dog. We'd like to buy him a new one,' she says.

'Frankie, Ma'am.'

'OK,' says Mrs Collins, 'I'll get him.'

She goes into the kitchen and the huge man just stands there. He doesn't look at us, he turns slightly and looks into the garden.

Frankie comes out and the minute he sees the man he cowers and puts his hands over his head.

'I done nothin' Da, I swear, I done nothin'.'

The man points to the footpath.

Frankie starts crying, not the horrible howling, more sniffly. He keeps his hands over his head and as he passes out the man he speeds up. The man nods at Mrs Collins and follows the boy. We all stand at the door and watch as they walk up the long driveway. Then, as they near the gates, the man holds the boy by the hair and kicks him so hard into his back that he crumples and staggers. Mrs Collins swears and Leah covers her eyes with her hands. Then the man closes his fist and thumps the boy with all his strength into the side of his head. He's saying something to him but we can't hear. Leah is crying and Mrs Collins puts a hand on her shoulder and pats her but she's still looking up the driveway.

I'm glad to be home early because Leah is in such a mood all day, banging doors and not talking and stuff and I so hate when she does that. Mammy got Ben the coolest Bart Simpson birthday cake and Sarah comes and Uncle Sean rings from Australia and Nana rings from Newcastle West. Ben is delighted and we all sing Happy Birthday even though Ben hates it – he hates birthday parties. He opens his presents – a PSP from Mammy and two games from me and fifty euro from Sarah and then she goes home and the phone rings again.

'Another call for the birthday boy, I bet,' says Mammy and answers the phone. I know it's Daddy by the way she stiffens up.

'Lanzarote?' she says in a low voice.

'On holiday?'

'I don't fucking believe it.'

'I won't let you speak to them, you liar.'

'You're such a liar, so pathetic,' she says, her voice louder. Poor Ben is standing there next to her, so I go to the table and pick up his PSP and turn it on.

'Show me how it works, Ben,' I say. He looks at me and comes over and Mammy goes into the hall with the phone. Ben starts playing the game and I ooh and aah but I can hear Mammy shouting in the hallway, shouting you bastard, you lying, cheating, two-faced bastard, burnt out indeed. She's screaming now and then there's a mighty crash and I run out and she's thrown the phone against the wall and smashed one of the good marble tiles.

'What's happened?' I whisper.

She looks at me, tears streaming down her face. 'He's such a bastard,' she says and then marches into her room and bangs the door.

Later she sits on the sofa drinking wine and not talking. Lucky plays with a little ball she's found behind the sofa. Ben is in bed. I flick the channels on the telly until *ER* comes on and I watch it while Mammy drinks. She's crying by the time it's over, even though nobody dies in the episode. And she smokes on the couch instead of at the patio doors – she never smokes in the room like that. I get up to go to bed, lifting Lucky off my knee. She holds on so tight with her claws that I have to pull her off.

''Night Mammy,' I say.

She pats the space beside her. 'Sit down a minute, Jane.'

I sit next to her. She smells of wine and her eyes are weird. Kind of puffy and watery.

'Do you remember the weekend Daddy left?'

I rub Lucky's ears and don't answer. She pours herself some more wine and asks me again.

'Do you remember the weekend your father left? Do you remember what happened?'

I don't know what the right answer is – yes or no – so I just shrug and keep rubbing the kitten. A noise like a roaring fire starts in my ears and my face is hot.

'For your own good, Jane, you should remember.'

The fire in my head feels like it's going to explode and I pinch the inside of my arm. The fire dies down a small bit. I pinch harder.

'Listen to me, Jane. Look at me.'

I turn and look at her. Her mascara has run a bit and I look at the tiny black blobs on her cheek.

'He walked around the house for two days threatening to hang himself . . .'

I shut my eyes. 'No, please.'

She grabs my arm tightly. 'You need to hear this, Jane. He walked around like a mad man and then he made a noose and—'

'No . . . stop . . .'

'And then, no, listen to me, and then he hung it from the kitchen door and he stood on a stool and put the noose around his neck . . .'

I try to get up but she has my arm and Lucky digs her nails

into my thighs and the roaring gets louder and louder in my ears. I shut my eyes tight again but when she says it I can see it in my head – the fuzzy thing that I thought I dreamt – I can see it and it's bright and shiny and real.

'Then you appeared in front of him, just as he was going to do it, and you had a razor and you cut your arm. Just sliced your arm right there in front of him . . .'

She starts crying then and she reaches for my hand and lifts it to her lips and kisses it.

'You need to know what he's like.'

Tears slip down my face on to Lucky's stripy back, making the fur change colour.

She lights a cigarette and wipes tears away with her hand.

'You need to know what he's like so that he can't hurt you any more. So that you won't care. Do you understand?'

I nod even though I don't understand. Lucky purrs on my lap and my head hurts.

She pours more wine and takes a long gulp. 'Do you know where he is?' she smiles as she speaks.

I shake my head.

'You spoke to him last week on the phone, Jane. What did he tell you?'

'That he was burnt out . . . that he needed time . . .'

She laughs. 'He's in Lanzarote with his girlfriend, sunning himself – how's that for burnt out?'

I get up and run out of the room and up the stairs and into the bathroom. I put Lucky on the white tiles and look at myself in the mirror and talk to myself. I look just like him and I'll be mad too when I'm older and I'll get a noose and do the same thing and there mightn't be anybody there to stop me and Mammy will hate me because I'm like him . . . and I so want to scream. But I say bollocks over and over instead because it's a really good word to say and then I have an idea. I open the bathroom cabinet and find it behind a box of Tampax. A blade. So light and innocent in my hand, like it couldn't hurt a thing. I breathe in and hold my arm over the sink. The blade feels delicious, like a new soap and it glints in the light. I rest it gently on my arm. There's a knock on the door.

'Janie?'

'What?'

Mammy tries to open the door. 'I'm sorry, Jane, I'm so sorry. I was mad with him and I . . . I'm sorry darling . . .'

I stare at my eyes in the mirror. My bright blue eyes, so like Daddy's.

'It's OK,' I say.

'Please open the door, Janie. I want to give you a hug. I'm so sorry.'

She starts crying against the door. I make a thin slice in my arm, a beautiful, thin, perfect slice and the pain is gorgeous, it comes in a wave, and a skinny sheet of blood, so thin you can see through it, runs down my arm slowly, like it has all the time in the world and then drips into the sink.

I turn around and smile at Lucky, who's purring on a wooden bath mat that's shaped like a boat. Another lovely wave of pain comes and I feel giddy and faint and brilliant.

'I'll be out in a minute. I'm just brushing my teeth.'

'I love you, Janie, do you know that?'

Six

Alison

There are two new messages for Jack on his Bebo page. One is from Hugsy, good old reliable Hugsy.

Jack, I just had to tell you I got Oxegen tickets and remember we swore last year we were going and that was that so I'm going for the two of us. Can't wait, Franz Ferdinand, Kaiser Chiefs, Red Hot Chili Peppers – oh my God, it's gonna be incredible!!! Just wish things were different . . . just wish I could talk to you just for five lousy minutes and I know what you're saying – not enough time cos I'd do all the talking!!! Love ya to bits my music man.

There's a row of hearts at the end of the comment. Hugsy's little signature.

The other comment is from Colinator.

Hey Bud. You're a pure legend. Never forget ya.

I smile at the contrast in messages – one so verbose and girly. The other boyish in its brevity. I check Jack's photo gallery just to remind myself of what these two look like. Hugsy is blonde and blue eyed, a teenage girl with a baby's face. She smiles at the camera, her face untouched yet by life. Colinator has a great head on him. That boy-man head, all cocky bravado and cool posing. An invincible, know-it-all teenager. So like Jack.

In Jack's gallery of top sixteen friends Hugsy and Colinator are in prime positions. Numbers one and two. They deserve it. They still keep in touch. They don't forget. I reluctantly close down the Bebo page and head upstairs to bed, my head swimming with snatches of Jack's life – his Bebo a virtual diary of who he was.

I don't sleep. I never sleep after Bebo and I really want to. I might dream about him. Might see his face tanned from a long summer, a hand shading his eyes, grinning at me. I might see a morning Jack, all moody and cranky, calling his sister a douche bag and telling Peter that he's gay. Or I might see a nightmare Jack, when he's somewhere and I can't get to him, a cliff, the sea, dying on a road. I don't care which one comes when I'm asleep. Any Jack is better than none.

'I need five euro for the class Christmas party and a cheque for swimming,' says Leah. Peter is sitting on a high stool munching cereal and reading a soccer magazine.

'Mam, what are you doing up so early?' he says as I start to make coffee. A sudden thump of guilt stops me. I look at my youngest child. At his lovely clear blue eyes. At his soft blonde hair so like his daddy's. Peter. Never a moment's trouble in his short happy little life. I can never imagine him being hormonal, banging doors, swearing at me, hating me.

'I wanted to see you two – anything wrong with that?' I say, smiling at him.

Leah rolls her eyes and bangs a cup down on the island.

'The cheque and the money?' she says.

There's a knock at the door and I know who it is immediately.

'He might as well move in, Peter,' says Leah. 'He can share your room. Or maybe he can have Jack's?' She smirks at me as I go to open the front door.

Frankie Ward stands there, grinning, like he's done most days this week.

'Come in, Frankie. Would you like some cereal?'

'Frankie's hungry,' he says, and walks into the kitchen.

Leah rolls her eyes and walks straight out. Peter nods at the boy.

I make Frankie a big bowl of cereal and some toast and I watch him wolf it down as I sip coffee.

'Are you ready, Pete?' says Leah from the doorway.

Peter jumps down from his stool and grabs his lunchbox from the worktop.

'Bye, Mam.'

'See you later, Peter,' I say and it's only when they're gone I realise that Leah left without the money or the cheque.

'So, Frankie, what are you up to today, then? I hope your dad doesn't catch you down here.'

Frankie stops shovelling cornflakes and speaks with his mouth full.

'Da is gone for the horses.' He grins as if this explains everything and starts shovelling again.

I make him a strong cup of sweet tea and we sit there sipping our drinks in silence. We grin at each other now and again instead of talking and it seems to suit us both.

My phone rings and interrupts us.

'Hello? Dermot?'

'Hi, Alison, sorry to disturb you.'

'Not at all. How are things? I heard you were in Lanzarote.'

'Long story. Listen, I know this is sudden but I'm actually just around the corner from you now – and I was going to . . . call in for a coffee maybe . . . now if . . .'

'Of course. That'd be great. I'll see you in a minute so.' I hang up and my heart starts racing for no reason.

'Come on Frankie, you have to go,' I say as I examine my face in the small mirror that's propped up on the kitchen window. I go and get my handbag and dump make-up out and start putting it on my face.

Frankie is smiling at me, cornflakes stuck to the edge of his mouth and snot beginning to run down his nose.

'Off you go, Frankie – see you tomorrow maybe.' I slick lipstick on my lips and root for the tiny perfume bottle that I remember seeing in my bag.

'Frankie,' I say, a little too loudly and he jumps up quickly and covers his head with his hands.

'I done nothin',' he says.

I walk over and take his hand and lead him out to the front door.

'I know, Frankie. You're a good kid. See you soon.' He walks away but keeps looking back at me. I smile and wave at him and close the door. Then I dash upstairs and change into trousers and a black and rust fitted sweater and brush my hair. I look at myself in the mirror and wonder why I haven't worn the sweater recently – it's a really good fit and looks wonderful. The doorbell rings and adrenalin pumps through my veins. I walk slowly downstairs and open the door.

He looks even more handsome than usual. His skin is a soft

golden colour and seems to glow against his dark navy overcoat. I want to touch his face. I want to trace his mouth with my fingers and smell him near me, even on me. I want to lean into his broad chest and bury my head there and . . .

'Alison, how are you?' He kisses me on the cheek, just long enough for me to feel the smooth skin of his face and then he follows me into the kitchen.

'Would you like coffee? I have Illy or Rombouts . . . oh, and I've decaf somewhere . . .' I turn around and laugh. A giddy laugh like a teenager's.

'It's great to see you,' he says, his eyes on me as I fill the coffee machine. A thrill races through me and I do the giddy girl laugh again. The coffee tin is empty and I search the presses for a fresh one.

'I missed our little chats. Really missed them and . . .' he stops and waits until I look at him. Then he shakes his head.

'What were you going to say?'

'Nothing, it's nothing.'

'Bet the weather was fabulous in Lanzarote, it's been the usual here, a mixture of everything.' My voice sounds squeaky as I try to make conversation.

'I'm glad I came to see you, Ali. Really glad.'

'So am I. I'm glad you came too.'

He beams and sits down on a high stool. 'You wouldn't believe the week I've had.'

'Tell me about it,' I say, glad of the distraction. I search for coffee cups.

'Oh where do I start? Did you ever feel, Ali, that everything is collapsing around you? You know, that things are going out of control and there's nothing you can do so you just sit back and let it all happen?'

I drop the coffee jug. 'I know exactly what you—'

'It started with Lanzarote. I mean it's so long since I'd had a break and then it just turns into this big scene with Evelyn – you know Evelyn, don't you?'

'Yes, I—'

'Well, I couldn't contact the children on my mobile – it wouldn't work over there and I had to ring the house and Evelyn went ballistic when she heard I was in Lanzarote.' He smiles sheepishly at me, like a little boy caught stealing sweets. He shrugs and I sit beside him and put two steaming mugs of coffee in front of us.

'Smells delicious,' he says. His body is inches from mine. I can feel heat from it and I look straight at him. His mouth mesmerises me. It's beautiful in an entirely masculine way. It's even a beautiful colour. I look away, flustered suddenly by the whole thing. He reaches out and touches my hand.

'She screamed down the phone at me and do you know what she did? She wouldn't let me speak to the children. Can you believe that? I wasn't allowed to speak to my own children.'

'Didn't they know you were on holiday?'

He looks hurt. 'It wasn't exactly a holiday you know. Have you any idea how stressful my job is? And when Fiona suggested a break I just decided here goes – you only live once, don't you?' His voice is defensive. Like Leah's when she feels wronged. Which is all the time.

'Have you seen the kids at all since you came back?'

He shakes his head and plays with his teaspoon.

I reach out a hand and put it on his shoulder. 'I'm sorry, Dermot. That must be hard.'

'This morning I felt so bad when I woke up. I didn't want to get up, I'm just so tired of it all.'

'I know that feeling.'

He looks at me intently. 'Do you really? Because . . . this is really strange . . .' he gives a little laugh and shakes his head. 'I can't . . . don't want to even say it . . .'

I tighten my hand on his shoulder and he pins me with those too-blue eyes.

'From the very first time we met . . . spoke . . . I felt there was a connection . . . I know it sounds corny but it's true.'

I smile at him, flattered like a giddy teenage girl at this. 'Me too,' I say and I know the second I say the words that it's a lie. I noticed no connection – just his perfect mouth and then his face.

'And then on our last day in Lanzarote, Fiona announces that she thinks we should cool it a little – just like that, Alison – completely out of the blue. I mean as far as I was concerned everything was . . .' His voice chokes with tears. 'So this morning when I woke up and everything was miserable I knew what to do.'

He reaches up and takes my hand from his shoulder and holds it lightly on his lap. I can feel the strain of his thigh muscle through his trousers and an exquisite rush of sexual tension rises inside me and makes my head feel light. Jesus Christ, it seems like years since my body craved sex like this.

'I knew I had to see you – just to talk for a while like this . . .' He lets go of my hand and takes a sip of coffee. 'She could stop me seeing them, you know.'

I try to tune into this turn in conversation.

'People don't realise it but she's very spiteful. She says I use the children – that I pick them up and discard them as it suits me . . .' He laughs and shakes his head. 'And she can talk – do you know, Alison, that she never stayed at home at night when we were together? Out every night with her sisters, her friends, her mother, anyone but me . . .'

His eyes fill up with tears and for some reason he reminds me of Frankie, so vulnerable and unable for the world.

'Hey,' I say and touch his face but he looks away as tears escape and flow down his cheeks. I catch his face in both my hands. 'Look at me, Dermot.'

He looks and then averts his eyes straight away.

I wipe his tears with my fingers. 'Dermot, come on, you're a lovely person, open and . . .'

He shakes his head and blinks. 'I'm sorry. I've never done that before – you know – start crying like a baby in front of . . . in front of someone like you.'

'Like me?'

He smiles tentatively now, the tears gone. 'Strong, beautiful, unbreakable.'

'That's not true . . .' I start to say.

He puts a finger to my lips to shush me. 'Yes it is. I know what you've been through, and look how you coped.'

He traces my mouth with his finger. 'So strong,' he whispers and leans forward and kisses me lightly on the lips. He tastes of coffee and I feel like I'm drunk and all I want him to do is to kiss me harder. He pulls away and smiles and for an instant he reminds me of Richard rehearsing for one of his plays. The smile and the set of him on the stool and then Brian's face pops into my head and I jump off the stool and run to fill the coffee pot again. 'I'll make some more coffee, those cups are tiny, aren't they? And mine's cold. I hate cold coffee.' I rattle cups and pots as I talk.

'I'm sorry, Alison, I overstepped myself. I'll leave.'

I stand by the sink with my back to him. Part of me wants him to leave, to just go because it's stupid and pathetic and . . . he's standing right behind me, I can feel his breath on my neck. I turn around slowly.

'I'm sorry,' he says again, 'I didn't mean to . . . look, I'll just go.' He leans forward and kisses me gently on the cheek and smiles a wry, boyish smile and I laugh.

'You've got a coffee stain right there,' I say and touch his mouth with my fingers.

But then he leans forward and kisses me again, his tongue pushing into my mouth. It's delicious.

He pulls away. 'I'm sorry, Alison. I shouldn't have done that. I'm so sorry.' He walks towards the door and all I'm thinking is please get back here right now.

'These things happen . . .'

'No. My apologies. I've had a shit time and you make me feel good so I—'

'No, really, it was nothing . . . I mean . . .'

'You're right as usual, Alison. It was nothing . . . it should never have happened. I feel so bad – I lost my job yesterday, Ali. I didn't tell you that bit of news yet.'

'Jesus, Dermot, I'm so sorry. What happened?' I walk towards him and he backs away.

'It was well on the cards – I knew before I went to Lanzarote.' He smiles and shrugs and I want to mind him like you would a small boy.

'I'd better be going anyway – I've an appointment with FÁS – big job hunt a couple of weeks before Christmas.'

I nod and walk to the door with him.

'Thanks Ali,' he says and bends to kiss me but pulls back quickly. 'I don't trust myself near you so I'll refrain from physical contact.'

I laugh.

'Ali, could I ask you a favour? No . . . it wouldn't be fair on you . . . involving you in my shit . . .'

'There's no harm in asking.'

'Well, if Jane is over here at the weekend – she texted to say she would be – well . . . could I maybe drop by?'

'Of course,' I say without thinking about it.

'You're the best, do you know that? Fiona, my girlfriend – she doesn't have children so she just doesn't understand at all. But you . . .' he reaches out a hand and rests it on my shoulder and then he's gone and I close the door and wonder what just happened. My head is full of it as I change into my tracksuit and head for the riverbank, delighted with all the new possibilities that my mind can play with.

There's a lovely mist on the river, so thick you can't see the bank on the other side. The air is damp with it and when I breathe I imagine mist filling my lungs. My phone vibrates with a message as I walk along the deserted woodland path and I know before I take it out that it's Dermot. And still when I see his name on the screen a thrill of danger races through me. But it's not scary. Not at all.

Leah and Jane are in the kitchen, making toasted sandwiches. It's Saturday night and Brian and Peter are watching *Match of the Day*. I can hear its familiar music and I can't bear it, the sound of it. Jack's ringtone. I pour myself a glass of wine and turn on the radio, switching the dial to Lyric FM. Leah and Jane roll their eyes and I laugh at them and then I notice Jane. Her face is a translucent, almost shiny white, and there are dark shadows under her eyes. She sees me looking at her and smiles. Leah throws daggers at me.

'How are you, Jane?' I ask.

'I'm fine thanks, Mrs Collins,' she says and turns back to making her sandwich. Leah glares at me and shakes her head. My phone signals the arrival of a message and I know it's Dermot again. I take the phone and my glass of wine and head into my study. He's texted me a chatroom address and I go online, calling myself Ali C. He knows me straight away and we chat for hours. I love the familiarity and anonymity all at the same time. A lovely little secret pleasure and nobody is examining me to see my reaction or gauge what they say. Nobody tip-toeing around me like they're walking on eggshells.

He texts again just as I'm brushing my teeth. A goodnight text I think and pray Brian doesn't hear the phone beeping. The text is strange. Cold and strange and gutting and exhilarating all at the same time.

Please understand that we can't have contact anymore. I find you dangerously attractive.

I read it twice just to check if I've missed the joke or something. I know that's possible because, since Jack, I don't seem to get jokes anymore. But no, it's loud and clear in its intent. I'm gutted but thrilled at the same time. Thrilled and flattered and . . . there's another word to describe it but it won't come to me.

I climb into bed beside a sleeping Brian and close my eyes. Sleep doesn't come for a very long time. And then the word comes. Distracted. Dermot distracts me. Makes me not think or feel.

Brian's easy, rhythmic sleep-breathing annoys me and I count his breaths like counting sheep.

A shrill, piercing noise sinks into my subconscious and I jump up in the bed. Brian is already awake and out of bed.

'What is it?' I ask, trying to open swollen, tired eyes.

'Phone. I'll get it,' he says and runs out to the landing and the shrill ringing stops as he speaks in a low voice.

'OK. I know. I'll tell her. Don't worry, I will.' He's looking at me through the open bedroom door as he talks and my heart flips around my chest.

'It's Mammy, isn't it?' I'm amazed that my voice works because my body is paralysed in the bed, stiff and rigid.

He hangs up the receiver and shakes his head. 'It's Rachel . . . no . . . wait . . . Ali . . .'

I'm sitting bolt upright now, holding my head and trying not to scream and the air is going and I can't breathe at all. There's no air left and I stumble out of the bed and start to crawl towards Brian, silhouetted in the soft yellow landing light. I'm gasping and spluttering for air and then Jack is in front of me, right there in front of my face and the lighthouse on Inisheer is right beside him and his head is down and as he lifts it his face is Frankie's and oh God I'm going to throw up.

Icy water splashes my face and then Brian is bending over me, holding a dripping glass of water to my lips.

'Ali, here, you fainted. Take some of this.'

I sip the water and realise I'm lying on the landing floor. Two small, tidy tears are rolling down Brian's cheeks.

'What's up? Please tell me – the not knowing is the worst. Tell me . . .'

'I thought you were . . . it's silly really . . . I thought for a second, Ali, that you'd close your eyes and that would be that . . .'

'Rachel?'

'She's fine.'

'It's the baby. The baby is dead and . . .'

'She started bleeding and Donal brought her to the hospital and the baby came . . .'

I shook my head. 'No. The baby isn't due for another month.'

'The baby came. A little boy, Ali. He's in an incubator and he's got breathing difficulties but he's a fighter and—'

'I want to go to her.'

'She wants you to go. I'll call a cab for you.'

'I can drive.'

'Are you sure? You've just fainted.'

'I didn't faint, it's those attacks – the panic attacks.'

'You told me they were gone.'

'They were but sometimes . . .'

'Are you sure you can drive?'

I nod and Brian puts his arms around me and sinks his head on to my shoulder. I smell his hair and can feel its springiness on my cheek. He stands up then and pulls me up gently and I dress quickly. He makes me coffee in a small, silver thermos and stands at the door as I pull out of the drive. It's dawn and the river mist has come up again and Brian stands there at the front door waving like some ethereal being.

She's sleeping. Little Rachel, baby sister. I kiss her and stroke her cheek and Donal hands me a tissue to wipe my tears. We share the coffee in the corridor and then we make our way to the neonatal unit and I feel the air tightening in my chest as we approach and I babble something to Donal and follow the signs for the loo. Inside I lean against the sink and gulp in air. I don't want to see him. I know that's what's wrong. I don't want to see him and maybe love him and then for him to be gone and to watch Rachel like a wounded animal looking for her dead baby. I close my eyes tightly and take deep breaths and the fact that I've thought the thought makes it easier to face.

I smile brightly at Donal when I come out.

'Show me the little warrior,' I say, and Donal smiles and rings for a nurse to open the door. There are six glass-sided incubators in the room, all wired up to machines. We move to the very end of the room and for some reason I can't look into the incubators as we pass. I can't look at the little scraps of human life fighting for breath.

He's bigger than I'd imagined. I almost laugh when I notice this. He's even got little folds of fat on his thighs like Jack had when he was born. Donal reaches in and holds his tiny pink hand, stroking it like it's precious silk. Tears stream down my face but I'm smiling.

'Has he a name?' I whisper.

Donal nods. 'Sean.'

'Sean. I like that. Hi, Sean.'

'Here, Ali, hold his hand.'

I reach in and hold his little star-shaped hand and he curls his fingers tightly around mine and opens his eyes.

'He's perfect, Donal. He's so perfect.'

'I know, Ali.' Donal's eyes mist up. 'Jesus, look at the two of us bawling our eyes out – Rachel'll kill us.'

I laugh and Donal hugs me. 'Ah, Ali, this is the best but Jesus it's terrifying too, isn't it?'

'Now you said it, Donal.'

'She's been asking for you all night. Do you know that?'

'Brian told me.'

'All night. And in typical Rachel fashion the minute she gets what she wants she falls asleep.' He laughs and a nurse comes to check on Sean and we leave.

Donal goes home for a shower and supplies and Rachel wakes as soon as I open the door. 'Ali?'

'Hi, Rachel.' I go and sit on the bed, and hold her hand. 'You've had a rough night.'

She smiles weakly. 'Did you see him?'

'He's gorgeous – lucky he came a month early or he'd be the size of a baby heifer.'

She smiles again and closes her eyes and I think she's asleep.

'None of us understood, Ali. Not a single one.'

She opens her eyes and looks at me. 'We thought we did. And we read all the literature on grief and I spoke to my therapist colleagues and I dispensed advice and do you know something?'

I shake my head.

'I hadn't a fucking clue.'

I smile at this because Rachel never swears.

'I hadn't a clue what it was like . . .'

'It's OK, Rachel.'

' . . . what it was like to hold your own baby in your arms. The smell of him, the way your heart feels like it's going to burst . . .'

'Sean is lovely, Rachel and he's going to be fine . . .'

'Your heart did burst, didn't it?'

I look away. There's an empty metal cot waiting for a new baby occupant. A long window and the misty morning outside. A water jug with three slices of lemon in it. God, they were getting very fancy in the maternity ward these days.

'Donal's gone home for a shower. He won't be long – he's going to pick up some stuff for you so tell me what you need and I'll phone him.' I smile at Rachel. 'We should tell Richard,' I add.

'I'm so sorry, Ali. I'm so sorry about Jack and last night in the middle of it all, it's Jack I kept thinking about . . .'

'Seriously, Richard'll go mad if he's not told . . .'

' . . . the night you had Leah and Jack stayed with me and I was tucking him into bed and I said, Jack what's you're new baby sister's name going to be . . .'

My hands are clenched into two tight fists and I stare at a tiny water stain on the wall in front of me.

'And his huge brown eyes are smiling up at me and he says, "I don't know cos they haven't thunk of a name yet."'

She smiles at me, her eyes spilling with tears.

'They haven't thunk of a name yet,' she repeats. 'And then the next morning Donal says to him at the breakfast table, he says, "Jack, what are you going to be when you grow up?"'

Rachel laughs now, and reaches out a hand for my clenched fist.

'"Up where?" says Jack. Isn't that brilliant? Up where?'

She's crying in earnest now, smiling and crying and clutching my fist and I can't look at her, not straight at her, because I'll see it in her eyes. She'll want me to make it all right. Make it all right that she has a son and mine is gone. Make it all right for her to love him.

'I'll ring Richard now, OK?'

'Alison . . . Ali . . . I'm sorry.'

My chest tightens but my eyes are bone dry. I shrug. I can't speak the words. I can't make it all right.

'He'll be mad as hell if he's missed all the drama – particularly if there's a happy ending,' I say but I see a flicker of hurt pass across Rachel's face.

'Do we have to?' she says, giving me a watery smile.

I nod. 'Oh come on Rach, don't you want the garage flowers and the wine?'

'He wouldn't bring wine. It'll be garage chocolates.'

I laugh. 'Wine, I'll put ten euros on it.'

'OK. Done. It's a bet.' Her eyes close again and she dozes off. I move to the armchair and fall asleep too and when I wake Richard is standing in the room, filling the room with himself. He's chuckling heartily like an off-duty Santa. He's holding a bunch of garage flowers in one hand and a bottle of champagne in the other.

'Rachel, Rachel. I've been up with Donal to see him. He's a fine strapping boy – he looks like our father – he's got our looks.'

'Fat and balding?' I say and Rachel laughs.

'The one thing us Careys have in abundance is hair. Now, where can we get a few champagne glasses around here?'

'Ten euro,' Rachel says to me, holding out her hand. We both laugh.

'I want to tell you about Sean.'

It's misty and I can barely see his face but I know it's him by the way he stands. By the way he leans slightly on to his right leg and drops his shoulder a little and tilts his head.

No answer. I take a step closer and he moves back a little. He's looking past me, as if there's someone creeping up on me. I look behind but there's nothing. Just a misty country road with grass growing at its centre. The mist seems to thicken and I can just about see his silhouette.

'Jack. Talk to me, please talk to me. This is stupid. Don't you want to hear about your new cousin?'

He shakes his head and walks backwards, away from me. I follow.

'Talk to me Jack. Don't walk away – the least you can do is talk to me. It's the least you can do.'

He stops dead still, mist swirling around him, bringing him in and out of focus. Even when the mist clears he still looks blurry and half-formed.

'The least I can do? The least I can do?' He laughs a mean laugh and shakes his head again. His voice sounds like an echo.

'Jack, just talk, have a chat, we'll catch up on all the news

– I miss you so much and this is . . .'

'The least I can do? Like it's my fault or something? Fuck off,' he says and turns his back on me, walking into the thickest part of the mist.

But I still don't give up, I follow him, calling and calling and calling . . .

Seven

Jane

Nana's cat is called Blackie. He's a big fat lump, the colour of coal and he's eyeing up Lucky from the windowsill in Nana's kitchen. He always sits in that exact same spot because the sun shines there all day. Lucky's trembling in my arms. I can feel her little heart racing and I'm sorry now that I brought her at all.

'Blackie's going to kill her, Nana,' I say, clutching Lucky tighter as Blackie stands up, arching his back and baring his horrible, sharp teeth.

'Not at all Jane, Blackie's a gentle old fella, he'll love the bit of company,' Nana goes and takes up Blackie in her arms and I wonder why she had to stop driving if she can lift a big fat cat like that.

'How's my best boy?' she says, stroking Blackie's head. Ben and I look at each other and Ben rolls his eyes. Nana can never admit that Blackie is horrible. Mean and nasty and scratchy and he's only nice when Nana's around.

'Come on, boy, you go out there in the backyard until Lucky settles down,' she says and puts him outside. I sit down at

Nana's kitchen table, all set for dinner, and I can feel Lucky relaxing in my arms. I put her on the floor and she prances up and down, then starts following her tail. We all laugh at this.

Ben goes to watch TV and I stay in the kitchen with Nana, watching her chop onions very fast and she doesn't even cry. The radio's on, people arguing about traffic and it feels like they're in the kitchen with us.

'I've made up the bed in Mam's old room for you, Janie, and I put on the lacy quilt that you love. You can take it home with you tomorrow if you like.' She dumps the onions into a steaming pot on the cooker. She takes some carrots and starts to chop them.

'It's OK, Nana, thanks.' Lucky's jumped up on Blackie's favourite spot and I can hear her purring happily, the sun on her stripy back.

'She told me about your dad going off to Lanzarote without saying a word.'

Lucky's eyes stare at me, lime green, closing and opening and then closing again.

'Anyway, she deserves a weekend away, doesn't she? Poor girl, I don't know how she copes with . . .' Nana stops chopping and smiles at me. The chopping starts again.

'With what, Nana?'

'I hope Ben likes stew, I'm making a big pot with mashed potatoes and I have an apple tart for sweet.'

'Copes with what?' I know she means Daddy but I want her to say it.

'Oh, you know – when people break up. It's hard to cope, that's all.' She puts the carrots in the pot and stirs it with a big, silver ladle.

'Let's have a game of Lives while we're waiting for dinner,' she says then and goes to the dresser for a deck of cards.

They're brand new and have pictures of the Cliffs of Moher on the back. I win the first two games.

'You're too good at this, Jane. When did you learn to be so good?'

I smile at Nan's kind face, with her tight-curled hair and blue-framed glasses. 'You're letting me win, Nana.'

'No, I am not indeed. You beat me fair and square.'

'I'm not a baby, Nana. I'm not Ben. I don't want to play if you're going to let me win.'

It's raining outside. I can hear it lashing against the small window and Blackie's crying at the back door. Nana lets him in, forgetting that Lucky's asleep on his windowsill. He makes a beeline for Lucky, who screeches and arches her back, spitting at Blackie. He paws her hard and she screeches again. Ben runs in to the kitchen to see what's happening. I try to get Lucky but Blackie scratches me on my hand, three long scratches that start to bleed. Nana lifts Blackie up and rubs him to calm him and I run into the hallway and then the bedroom with Lucky in my arms, her fur standing up and her heart pumping.

The bedroom is exactly like I remember and I lie on the soft quilt looking up at the wallpaper with tiny lilac flowers. The same wallpaper that Mammy looked at when she was my age. There's a doll's house on a chest of drawers in the corner. A perfect house, with all the furniture inside, even a mother and father and a tiny baby in a crib. I go over and open up the house and straighten some of the pieces. Next to the house there's an orange-and-cream-striped box. I bring it over to the bed and open the lid. Lucky tries to climb in but I hunt her. Inside are some photos and reports. Mammy's reports from school. I read them, but feel guilty, like I'm spying or something, and I open a bunch of photos tied with purple string.

First I don't recognise the people in the pictures, They're so young, not much older than me, but then I realise it's Mammy and Daddy. She's in her school uniform, dark green with a long skirt almost to the floor. She's laughing at the camera and he's standing behind her, his arms around her. And then I notice he's tickling her and that's why she's laughing. The next photo is at the beach. They're looking at each other and you can see the long shadow of the person that took the photo on the bright yellow sand.

They're older in the next one. It's a Debs picture and Mammy looks so beautiful except the dress is a bit old-fashioned, all ruffles and stuff. Daddy's gorgeous though in a black suit and snow-white shirt. The last picture is the biggest. It's Mammy and Daddy and another man that looks very like him except his hair is blonde. Kieran. My uncle Kieran. Daddy told me about him. About how he died suddenly when he was only twenty-two and just finished college.

Nana knocks and walks in, the exact way Ben does at home.

'Dinner's ready, love, and I locked Blackie into the sitting room so you don't have to . . .' She looks at the picture in my hand.

'Poor Kieran,' she says, 'such a tragedy.'

'I know. Daddy told me about it.'

'You just don't know, sure you don't, what's going on in someone's head.'

I don't know what she means but I keep quiet. Let her keep talking.

'Such a terrible day. And to do that to his mother . . .' She touches the picture, like it'll help her to remember better. 'To hang himself like that in the garden shed . . .'

I can't hear the rest, just my heart thumping and rain on the roof. I drop the photo on the red lino floor.

'Jane, are you all right? I'm sorry, I thought you knew – you said your dad told you so I thought you knew . . .' She hugs me tight to her chest and rubs my hair. I can smell stew and perfume.

'I'm fine, Nana, I'm fine. Daddy told me ages ago.'

Nana pats my shoulder. 'He was a lovely boy, you'd never think there was anything wrong in his life. It's the last thing you'd think, God rest his soul.'

My head is pounding and I want to tell Nana about Daddy and the rope thing and then I think maybe she knows already, maybe Mammy told her but I know deep down she didn't. I just know it. And Daddy isn't Kieran. Daddy has us so he'd never do that. And he was just sad that time because they were breaking up. That's all. Sad.

'Nana, I'm starving. Can we have dinner now?'

We have to watch the *Late Late Show* with Nana after dinner but I don't mind. We're all cosy and the fire is crackling and Nana makes jokes all the time about all the guests. Ben is snuggled up against Nana, the heat from the fire making his face red. My phone rings. It's Daddy.

'Where are you?' he asks without saying hello.

'In Nana's house.'

Nana's pretending to watch the TV but I know she's listening. I walk out to the kitchen, Daddy's voice in my ear.

'Why didn't you ring me back last night, Jane? I left three messages and you just ignore me . . .'

'I'd no credit, Daddy, and—'

'Always the same stupid excuses. Treating me like dirt to please her . . .' his words jumble in my head so I say nothing, just listen. Blackie's asleep on the rug and I can't believe it when I see Lucky curled up right beside him, her head on his paws.

' . . . and I've a good mind to drive out there now . . .
actually pack your stuff, Ben's too, I'll be out in half an hour.'

He hangs up and I'm crying and then Nan's beside me.

'What did Daddy say, Jane?'

'He's coming to get us, that Mammy has no right to dump
us . . .'

'It's OK. I'll sort it out. I'll ring him. You go back in and
keep an eye on Pat Kenny for me.'

She doesn't come back to the sitting room for ages but when
she does she brings lemonade and Taytos and a giant bar of
fruit and nut chocolate. Ben cheers and Blackie and Lucky
follow her into the room and curl up together again next to the
fire.

I look at her, wondering if Daddy's going to come soon,
honking his horn outside and making a scene. She smiles at me
then, and pats my hand.

'Who's for chocolate then?' she says and I know it's all
right. I love that about Nana. The way she makes things all
right without saying a word about it.

Eight

Alison

Brian is back in therapy. His diary is in front of me and there it is as plain as day, and I just know straight away what it is. Can that be possible? That there's a pattern to a particular therapist's appointment dates? I feel sorry for him. I feel sorry that he still thinks that other people can make him better. We were together for those first long sessions and I knew immediately that this bullshit wasn't going to help – not one little bit.

Friday. 10 December. 10 a.m.

Today. This hour. Right this minute. He's in there with her and her lovely, comfortable terms for agony. That's what she does best – gives names to things you feel – like it's the solution when it's just a fucking word. You could call it cat shit and it would still hurt. I kind of pity Brian for his dumb acceptance but I hate him for it too. The stages of grief: transference, displacement, foreshortened future. Bullshit terms to make the heartache 'acceptable'. Like if we label it all we can pack it up in nice bite-sized pieces of hell, nice, antiseptic, inoffensive professional terms that fix everything up. I look up at the clock on the kitchen wall: 10.25.

That's what he's talking about now with her. Foreshortened future. That's how she described my aversion to Rome. My panic attacks. My solitude. And then one day I told her to fuck off with her foreshortened future and her stages of grief and all the other terminology that cloaked her sessions. I screamed at her and Brian tried to hold me back but I screamed and screamed so that the waiting room full of sad, dead people could hear me. I screamed it out at the top of my lungs. What the fuck ever happened to a good old-fashioned broken heart? What the fuck happened to that? I know what happened – it can't be fixed so nobody mentions it. Right? Right? Right? And then I ran and the air evaporated and Brian came after me.

And now he's having some more. Another dose of bullshit. A spoonful of sugar. I laugh out loud and it echoes around the empty kitchen. Poor stupid Brian. Clinging to the bullshit like a big fool. If there was a tablet for it he'd be double dosing. I laugh out loud again.

Then I realise I'm crying when I pour myself more coffee and see my reflection in the stainless steel kettle. I sit down on a stool with my coffee and consider going back to bed. But sleep won't come. It doesn't come at night so it's not going to come now. The radio is on low and I hear a Christmas carol – 'O Holy Night' – and that makes me cry more. The thought of Christmas makes me feel sick and I realise I haven't eaten anything since yesterday. I get up and throw bread into the toaster and the doorbell rings. Richard, I think, as I go to answer it.

Dermot stands there in a navy overcoat and matching striped scarf. He grins like a bold child.

'Am I forgiven?'

I spot Frankie out of the corner of my eye, hiding behind a cherry blossom near the driveway entrance. He's holding his hands over his head. Dermot follows my gaze.

'Oh him. Spotted the little fucker sizing up the place so I told him what for. Am I forgiven, Ali?'

'For what?' I want to hear what he has to say.

'For my lack of communication.'

'Come in.' He follows me into the kitchen.

I make fresh coffee and he remains standing but takes off his coat and lays it carefully across the back of a stool.

'I've had a horrible week.' He smiles wanly at me. 'Forgiven?'

I continue fiddling with the coffee making. 'Why?'

His jaw seems to stiffen. 'Why did I call? As I said, my week's been rubbish and—'

'No. Why did you send me that text? The noble one where we couldn't have contact anymore and then – hey presto – here you are in my kitchen. Why?' I rinse two coffee mugs under the tap and dry them on a stained grey tea towel.

He drops his eyes from mine. 'I meant it at the time.'

'So what's changed? What's changed that you feel you can have contact with me now?'

He looks at me now, his eyes a piercing blue, exactly like Jane's. Except hers seem older, more knowing. 'I meant it all. I find your company irresistible. Is that bad?'

He smiles and it changes his whole face. Makes him almost boyish in appearance. I examine his mouth, fascinated by the deep smile lines on each side. I want to touch them.

The air changes between us. He reaches out a hand, then pulls it away fast, like he's touched something hot.

'I couldn't resist calling, Ali. Every day I've wanted to contact you, text you, see you and then today . . . where's Brian?'

'Why? Would you like him to join us for coffee?'

He shakes his head. 'No. I was just asking, that's all. I consider you a friend, a really good friend, and some husbands mightn't be OK with that.'

'Brian is fine with that. Trust me. Is that why you sent the text?'

'That and other reasons.'

'Like?' The coffee pot screeches but I ignore it.

'All sorts – there's Fiona and . . .'

'But we're just friends – right?' I smile at him, enjoying the challenge of the conversation now.

'Touché, Alison. I did it really to protect myself. God knows I have enough complications in my life . . .'

'So friends are complications now?' The coffee pot is making hissing sounds like it's going to explode any second but I know if I turn around the thread of conversation will be lost.

He laughs and reaches out and touches me lightly with his hand. He smells lovely, spicy man smells and damp winter rain.

'Friends like you are complications.' He moves closer. Now I can smell his minty breath, see soft shadow on his newly shaven jaw. I'm just the right height to lay my head exactly under his, for him to wrap his arms tightly around me and distract me into a new world, a different place.

I answer the gurgling call of the coffee pot, pouring coffee, searching for milk, sugar, clean spoons. I hand him a steaming mug of coffee.

'I don't want to be a complication, Dermot, it's not very sexy,' I say, smiling and amazed at my long-forgotten ability to flirt with the best of them.

He laughs. 'That's the problem. The more complicated it is, the sexier it is.' He winks, flirting right back at me. My stomach does a little flip. I hold my cup to my lips and he watches me sipping the hot liquid. I can feel my face reddening like a schoolgirl's.

'I feel better already, just being here, do you know that?'

I keep sipping the coffee but it tastes burnt.

'The last couple of weeks were a nightmare – do you know how hard it is not to see your children?' He looks away. 'It's hell, Ali, that's what it is. Not to be part of their lives, see them in the morning, hear their news in the evening when I come home.'

He takes a gulp of coffee. 'I look at them now sometimes and they're like two strangers to me, and then just as I'm getting to know them all over again they go back to her . . .'

'They love you, Dermot, don't you know that?'

'I think so. I try to believe it but when I don't see them I doubt myself, I doubt it all.'

'I've had a shit week, too.' I look at him and a small tear escapes down my cheek. He puts his cup down and comes over and wipes it away with his thumb.

'I'm sorry, Ali. I shouldn't have sent that text, I should have been there for you – that's what friends are for, right?'

'I wasn't here for you either. I could have helped you to see Jane and—'

'It doesn't matter now. Honestly, it doesn't.'

I shrug. 'I was in the hospital and . . .'

'I know. Don't worry about it . . .'

'And then I wanted to text you to explain and . . .'

'But you couldn't because I'd told you not to . . .'

I'm crying now, big fat tears streaming down, my nose beginning to drip.

'You see, Ali? It's all my fault – I can't even manage a friendship – let alone anything else.'

A tear runs down his face, a perfect designer one that doesn't even leave a water track.

'I'm not a nice person and I don't deserve friends like you, children like mine. I don't deserve anything.'

He's crying now too and trying not to and I feel sorry for him.

He smiles his little boy's smile and cocks his head to one side. 'Forgiven?'

I touch his face lightly and nod. 'Of course.'

'Thank you, Ali.'

He leans down and kisses me on the cheek and whispers in my ear.

'Where is everybody?'

'Not here . . .'

My heart pounds in my chest as he bends to kiss me again, this time on the mouth. But then he jumps back, hands in the air like a man being arrested. 'I'm sorry, Alison, sorry. I did it again. I can't help it around you . . .'

I laugh. 'It's OK.'

'Great. I'll stand six feet away from you at all times and just drink my coffee – how's that?'

We both laugh now and the tension relaxes a little.

'How was Jane?' he asks suddenly, in that weird way he has of jumping unexpectedly in his line of thought.

'She seemed fine.'

He shakes his head. 'I miss them so much – I can't cope without them and that bitch knows.'

'You'll have to talk to her, try and work something out.'

He looks away and I know he's on the verge of tears again. I reach out and touch his hair. 'I'll come with you, I'll help.'

He turns and looks at me with watery eyes. 'Would you? You'd do that for me?'

I nod. He has the little-boy look again, the Frankie look. I hug him to me and his arms tighten around me. He smells of man and sex and safety.

'We're breaking the six-feet rule,' he says into my hair.

'I don't care,' I answer, pulling away from him and looking up into his face. He's smiling and I lean up and kiss him lightly on the mouth. He groans and I kiss him again and his tongue probes my mouth and his hands roam up and down my body and I want him now, I want the release of it, the beginning, middle and end of it, the being lost in it and it's so close as I feel his hand on the top of my trousers. Sexual energy races through me, familiar and new all at once. He slides his fingers under the elastic of my knickers and I groan softly. Then his fingers are slipping inside me and I can feel my wetness and my head is full of sensation. Then he takes his fingers out and looks at me as he licks them slowly.

'I wanted to do that for so long. I wanted to taste you.' He smiles and we begin to kiss again and I wonder why I haven't done this in so long because it's such a fucking great feeling and I want him inside me now and not just his fingers. I press my body against his, prising my knee between his legs. He groans and lowers his mouth and begins sucking my nipple, first through my clothing and then pushing that away too. I open my blouse as he sucks.

Then he pushes me towards the kitchen table and perches me on the edge of it. He's still sucking my nipples, going from one to the other in a delicious kind of eeny meeny miney mo. I throw my head back and give myself up to the sex. He starts kissing my mouth again and I fumble with his trouser belt until his pants drop on to the floor, followed by his boxers. He's still kissing me. Nothing else, just kissing. And I kiss him back for a while and then take the initiative. I lower my hand to guide his penis into me. It's small and soft in my hand. He keeps kissing me and I pull my face back.

'Oh,' I say in surprise. He ignores me and keeps on kissing my nose and my cheeks.

'Slight problem, Dermot.'

He kisses my neck.

'What's up?' The minute I say it I know it's the wrong thing.

'Are you being smart?' He says, into my neck.

I pull his face up and look at him. 'No, I'm not.'

He shrugs and starts the kissing again.

'What's wrong?'

He looks away. 'I don't know. It never happened before until today.'

I know he's lying. I can see the lie in his eyes. The little boy caught stealing.

'Jesus, Dermot . . .' I look past him to the kitchen window. Frankie's standing there, watching, tears and snot running freely down his nose. He ducks away when he sees me and I want to run after him and explain.

'Hey, it never happened to me before, ever.'

'Oh right. My fault – I should have guessed.' I bend down and pick up my jeans and begin to pull them on. I feel suddenly cold and Frankie's face is still bothering me. He must have been there for ages, just watching. I shiver.

'I . . . it's happened a few times before . . . stress . . . I don't know . . .'

I feel completely deflated and I know it's not just the bad sex. It's something way bigger than that.

'You don't know how hard my life is . . .'

Tears stream down his face and I know I should comfort

him in some way but now I find the tears and the self-pity repulsive. Indulgent. Childish. What I really want is for him to be gone.

'I've lost my job and my children and now my girlfriend has called it off . . .' He sniffles and I pat him on his bare, golden-brown shoulder.

'Get dressed, you'll get cold.'

More tears.

'It's not the end of the world you know. Things could be a lot worse.'

He laughs through his tears. 'How? That's impossible.'

I look at him standing there, leaning against my kitchen table. The waxed oak table that Brian and I had painstakingly chosen one cold November day when Jack was just a toddler. I'd wanted a snazzy, modern, glass affair but Brian insisted on the oak, saying it would be there long after we'd gone. He'd been right about that.

I see him now without the mask – the Dermot mask of lovely wool overcoats and well-cut suits and a perfect mouth able to talk the talk.

'You still have your children.'

'Do I?'

I wish he'd put on some clothes – standing there in his limp glory.

'Yes, you do. Two beautiful children.'

'That I'm not allowed to see.'

'Stop making excuses – you could see them if you really wanted to . . .'

'No, I couldn't – she won't let me . . .'

'Oh, for God's sake. If you really want something then there's always a way.'

His face takes on a petulant look that reminds me of the

spoilt Sebastian in *Brideshead Revisited*.

I notice I'm shivering. I bend down and pick up his shorts and throw them at him. 'Let's get dressed.'

And then I look up at the doorway and Brian is there.

'I . . . Brian we . . . Jesus Christ.'

He looks at us, both of us, and says nothing, and it seems like time stands still in the room. I can hear the low hum of the fridge and light rain falling outside. A sniffle from Dermot. A small cough from me.

'Don't rush yourselves on my account – forgot something – won't be a minute.' He holds my eyes with his before he leaves, his face tight, like as if he has to concentrate really hard to hold it in place. It's a look of his I recognise. The last time I saw it was in a cold morgue on a sleety January afternoon.

Nine

Jane

I hate Daddy so much now that I even tell Leah about the rope. We're in her house after karate and we're having a great laugh and stuff and it just comes out of me before I can stop it.

'My dad tried to hang himself.'

Her dark eyes are round with disbelief.

'No way. When?'

'Last year.'

'Oh my God, Jane, were you like there?'

I nod. Now that I've said it I want to take it back.

'Oh my God. And was it like terrible?'

'Please don't tell anyone.'

She hugs me close to her. 'You're my best friend, Jane. I'd never tell if you asked me not to. Never. I swear on Sandy's life. It's our secret.'

I believe her and I'm glad now that I told.

'And do you know the really weird thing?'

Her eyes are round again. She shakes her head. 'No. What's the really weird thing?'

'My uncle Kieran actually did it. Hung himself in the shed.'

And then she just says it out – the thing I've been thinking in my head all the time since Nana's house. She says it straight out.

'Can you inherit it? I mean, wanting to do something like that.'

I don't answer her. I pick the pale pink polish from my nails and don't even look at her.

'Joking, you fool,' she says, laughing, but I know she isn't. 'Sleep here tonight – please please please,' she says, pulling my arm and jumping up and down.

'I have to go to Dad's later. I like have to go.' I shrug.

'That's stupid. You shouldn't have to go somewhere if you don't want to. That's like taking away your human rights and stuff.'

I laugh. 'I'm used to it now.'

'Please Jane – we'll have a laugh. We can go on Bebo – my dad let me join – please?'

'I can't.'

'Come on, you can join up too and Darren Tierney's on it – we'll have a great skit.'

'Honestly, Leah. I have to stay at my dad's.'

Just as I'm getting ready to leave we're in the kitchen and Mrs Collins starts giving me these like weird looks and asking me am I OK and stuff but Leah swears she didn't tell. I hate when Mrs Collins does that. Looks at me like she knows what's inside my head.

Daddy still has a suntan. It's the first thing I notice when we go into the flat. It's weeks since we stayed and it's so weird and the flat smells damp and it's so cold. He's all happy and jolly but it's pretend happy and I don't smile at him – not even once. Ben of course whoops and throws his arms around him and hugs him and I watch and hold Lucky close to me and I promise myself that I won't talk to him – not for the whole weekend.

I mean it was cool the last few weekends because I got to go to Leah's and we went swimming with her dad and had a mad laugh in the pool and stuff. And I got to see Nana and that was brilliant even though I thought it'd be really boring because Nana's house is in the middle of nowhere.

I hate this flat and I hate Daddy too. And I bet we wouldn't ever have to come here again except for stupid dumb-ass Ben, crying to Mammy and telling her how much he wanted to see Daddy. And then she gives in and tells us this morning that we had to come. I haven't answered Daddy's phone calls or texts since the night at Nana's. She told me not to and it works. Just don't answer, Nana says. If you don't want to talk then just don't answer. And I don't want to talk to him. Or see him or be in the same room as him.

But Ben wants to talk and he's talking to Dad now like it's going out of fashion and I go into the bedroom with Lucky and bang the door – not too hard – so if he says anything I can still pretend it's an accident. The room is freezing and I lie on the bed and it feels damp. Lucky curls up beside me and stares at me with her bright green alien-eyes and then she nods off just like that.

I look at the cracks in the ceiling. There's one really big one that's spreading down to the wall. I close my eyes and wish Nana was here. I think I should have told Nana everything instead of Leah but she hasn't been around and if someone doesn't know all the stuff then it's too long and hard to tell. Leah understands. Especially now because there's stuff going on in her house as well. She doesn't say anything – nobody does and they all carry on like it's all normal but I can feel it the second I go into the house. The second that Mr and Mrs Collins are in a room together. And Mrs Collins is totally weirding out but I can't say that to Leah . . . I mean all that stuff with the Traveller boy and . . . just even the look of her. Weird.

'Jane?'

Daddy's knocking on the door and then he just comes in so I don't know why he bothers knocking in the first place.

He sits on the edge of the bed and strokes Lucky's sleeping head.

'I lit the fire.'

I don't answer.

'I'm making some hot chocolate for Ben – would you like some, Hon?'

I shake my head and stare at the crack in the ceiling. It looks like it grew already.

'Janie . . .' He touches my arm and then pulls his hand away. 'I'll make you some chocolate.'

When he's gone I cry. But quietly, so that they don't hear.

In the morning I wake up but I lie in my bed with the duvet pulled right up to my chin. I hear Ben and Daddy in the sitting room talking about Lanzarote. And Ben is so stupid and believing everything Daddy says and I get mad and before I can stop myself I march out and sit next to Ben on the couch. Daddy has an atlas and he's pointing out Lanzarote to Ben.

'Hi, Hon, do want some breakfast?' he says, smiling at me.

I shake my head.

'Did you go on a camel?' Ben asks, still studying the map.

Daddy smiles and nods. 'I just got the photos back yesterday. Hang on a tick,' he says and goes to the sideboard and rummages through a stack of papers.

'Here we are guys,' he says, waving a packet at us. He squeezes in between Ben and me and I move away a little. He takes out a bundle of photos. I search for the remote and flick on the TV. Mass.

Ben is laughing with Daddy as they look at the photos. I watch Mass.

'Here, Jane, that's the local market. And look at this one, that's Fiona and me in front of the ancient town walls and . . .' he starts laughing and shaking his head, 'that's your old dad on a camel.' He pushes the pictures at me so I'm forced to look. I don't want to see them. Pictures of him and Fiona smiling at the camera in the bright sky-blue sunshine. Him with his arm around Fiona, her looking up into his face, tiny like a child next to him. Like a little girl. I hand the pictures back and turn up the sound on the TV.

'That's such a cool photo, Daddy, I wish I was there on a camel's back,' says Ben.

Daddy laughs. 'It was pretty cool all right.'

'I bet it was,' I say, surprising myself with the sound of my voice. 'Just the place to go with your girlfriend when you're burnt out.'

'Jane . . . you don't understand.'

'No, Daddy, Ben doesn't understand. I understand it no problem. Tell him why you brought your girlfriend and not him. Tell him why you lied to us.'

He puts his hand on my shoulder. 'Janey, please . . .'

I shake it off and tears come, even though I'm trying to swallow them back. I try to stop my voice from shaking when I speak. 'You're a liar. You went off with your girlfriend, sunning yourself and having sex and you lied to Mammy and you lied to us and it was Ben's birthday – tell him, Ben, tell him that you were mad, go on, tell him!'

I'm standing up now, right in front of the two of them and Ben has dropped his head and won't look at me and his shoulders are shaking and I'm sorry but I still can't stop myself.

'You're a liar and your girlfriend matters the most and . . . I hate you . . . and I wish you were dead.' I scream this and my throat hurts and then I run into the bathroom and lock the door and collapse in front of it. The tears are hot on my face and my whole body shakes. Daddy knocks on the door and I know what's going to happen. It'll be exactly like Mammy, first telling me the awful stuff about the rope and then telling me how sorry she is, and sure enough Daddy is saying sorry now, sorry for upsetting me and that he loves me and I should know he does.

I go to the shelf and look for his razor and find it behind a jar of men's moisturiser. I open the head and slip the blade out and my heart thumps when I see it. I lean against the sink and roll up my sleeve. The crisscrosses from the last time are nearly gone. I look at the smooth, white skin and pick a spot and slice but I do it a bit too hard and almost scream as the pain and blood come in a rush of red on my arm and in my head. It's so bad that I want to faint and my stomach starts to churn and then I throw up, just making it to the toilet, and I hear Daddy calling, saying 'Are you all right Hon, are you all right?' I try to stand up and the wall in front of me moves and then when I open my eyes again there's a giant map of Lanzarote on the wall and then the pain swallows me up and it's so beautiful that I want to laugh and cry all at the same time.

Dad brings us to Milanos for dinner. He's so nice to me and my arm hurts so bad but I feel grand. Like as if the minute the blood came all the bad stuff went out of me. I feel so calm sitting here watching Ben and Daddy talk and Ben so wants me to be happy too and I am really inside me, it's just that I'm a bit tired. But I am happy and even when Daddy says Fiona is coming to join us I'm still happy. We wait and wait but there's no sign of Fiona and Daddy tries to ring her but she doesn't answer so we eat our pizzas and order our chocolate fudge cake and Daddy keeps looking at his phone even though it's right beside him on the table. I wish he'd put the phone in his pocket because it's making him so nervous and fidgety. The chocolate cake arrives and Ben's face lights up.

'This is just the best,' he says through a mouthful of cake and I laugh but Daddy isn't really listening. He hasn't touched his cake and the ice cream is melting.

'You should eat that before it melts,' I say but he doesn't really hear that either.

Then he speaks to me. 'There's been a bit of a blip at work and . . . well . . . I'm looking for a new job,' he announces. Ben smiles at him like he's just said something great.

I swirl cake around my plate, trying to keep it separate from the cream.

'It's nothing to worry about really. I'll get a new job, a better one soon and it will all be fine,' he says and I feel his eyes on me.

'I thought you loved your job. You said it was the best company you ever worked for,' I say but I don't look at him. I keep separating the cake from the cream.

He laughs, that girl laugh he does sometimes that makes him sound mad. 'Things change, Jane, they burnt me out, that crowd, piling the pressure on me . . . Anyway I've something else in the pipeline.'

'Can I still go skiing?' I look at him now, straight into his eyes, so like my own.

He shakes his head. 'We'll have to see about that. Christmas is coming and Ben isn't getting any fancy trip. We might have to tighten our belts for a little while.'

'Did you know before you went on your holidays?' I ask and am glad when I see hurt in his face.

'Of course not, Jane,' he says.

My arm throbs. 'Can we go now?' I ask.

His phone rings and he jumps and picks it up. 'Hon?' he whines into it, 'Where are you? I've been ringing all night.'

I can hear the tinny sound of 'Hon's' voice replying to Daddy and his face changes as he listens. Ben has cleared his cake and is spooning up the remaining crumbs with his finger. Daddy's mouth is in a hard line and his jaw is sticking out the way Ben's does when he's angry. He hangs up the phone and stirs his coffee and looks all sad and hurt and I'm delighted.

It's the night before my Brown Belt and my stomach is jittery with nerves. I'm sleeping over in Leah's so we can get in some last-minute practise but she doesn't need to. I sit on the bed and watch as she goes through her moves and I'm jealous of her.

'You're brilliant. He'll give you a Black Belt tomorrow, not a Brown.'

She smiles at me. 'I'm so nervous, Jane, and do you know what always happens to me when I get nervous?'

I shake my head and stroke Sandy's lovely marmalade fur. She licks my hand exactly the way Lucky does.

'I get the runs.' She puts her hand over her mouth and giggles.

'The runs?'

'You know. The runs. The Sonias.'

'Sonias?'

She jumps on to the bed beside me, scaring Sandy. 'That's

what my dad calls them. He says that Sonia O'Sullivan was a great runner and then during like a really important race like the Olympics or the Worlds or something she got like the worst dose . . .'

'No!' I scream. 'Disgusting!'

'It's true. So Dad calls them the Sonias now.'

'My nana calls them the squits.'

'Oh my God, that's worse! That sounds so like . . .'

'Stop, Leah,' I say, covering my ears with my hands. 'Too much information, too much.'

'Hey, do you want to sleep over again tomorrow night after the competition? Dad said he'll take us to the movies on Sunday at the new Omniplex, not the scumbag one where you come out all itchy.'

'I can't. I have to stay at my dad's again this weekend.'

She jumps off the bed and stands in front of the mirror and mock-karate chops her reflection. 'Again? You stayed there last weekend. I thought you hated it.'

'I do but he wants more access now if you don't mind cos he got himself fired.'

She turns to face me. 'What? You never said.'

I shrug. 'He says the job burnt him out but Mam says he couldn't hack it as usual and they got wise and fired him.'

'So he has no job so he decides he wants to spend more time with you? That's so not fair,' she says and pulls a go-go from her pony tail so that her hair falls around her face and shoulders.

'Yeah, I know. Anyway, forget about him.'

'Want to know something?' she says, taking a hairbrush from the locker. She runs it through her dark, shiny hair, all razor cut at the ends.

'Yeah. What?'

'Something about your dad . . .' she turns away and looks at herself in the mirror.

The air in the room is very still and I can hear Sandy purring loudly. I reach out to bury my hand in her fur but I can't find her on the bed. Leah starts to brush her hair again.

'What about him?' I ask after a while.

'Nothing, just joking,' she says and smiles at me in the glass.

'What about him, Leah?' I ask. I know this is risky, that Leah might go off into one of her horrible moods, but I think she's lying to me. Well, not lying exactly. What she's doing is saying look here is a secret and I'm going to show you the outside but not the important part, not the inside.

'He's a fool, that's all. They all are.' She smiles at me and I smile back but I know she's lying.

'All?'

'Yeah. Mothers, dads, brothers . . . come on. Let's watch a film.'

Daddy turns up for the competition. I'm not surprised. He's sent me loads of texts about it during the week, asking what time is it on, is Mam going, is Leah's mam going, so I kind of had a feeling he'd show up. He's inside in his karate suit talking to the instructor and the external examiner and I pretend I don't see him and roll my eyes at Leah and we both laugh.

Mrs Collins comes in to the hall with us and then all of a sudden says she has to get something in the shop and is gone back out the door. Leah rolls her eyes at me this time and we laugh again. Mr Collins arrives at the same time as Mam and Ben and they sit together on the benches that are arranged in front of the mats.

We all practise on the floor and I can hear Daddy's voice above everybody else, really high with this laugh at the end of it. I feel my face going red so I move away to the far corner of the room. Leah is practising with Darren Tierney and she's so much better than him and he looks like he's in love with her but maybe it's just jealousy. Why did Daddy have to wear his stupid karate suit? I mean it's not like he's in the competition.

Mrs Collins arrives in late, just as Ben's group go on the mats. She stands over by the door and I can see Daddy waving at her and pointing to an empty space on the bench but she just waves her glove at him and stays standing. Ben makes a dog's arse of his assessment and I get that feeling I always get about Ben. That feeling of wanting to hug him and murder him at the same time.

Daddy grins at me and gives me the thumbs up as I take my turn on the mat and I try to not let him bother me. I try to block everything out – Mammy's cross face, Ben sitting next to her with his head drooped, looking up every so often only to drop his eyes quickly again. Leah sitting cross-legged on the floor, Darren Tierney beside her, knees touching. Leah's brother Peter smiling at me and waving a Spurs scarf in the air. I try to block out the stinging pain in my arm, the yellow gunk that keeps coming out of it no matter how much Dettol I dab on, but most of all Daddy and his eager stupid face and his high voice talking to the coach. Even though the coach isn't even listening.

It feels like a dream, facing my opponent, going through the moves, listening for the bell. And then it's over and I think it's OK because the coach is smiling at me. Daddy is still yapping into his ear but he's smiling at me and mouthing well done and he makes me feel so great.

We get a takeaway for dinner and go back to Daddy's flat, clutching the greasy bags of fish and chips and burgers, the smell filling up the car and making us all hungry. Daddy lights a fire as Ben and I dump chips on to plates. Ben is smiling because he got his Brown Belt even though he wasn't great – the coach said he was good enough to pass and of course Leah got like the highest marks in the history of karate.

Daddy is weird. I watch him now as we eat and he can't seem to sit down and when he talks it's a whole pile of stuff like when you have to talk in school about a subject off the top of your head. And he doesn't sit down at all, he walks around eating and talking at the same time and checking his phone in his pocket.

'Put it on vibrate, Daddy, then you won't have to check it,' I say as he takes it out for the millionth time.

'You were brilliant today, Hon, the coach said you were the most improved – did I tell you that?' He goes to the fireplace and pokes at the briquettes. 'What happened to Ali? She was gone as soon as the competition finished and I really wanted to say hello to her – just to be nice. Polite. Say hi – that's all.' He juts his jaw out like a bold Ben.

I shrug. Leah's dad was taking them to Luigi Malones for dinner and her mother was doing something else. No big deal.

Later we watch a really dumb movie that Ben loves about three cowboy bank robbers that find a baby in a desert. There's even singing in it and Ben throws a cushion at me when I say it's gay. Daddy is on the phone for ages. He's in the kitchen, then the bathroom, and then the kitchen again. He's talking to 'Hon'. To Fiona. And then after the movie there's a knock on the door and we all jump. Nobody calls to the flat ever. Daddy goes to answer the door.

Fiona arrives back in with him, her face shiny from rain. 'Hi, lads, how are you?' she says as she shakes the rain from her hair.

'Fine,' Ben and I say in unison and then we laugh.

'Coffee, tea, a beer? I've cold beer in the fridge. And I have some wine. Would you like a glass of wine, Fiona?' Daddy says, but he's all weird still – like there isn't enough time so he has to say and do everything much faster.

Fiona looks at him. 'I told you already Dermot. I can't stay. I only came because it was . . .'

I can feel her looking at us as she stops talking.

'Come on Ben, bed,' I say.

'Do we have to? There's another movie on . . .'

'Bed. 'Night, Daddy, 'night, Fiona.' I go into my bedroom and shiver as I undress. Ben climbs into bed with his clothes on and I don't blame him. It's freezing in here. The duvet smells musty and damp and I wish I'd brought Lucky in with me so that I could feel her warm body and listen to her soft purr, which always makes me sleepy. I don't want to go back out to get her now. Not while they're talking.

But I might as well have stayed in the room with them I can hear their voices so clearly. I put the pillow over my head but it makes no difference. Fiona is telling Daddy he's depressed. She's not exactly saying it like that but it's what she means. Her voice is low and calm and quiet – *we're going nowhere, the relationship is nose-diving, oh for God's sake, Dermot, the writing was on the wall in Lanzarote. Don't talk about it like it was some perfect, idyllic holiday. You spent the time bitching about your ex-wife. Do you ever move on?*

And then Daddy and his fast-forward voice, *Hon, give our relationship a chance. It's hard with the children and now the job but I'm confident . . . no, that's unfair. I didn't say I slept with her exactly, we got close, she understood and I . . . I should never have told you, Hon, it meant nothing, but I respect you and I trust you and that's why I told you . . .*

Daddy's crying now and I pinch my arm where it's sore. I want it to stop. I want Fiona and her tight, calm voice to go and let Daddy alone. She's making him cry like a little kid, like Ben.

Look, Dermot, it's over. I've told you why a hundred times. It's over.

Ali offered support when I needed it . . .

Ali. The name is a chant in my head blocking out Daddy's voice. Ali Ali Ali. I must have heard it wrong. I had the pillow over my ears and the words were muffled and it's so not true. I just know it isn't because it's too disgusting and gross and I can't even think about it. But something Leah said about Daddy keeps popping up, keeps trying to tell me something but I force it away. I take the pillow from my head and sit up, listening on purpose now.

It's over, Dermot. I . . . it's all too much for me. I've never dealt with anything like this before . . .

You don't have children, you see. That's what it is – we can work through this . . .

It's not the children, it's you, Dermot. You need, I don't know, you should see someone, a therapist, I don't know.

I can hear her high heels on the lino as she leaves. Then the sound of the door closing softly. The sound of rain on the window and Ben snoring and Daddy crying. There's something about the crying – it makes me think of the rope. Of that day, watching them fight, listening to Daddy, and that high voice, and Mammy not realising what was going to happen. But I did and then he was there in the doorway, the bright blue rope around his neck, and I had to think of a way to stop him.

There's a mood building up inside me, a black one, worse than any of Leah's and I close my fist tight and then punch the wall so hard that I have to swallow a scream. My knuckles throb under the quilt, first with no pain and then a huge wave of it that fills my head. But it makes me think straight. Daddy needs me.

I get up and go quietly into the sitting room. Daddy's on the couch with his head in his hands and when I come in he looks up at me and he looks so like Ben did today and I feel the exact same thing. I want to love and hurt him all at the same time.

'Janie,' he says, wiping his face with the back of his sleeve. 'You're still awake? Do you want hot chocolate? I'll make hot chocolate for both of us and we'll see if there's anything on TV and I'll get my quilt and . . .' He smiles at me eagerly and rushes off into the kitchen. I follow him and watch as he pours milk into a saucepan.

'Cocoa, we'll make cocoa. All the hot chocolate is gone and I never thought of it today when I did the shopping and . . .' a tear escapes and rolls down his cheek and he takes a deep breath and shakes his head and then gives me that mad smile again. I touch his arm.

'You'll be OK, Daddy, won't you?'

He hugs me to him so tightly I can't breathe and kisses the top of my head over and over and he feels so strong.

'Of course I will, Hon, of course I will. Don't mind me. Just a minor blip in life, that's all. I'll be fine, you wait and see.'

We have no school today. It's a training day for teachers but I wake up early anyway. Ben is still snoring as I pad out to the kitchen. While I'm putting on the kettle I notice that Lucky's not in her basket. I search the whole flat for her but there's no sign of her. I try not to panic but she's still only a baby and I'm worried that if she got out into the street she'd get herself lost or something. Daddy comes into the kitchen, his eyes dark and swollen.

'Daddy, did you see Lucky? I searched everywhere and I can't find her and . . .'

Daddy looks at me like I'm talking Chinese or something and goes to make his morning coffee. He doesn't say one word as he fills the pot with coffee and water.

'Daddy?'

He doesn't hear me. It's like he's used up all his talking last night and has none left for today. And then I hear it. A tiny little miaow.

I run out to the hallway and it's louder now, right outside the front door. I open the door and Lucky's lying there, so small and damp from rain. I pick her up and she screeches in pain. Tears are running down my face and I run into Daddy with the kitten in my arms. I'm trying to hold her gently and it must be working because now she isn't crying. She's just lying there like she's asleep.

'Daddy, something's happened to Lucky. She's hurt, Daddy. Do something.'

He looks down at the kitten and takes her in his arms. She's limp. Her head falls back and a tiny pink piece of her tongue is sticking out.

'Jane, I think she's . . . I think she's dead. Jesus . . .'

'No she's not. She's not dead, you liar, she's not dead. You're lying to me, you're just a liar.' I scream this at him and Ben is in the kitchen now and he's crying too. I try to take the kitten back from Daddy and scream liar liar liar at him.

But Lucky is dead. Part of me can't believe it. I still think that she'll come bouncing in through the door in a little while, the bell on her collar jingling her arrival. She'll purr at my feet and dig her claws so hard into my socks and when I move she'll slide along the lino floor. I still think that when I curl up on my bed tonight to read Mammy's *Hello!* magazine, she'll sit on the pillow staring at me with her lime-green eyes and then her eyes will droop and she'll purr herself to sleep and I'll bury my hands in her silky fur like Ben used to do with Blanky, his baby blanket that Mammy had to bribe away from him a few years ago.

Why Lucky? If a kitten had to die, if God wanted a kitten to die, then why not Sandy? Leah barely looks at Sandy now, barely even rubs her or feeds her and Mrs Collins hates her and only Mr Collins bothers and why had it to be Lucky?

She's in the kitchen now in a blue shoebox. Her stripy body is cold and stiff and her lovely lime-green eyes are shut tight. I'm going to take her home and bury her near our treehouse.

I won't talk to Daddy. It's his fault she's dead. He must have let her out during the night and I hate him. He came a while ago and said we'll get you another kitten, these things happen, it's terrible but they do, and I screamed at him and told him to fuck off for the very first time in my life and that made me cry even more.

I tell Leah in school the next day and I don't even cry now. I'm used to it, to the picture in my head of Lucky's stiff body like somebody had frozen it solid. I tell Leah but she doesn't understand, not really, because she doesn't love Sandy the same way. She pats my arm and says I can always get another one, kittens are so easy to get and then she offers me one of her salsa wraps – her dad's special recipe.

I don't really talk to her for the rest of the day and then we're standing outside the school gates and she asks me to sleep over on Friday – her dad wants to take us shopping for ski clothes, there's a sale in River Deep Mountain High.

'Please, Jane, please sleep over – there's like fifty per cent off all the ski wear – and there's this pink jacket with a white fur collar – it's like the coolest jacket ever and . . .'

I don't want to go shopping for pink jackets. I want Lucky back. I want Leah to know how sad I am.

'And we're going to Copper and Spice too – Daddy's treat for being away all week. We'll have a ball, please, Jane, please?'

She smiles at me like she hasn't a care in the world.

'I can't.'

'Why not? Give me like one good reason why not.'

'Because I don't want to.'

She looks at me like I slapped her.

'Be like that so. I don't know why I'm friends with you any more. I mean, you're not like my only friend in the world – do you know that?'

She has her hand on her hip, her eyes slitty and moody.

I just shrug. 'Ring one of your friends so. I'm sure they'll sleep over, go shopping.'

'I might just do that because you're gone really weird lately – always weirding out – I mean OK, so your kitten died. I'm sorry but I didn't make her die, did I? And you think you can just take it out . . .'

'Why don't you sleep in mine?'

'I . . . well, Daddy's taking me shopping and then we're going to see . . .'

'So you can't?'

She doesn't answer.

'Why do we always do what you want, Leah? Why is it always your house, your shopping trips, your plans?'

'That's not true, Jane. You're just being a bitch because your cat died and I told you I was sorry this morning, didn't I? I told you twice actually.'

'You're so sympathetic. You said sorry twice. Wow.'

'Do you know something, Jane? I hate you sometimes and I

don't even want you to go skiing now, you'll just be mopey and weird all the time.'

'I don't want to go skiing, Leah, so why don't you do me a favour and fuck off right now?' I smile at her, like I couldn't care less and I'm pleased when I see the anger and hurt in her face.

'I know a secret about your dad and you're going down the same road.' She smirks then and marches off.

'Say it then – go on, say it out to my face, you bitch,' I shout after her but she keeps walking away. I begin to walk in the other direction, tears streaming down my face.

In bed later I pinch my arm so hard I have to stuff my hand in my mouth to stop myself from screaming. But the pain doesn't make the black thing inside me go away this time. It just makes it worse. I pinch again. Really hard and keep pinching and pinching without stopping, keeping my eyes shut tight. I see her face in my head and I'm mad with her and God and I hate the two of them.

I hate God more because he keeps changing things – making me think that I'll have something for ever and then just taking it away because he feels like it. He keeps breaking things up. Giving them to me and then smashing them and I can nearly hear his voice like Nelson in *The Simpsons* saying ha-ha, ha-ha, fooled you.

I bring my arm up to my mouth and bite down hard, as hard as I can, and I'm mad inside now and I know one thing for certain. I hate God. God is a bastard. I say this out loud and it makes me laugh. And then I say something worse. I say it really loud so the whole house can hear. I scream it out at the top of my lungs: God is a cunt. A shitbag.

Ten

Alison

'Nothing happened with Dermot Harris. He's depressed, he's got issues . . .'

'Spare me, Ali. Spare me the sympathy card – poor Dermot, he's depressed so he gets to waltz around my kitchen naked.'

'That's not what I—'

'Naked, mind you – oh, and with my wife – did I forget to add that little detail?'

I kick at a box of Christmas decorations waiting for a week to be hung. 'Do we have to have this conversation again?' I turn around and look at Brian.

He puts up a hand. 'No need to shout. I'm just saying I'm leaving, that's all. I never mentioned his name.'

'Oh, for fuck's sake, Brian, you don't have to. I see it in your eyes, in your face every morning, in your body in bed at night.'

'And what do you expect, Ali?' He stands there, hands dropped to his sides, eyes questioning me.

'I don't know, Brian. Some of that communication that you always talk about, a little understanding – for Christ's sake, nothing happened. I told you that. Nothing fucking happened.' I kick the box again and two star-shaped glass ornaments fall out. They bounce across the tiles without breaking.

He folds his arms across his chest and tilts his head to one side, looking straight at me. Exactly like Jack does. Like Jack did.

'Did I even come into the picture? When you decided to have sex with him, did you even think of me? Of the kids? Our life?'

'I didn't decide anything. Things just happened and . . .'

'Ah for fuck's sake. You're as fucking mad as him.' He throws his hands in the air and goes to walk out of the sitting room.

'I'm sorry.'

He stops and turns back towards me. 'Really?'

I nod, a small tear escaping down my cheek.

'OK, you're sorry. Sorry that you did it or sorry that I arrived home and caught you? Sorry that we're at rock bottom, you and I, sorry that you've opted out of everything? Ali, what exactly are you sorry about?'

I hold my head in my hands like as if an answer will come if I think hard enough. I shrug. 'I don't know.'

Brian laughs, a mean dead Jack laugh. 'Look, I'm not going into all of this again, none of it matters anymore. I'm leaving, Ali. Once Christmas is over, I'm taking the kids skiing and I won't be coming back here. End of story.'

He walks away, and I pick up a small stuffed Santa from the box and throw it at him.

'Go, I don't care, I don't give a fuck anymore what you do, so go, please, be my guest,' I scream, tears running down my face.

He turns as he reaches the door. 'I know you don't care.

And you don't care because you need serious help. Not even therapy, Ali, you're way beyond that.'

'Oh, I get it. You had the therapy so you're all better now. You have fancy names for all of it – nice, neat names that make it all go away.'

He comes back into the room, eyes blazing now. His voice, when he speaks is low and mean. 'At least I'm trying to get on with it, Alison. For the sake of our two living children, I'm trying to move on . . .'

'Move on? Trying to move on?' I shout, my heart thumping in my chest. 'Trying to forget is a more accurate description, Brian. Camper vans, skiing trips, weekends in Rome. At least I deal with reality, miserable and all as it is – at least I have the guts to do that.'

He's so close to me now that I can smell him – garlic and aftershave and beer.

His face is twisted, ugly even when he speaks. 'I'll try your way so, Ali – I'll tune out of life for months and when a little extra-marital sex presents itself in the shape of the first lunatic you see – in this case, Dermot Harris – I'll have a little helping of that and then I'll walk myself stupid in the woods every day while my children pine for me . . .'

Before he can finish I slap him hard across the face. So hard that my hand throbs.

He catches both my hands and pushes them down by my side. 'You're sick,' he says, his voice barely above a whisper. 'You're sick and you blame yourself for Jack's . . .'

'Don't you fucking even go there, Brian, don't you dare or I swear I'll kill you, I will,' I scream, launching myself at him.

'Listen to yourself, Alison, just listen to yourself.'

He walks out the door and I follow him, but Leah is standing in the hallway with Pete. Her hand is on her brother's shoulder, her eyes huge and dark and disbelieving. Brian runs upstairs.

'Leah, Petey, we were just . . .' I say but already she's shaking her head at me, not wanting me to say anything.

'Leah . . .'

But she's gone off after Brian and Pete follows his sister. I wipe my eyes and I know I have to get out of there. Grabbing my handbag and keys, I run out the door and into my car and reverse noisily down the drive.

I end up in the woods. Winter woods, with straggly, bare trees and a mist over the river, and it looks eerie and beautiful. The colours around me are browns and greys and silvers. I walk along the riverbank, my heart still pounding in my chest, and take deep breaths. My phone rings but I ignore it. I come to the red bridge, its silhouette reflected perfectly in the still evening water. I sit down on a damp tree stump and shiver in the cold December evening. I want to cry. For Leah and Pete, for Brian, for all of it, but no tears come and I think now that this is it, this will be my life now. Always in this place where you're there but not there. Limbo. The place you end up rather than choose.

It's the last light of evening when I leave and I walk through the woods towards my car wondering what I should do. Go home. Go to Rachel. Richard. This thought makes me laugh. These people are like Brian. They are the move-on brigade, the let-it-go brigade. The advocates of the therapy tablet. But I know something they don't. I know that this really is limbo, and bar turning back time, there is no escape.

A sudden noise behind me pulls me out of my head and I look back quickly. There's only a whispery rustling of branches and a faint purr of water flowing from the river. Familiar sounds. Just as I turn back I imagine I hear someone laughing.

'Frankie?' I call out. But there's silence. I walk on, my boots crunching loudly on the soft earth path. And then another noise, louder this time.

'Who's there?' I ask the darkness behind me. I stand there for a minute looking back towards the bridge. Nothing, just the usual sounds. I'm not scared but I walk faster all the same. I can see the faint, orange glow of street lights through the bare trees as I reach the edge of the wood. And then suddenly I hear it again, a crackle like somebody stepping on dry twigs.

'Frankie?'

And then he's right in front of me, scaring the life out of me.

'Jesus, Frankie, you scared the shit out of me.'

'Shit, shit, shit,' he says, laughing.

I laugh now too. He falls into step beside me and reaches for my hand like a small child would. I grasp it and we walk along the riverbank, the dusky sky around us darkened by the minute.

'Frankie, life is a ball of shit that you must push up a hill,' I say, as our feet crunch on dead leaves.

'Shit! Shit!' he repeats again, delighted with himself.

'Yeah. Shit. And you have to keep pushing it and sometimes the shit will fall on you anyway – no matter how hard you push, no matter what you do – the shit will fall on you. But do you know what the trick is?'

'Charlie can do a trick with cards. Magic trick.' He smiles like he's bestowed the greatest gem of wisdom on me.

I stop and touch his face. He nuzzles against the touch of my hand like a cat.

'The trick is to keep pushing the ball of shit even when it's raining down on you.'

He reaches out and touches my locket. The one Jack bought.

'And do you know something, Frankie? I'm tired of pushing. I'm so sick of pushing.'

He holds the little heart-shaped locket in his fingers, stroking it like it's a precious stone.

I take the locket off and put it round his neck. He beams at me and looks down at the locket, and starts to stroke it again.

'I like this, it's nice. Charlie likes it too. She likes it.'

I smile at him. 'My boy bought me that one Christmas. He picked it out in Argos, all by himself.'

'Christmas is jingle bells.'

'He died, Frankie. He upped and died on me.'

'Joe Mac died. My Joe died under the car and I was cryin' all the time.'

'I know. It's sad, isn't it?'

He nods solemnly and rubs the locket again. Then he tries to take it off but he can't open the clasp.

'No, Frankie – you keep it. It's yours. For keeps.'

He's puzzled, I can see it in his eyes.

'Come on, let's turn back, it's getting dark,' I say, catching his hand again and pulling him along until we break into a run. He laughs infectiously as we race down the path, heading towards the street lights. I laugh too, and we don't stop running until I get a stitch in my side from the exertion and the laughing. I bend over, trying to get my breath back, gulping in mouthfuls of cold December air. Frankie's still laughing. When I stand up he's serious again.

'I like you. We're friends,' he says, and reaches out to hold my hand again.

'I like you too, Frankie,' I say and pull him into my arms in a huge Mammy bear hug. He hugs me back and I can smell his dark springy hair near my face. A turfy smell. Earthy.

'Get the fuck home,' a voice says from behind us. It's

Frankie's father. I jump away from Frankie, who's paralysed with fear.

The father pushes past me and grabs Frankie by the hair. 'Get home you fuckin' cunt, I've been out lookin' for you you bastard.'

'Leave him alone. Don't hurt him,' I say, trying to keep my voice steady.

The father completely ignores me. It's as if I don't exist. He pulls Frankie along by the arm, punching him as he tears him up towards the Travellers' caravans. I follow him now, filled with indignation. I have to run to catch up with him.

'Leave him alone, he was doing no harm,' I say to the father's broad back. Frankie's crying now, a low, resigned sound in the still night.

The father turns around to face me. A thrill of fear runs through me as he looks at me with hate-loaded eyes. 'Missus, why don't you fuck off away from us and mind your business?'

'We were only having a little chat . . .'

'Fuck off. Come on, you little bollocks, bringing trouble to us.' He pushes Frankie roughly in front of him and the boy half-stumbles as he tries to walk. I follow them. Follow them right up to the caravans. The dad doesn't glance at me as he pushes Frankie up the steps of a shiny, new caravan.

'Don't hurt him. Please, don't,' I say, but already the caravan door is slammed shut. It's started to rain, a light drizzle that quickly turns into the *Angela's Ashes* type. There's shouting from the caravan and the little girl, Charlotte, comes running out followed by another child, a young boy of about four, with bare feet and a T-shirt that says Hawaii across the front. And then the beating really starts. I can see shadows inside the caravan – the bulk of the father bearing down on Frankie and

Frankie's voice saying over and over 'I was good, Dad, I done nothin'.'

Charlotte and her little brother sit on the steps of the caravan, looking at me. Frankie's screams fill the air but the children just keep looking at me. I want to do something but I don't know what to do. I run to the caravan beside it and bang frantically on the door. The caravan door opens and a thin woman in a grey velour tracksuit glares at me and then nods at Charlotte and her brother to go inside. The little girl moves instantly, pulling her brother behind her.

'Please you have to stop him, he's beating the shit out of Frankie, please can you get him to stop – he'll kill him,' I shout. My face is slick with rain and it drips down the back of my neck.

She doesn't even look at me as I speak, she just goes back inside, banging the door hard behind her.

I try the next caravan. No answer. And the next. No answer. Frankie's screams fill the night now, drowning out the hum of the generators and the yelping of the dogs. I can see his silhouette through the blinds, and his dad's relentless fists pummelling and pummelling. A couple have gathered on the green opposite the encampment, standing there in the rain with their umbrellas like it's a TV progamme that they'd been waiting to watch. I bang on the caravan door, screaming at the top of my lungs.

'Stop it, you fucking bully, you big fat fucker of a fucking bully,' I scream it so loud that my throat hurts. But it doesn't make him stop.

I look over at the spectators, dressed for the occasion in their raincoats and hats.

'Are you just going to stand there or are you going to help me stop it?' I shout. A neat, middle-aged woman who looks vaguely familiar looks down at her shoes.

171

'Why don't you fuck off so if you can't help?'

The swearing has the desired effect and both look at their shoes now.

And then I have an idea. I search the sodden ground for a rock and find a fist-sized one and then I hurl it with all my might through one of the tinted caravan windows. The crash is almighty and an eerie silence follows. I can hear Frankie crying softly and the two silhouettes are frozen in the window for a second. Then the door bursts open and the dad barrels down the steps, his eyes wild and angry.

'Go away and fuck off, go fuck yourself,' he screams, his face inches from mine. Spit flies from his mouth and I think he's going to punch me the way he punched Frankie.

But I don't flinch at all. Adrenalin pumps through me and fills my body with an icy calm.

'Leave him alone or I'll call the Guards.'

More people have joined the spectators. I can hear their whispers behind me.

The dad grabs my arm, grabs it so tight I almost scream.

'Go home about your business.'

I try to pull my arm away but he leans into me, pushing his face right up to mine. I pull back again and he lets go suddenly and I stumble backwards, landing heavily on the slippery, wet mud. He stands over me and I wait for a punch, a kick, pain of some sort. But he just walks away down the road. I stagger to my feet as a Garda patrol car approaches. I ignore it and climb the steps to the caravan. Frankie's lying on the plastic-covered seating under the window. A woman, his mother I presume, leans over him, mopping blood from his face. He's groaning, small little groans every time she touches the bloodied rag to his face. She doesn't hear me come in.

'It's all over now, Frank, there's a good fella. I've stew in the pot for you and all. There's a good fella.'

She turns to rinse out the rag in a bowl of water on the floor and spots me. She doesn't say anything and goes back to her task of cleaning up her boy's battered face. I realise I've dripped mud on the spotless, peach-coloured carpet.

'Is he OK?' My voice is shaky.

'No thanks to you,' she says without turning around.

There's a policeman tapping at the open door.

'Is everything all right in here?' he asks.

She keeps wiping blood from Frankie's face.

The garda, young-looking enough to be my son, addresses me then.

'Is everything OK? We got a call about a fracas here.' There's a policewoman behind him now trying to push into the tiny space.

'Hi . . . I . . .'

The mother glares at me, daring me to put it into words.

'It's fine. It's OK,' I say.

'Are you sure?' He leans in to have a closer look at Frankie.

'It's between him and his father,' the mother says, still not looking up, still wiping blood and snot from Frankie's face.

The policewoman's radio crackles to life and she lifts it to her mouth and speaks into it.

'Yeah, we have this one. No. No need. Just a domestic – that's all.'

The young guard nods at me and they leave.

'Hey Frankie, are you all right?' I ask. The two young children are standing in the doorway now, rain shining on their faces and hair.

Frankie tries to open his eyes. One is so badly bruised it's closed tight. He groans in pain.

'You can leave now too,' the mother says.

'I . . . can I do anything? Can I help? He might need stitches on that eye, it looks . . .'

'You can leave now,' she says again.

I walk out, my head reeling.

I'm just down the steps when she calls me.

'Hey.'

I turn around. She shoves the locket into my hand and closes the door loudly behind her.

I wake suddenly and don't know where I am and think I'm in the woods. I sit bolt upright. Leah and Peter are standing above me in their pyjamas. I'm lying on the couch in my muddy clothes. My body is stiff and sore. There's a half-full glass of wine on the coffee table in front of me.

'Hi, Mom, why aren't you in bed? Did you pull an all-nighter?' Leah says, a sneer in her voice. She has dark circles under her eyes and I want to hug her to me like I did when she was small and tell her it will all be fine. Kiss it better. Those were the days.

'I fell asleep here last night. No school?'

'It's Sunday,' says Leah.

'And we're getting our Christmas holidays in three more days, Mom. Did you know that?' says Peter, grinning at me.

'Of course I knew that, Honey,' I say, smiling at him.

I'm trying to remember what woke me, something I remembered about last night. And just as it comes back to me, Brian comes into the room.

The children leave silently, as if it was prearranged with their daddy.

'Rough night?'

'No. Why do you say that?'

He picks up an almost empty wine bottle from the floor and puts it on the coffee table.

'I had a glass of fucking wine – is that a problem?'

'No. Not at all. But fighting with the Travellers could be.'

'Good news travels fast around here. Who told you?'

'Does it matter?'

I swing my legs on to the floor and my head starts to pound. There's mud encrusted into my pants.

'I won't even ask what happened – I know better.'

'Good. Glad you're finally learning to shut up.' The room spins a little and I shake my head in an effort to clear it.

'And you left the front door open when you came in, did you know that?'

'That's a stupid question, Brian. If I'd known the door was open I'd have closed it, wouldn't I?'

'I have no idea, Ali, what you would or wouldn't do these days. But do you know something? Nothing you do would surprise me.'

'Would it surprise you to know that I tried to stop a man from beating the living shit out of his son?'

He's silent for a second, staring down at me accusingly. 'Why don't you look after your own children instead of running around interfering with other people's?'

'You're a heartless bastard sometimes, Brian. A heartless fucker.'

He guffaws as he leaves the room.

I remember then the thing that woke me. It was the policewoman's glib description of what had gone on inside the caravan. *Just a domestic – that's all.*

Eleven

Jane

Mammy has a boyfriend. A real one this time and she's mad about him and all girly and stuff and he's coming in a while to take us all out to dinner.

Ben likes him, even though he hasn't met him yet. Ben likes everyone – he never wants to make a fuss and he just likes Gordon's – that's Mam's boyfriend's name – car. Mam told Ben it was a convertible and that he might give him a spin in it later. And that's another thing about when people break up. You get to go to all these restaurants all the time and first it's fun but then it's boring.

Mammy's really annoying. She's getting ready for hours – waxing her legs and doing her nails, toenails too, and I don't know why she's bothering going to all that trouble because she's wearing trousers. I know she's nervous because she keeps asking me what I'm wearing. And I'm still not ready – just sitting on my bed with a pile of clothes dumped around me. I'd love to shock them – do a Slutty McMuffin. She's a girl living down the road from Leah and that's Leah's brilliant nickname for her.

She's got this awful muffin top but she still wears skin-tight belly tops and miniskirts and it makes Leah and me crack up.

The restaurant is really fancy. The tablecloths are snow white and not paper and all the waiters are dressed in black and there's a man playing the piano in the corner. Ben's eyes are round in his head. Mammy is checking her watch and looking at the door.

'He's late, Mammy, and you made me rush,' I say.

'Jane, please,' she says, her eyes darting around looking for Gordon.

'Maybe he forgot,' I say and smile at her.

She glares at me. Ben is trying to read the menu but it's all in French.

'Maybe he thinks it's a different restaurant,' I say.

She glares at me again.

'A good one, like McDonalds or The Chicken Hut.'

Ben cracks up laughing and I smile innocently at Mammy.

'Behave yourself, Jane,' she says.

Then she starts waving as a knot of people come through the door.

'There he is,' she says, like she's his proud mother or something.

A tall man in a dark suit walks over towards our table. His hair is cut really short and he has two bumps on his nose. His eyes are dark brown, darker even than Leah's.

'Evelyn,' he says, kissing Mammy twice. 'You look gorgeous. And who have we here?'

He smiles down at us and I want to say out loud who do you fucking think we have but I just look at him, letting him make the next move.

'Gordon, this is Jane.'

'Hello, young lady, how are you?'

'Hungry.' It's out before I can stop it.

'Jane! Don't be so rude,' says Mammy, her face like thunder.

But Gordon laughs at this. 'And you must be Ben,' he says, sitting down next to Mammy. Ben smiles at him.

'I'm sorry I'm late, darling, I was delayed in court – unbelievable day. You look lovely this evening, I must say.'

Mammy goes all girly and shy and flutters her eyelashes at him. She looks so dumb trying to be a young girl again when she's married already with children.

'Gordon is a solicitor, a very important one,' she says to us. He nuzzles her neck with his face. She giggles and pushes him away.

'Why? Are there unimportant ones too?' I ask.

Gordon tilts his head to the side and then starts laughing.

'You're funny, Jane – I like a kid with a sense of humour.'

'I'm not a kid.'

'Of course you're not. Now, let's eat. What should we order? Let's see.'

'I'll have a burger and chips and Ben will have the same but with extra ketchup and onion rings.'

Mammy's really mad now. I can see it in her eyes but I don't care.

Gordon smiles at me. 'That, my dear, can be arranged. We'll have French burgers all round!'

The meal takes hours. There's starters and then the dinner and then a kind of ice thing, a sorbet, Gordon calls it, and then desserts that don't look like desserts at all. They look nothing like Nana's sweets and even Ben doesn't like them. And then they have coffee and that's another hour so I take out my phone and start texting Leah. We're friends again since yesterday. She wants me to take a picture of Gordon without him knowing but Mammy will be really cross then. And Gordon talks non-stop – even more than Daddy when Daddy's in his talking moods. Non-stop, all about his day and his work and his golf and his holidays.

'Put away your phone at the table, Jane,' she says, when Gordon goes to the loo.

'I'm bored and we've been here hours.'

'Can't you be pleasant for one night after Gordon made such an effort?' Her eyes are blazing with anger.

'What effort? He was late and he hardly cooked the dinner himself and anyway it was horrible.'

Gordon arrives back and notices Mammy and me glaring at each other.

'What did I miss?' he says, beaming.

'Nothing,' says Mammy, fluttering her eyelashes again. And I notice now that she's wearing way too much make-up. And that her top is very low – so low you can see her red bra sometimes when she bends down even a little. She doesn't look like Mammy – she looks like Slutty McMuffin's mother.

'I want to go home. Ben's tired and I'm bored.' I stare back at Mammy, watching her get angrier and angrier.

'No, I'm not,' says Ben.

'Jane, behave yourself. You're being very rude.'

I roll my eyes. My phone beeps a message.

'Do not answer that,' says Mammy.

I pick up the phone from the table and read the message. It's from Leah. *Where's the pic of bumpy nose?*

I start to text back, not looking at the screen. Just staring at Mammy.

She reaches out and tries to pull the phone from my hand but she knocks over a glass of water instead. It darkens the white tablecloth, dripping over the edge of the table.

'You are one selfish little bitch,' she says. 'Come on, let's go.'

I blink back tears as Gordon pays the bill, laughing and joking with the waiter. Mammy's really cross, the maddest I've ever seen her.

Outside, Gordon and Mammy talk while Ben and I wait in her car. Then she climbs in and glares at me before starting the engine.

'Can I have a spin in the convertible,' says Ben.

'There's been a change of plan, Ben. Thank your sister for it,' says Mammy. She drives into the line of traffic and I can see how angry she is by the way she drives. There's silence the whole way home.

Just as I'm about to run upstairs to my room she grabs me by the arm.

'I expect an apology for your behaviour tonight, Jane.'

I roll my eyes. 'I didn't do anything wrong.'

'Is that what you think? You were beyond rude, Jane. I was ashamed of my life. I was mortified.'

I shrug.

'What's your problem anyway? Am I not allowed to have any life? And the worse thing is that the whole night was Gordon's idea. He wanted to meet you, be friends. The whole night was about you.'

'No it wasn't. It was about you.' I pull away from her grasp and try to run upstairs but she grabs me again.

'You are one selfish little bitch and do you know something? You're exactly like him. Exactly like your father.'

She walks away into the kitchen, banging the door behind her. I stand there on the bottom step, pinching my arm so that I don't cry. Pinching really really hard.

She comes into my bedroom later and I pretend to be asleep.

'Jane?' she whispers. 'Jane?'

I keep my eyes shut tight. She rubs my forehead and bends down and kisses me.

'I'm sorry,' she whispers. 'I'm sorry I was mad. I love you little Janie.'

She's meeting him again tonight and I'm allowed stay at Leah's even though it's a school night and Ben is going to Daddy's. Mammy never does that – lets Daddy take us when it's not his turn so that's how I know this boyfriend's for real. And he's a Protestant, like Mammy is. And he mustn't have thought it was that horrible last night if he's going out with her again tonight. If it was as bad as Mammy tries to make it out to be he'd have run a mile by now.

And Leah's so nice to me since our huge fight and I thought she'd be like moody for weeks but she pretended it never happened and I think maybe in future I should fight with her instead of putting up with her moods and stuff. And anyway I know she's dying to hear all about Gordon because he's like loaded and stuff. I heard Mammy and Anna talking about him weeks ago. I didn't know then who they were talking about but I know now it was Bumpy Nose.

So after school we walk home to Leah's house with Darren Tierney and his friend Josh, and Leah is like so full of herself, telling them about going skiing and stuff and I want to fight with her all over again and I'm nearly sorry I said I'd sleep over and then I remember what decided me. Sandy and her lovely soft body and not having to see Daddy.

We finally get to Leah's and the camper van is in the

driveway and it's so cool. I don't say this to Leah in case she thinks I'm jealous.

Her dad is cooking something that smells really good in the kitchen.

'Hi guys, dinner's nearly ready,' he says. 'Sit yourselves down there and tell me all the news. Any boyfriends?'

We both laugh and I go bright red.

'Ah ha – Jane isn't telling us something. Go on, Leah, you tell me – spill the beans like a good girl.'

Leah smiles and shakes her head. 'Never tell on your best friend Dad, that's the law.'

'Always tell your father everything – that's another law. Hey, I got the camper van back, did you see it outside?'

'Yeah, we couldn't miss it,' Leah says and Mr Collins mock-glares at her.

'You'll be glad of that van in the summer when you're in some exotic place like Cannes and all the hotels are booked out.'

Sandy rubs up against my legs and for a second I think it's my kitten. I bend down and stroke her small, ginger head.

'Where's Mam?' Leah asks as she sits down at the table. Peter comes in just as Mr Collins is piling stew on to plates. Like he knew it was time for dinner.

'Mam is in bed, she's not feeling great. Ta-Da!!' He puts a steaming plate of stew in front of me. 'Collins au Vin,' he says in a very bad French accent. We all laugh.

Later when we're playing cards in the sitting room Mrs Collins comes in and sits on the couch and just stares at Mr Collins. Keeps staring at him and I pretend not to notice and Leah does too, turning her back so she can't see her mother's eyes. But it feels really weird pretending she isn't staring and it's very hard not to stare back and I keep telling myself not to but then I do.

I look at her, straight at her, and she looks at me and she knows I know something because her eyes fill up with tears and they spill down her face without a sound and everybody just keeps on playing Lives. I excuse myself and go to the bathroom and pinch my arm, the gooey part until it splits open again and I have to use loads of toilet paper to make it stop bleeding. The blood has yellow disgusting stuff in it.

We have to go to bed early because we've school the next day and then we're nearly asleep and all and my phone rings and it's Daddy. His voice is loud and I know Leah can hear but if I go somewhere else it's worse because that's like saying she's not really my friend. So I sit up in bed and try to understand what Daddy's saying.

'Who is this new boyfriend? She said nothing to me about boyfriends, she said it was an emergency and your brother tells me it was a date, and that whore has the cheek to criticise me. Where has the shitbag gone?'

Leah is sitting up in her bed now, her eyes huge in the soft glow of the night light. I let Daddy rant on the phone because I don't know what else to do and I don't want to say anything in case it's wrong and he'll get madder and poor Ben will be upset. Stupid Ben for opening his dumb mouth.

'Mark my words, Jane, there's going to be big changes now, I promise you that. This isn't just *Schadenfreude*, this is me reclaiming my life from that bitch, that slut. Hasn't the manners to answer her phone even – I told you she doesn't care about you – I told you that.'

I close my eyes and squeeze back tears. Leah comes over and hugs me and then I let the tears come and they're hot on my face and Daddy's voice just goes on and on. It's high, like a girl's and I hope Ben can't hear but I know in my heart he's probably right there in the room with him and then the voice stops all of a sudden and I look at the phone, waiting for his voice to start again. The phone feels warm in my hand.

'God – parents,' Leah says, 'we'd be better off if we were orphans.' She smiles at me and we burst out laughing.

'Take no notice of him, Jane. He's . . . my dad says . . .' she stops, and climbs back into her bed, but I see it in her eyes, the secret she won't tell.

'What does your dad say?'

'Nothing. Look, let's not talk about parents, it's like way too boring and depressing and stuff. Let's talk about Darren – wasn't he just so cute today? I wonder if he ever kissed a girl? Ciara Hanly says he kissed her – and he used his tongue and all!' Leah puts her hands to her face and half-laughs, half-groans. 'I mean she has braces – how gross is that?'

'What did he say about my dad?' Leah looks at me. 'Tell me,' I say.

'Nothing. God, what's wrong with you lately, you're like so moody, and you can't even have a laugh or anything. I'm going to sleep. Goodnight,' she says and pulls the quilt over her head in a big huff. She's back to her old moody self. It takes me ages to go to sleep. Every time I close my eyes I think I hear Ben crying.

Next morning she's really in a mood, banging things and glaring at me like it's my fault. I ignore her. Her dad gives us breakfast, a big fry up that nobody eats and I can't wait to get out of the house and away from her.

We walk to school and Peter skips ahead of us, his Spurs schoolbag jiggling on his back.

'Are you going to basketball today?' I ask, just to make conversation.

'I might. I might not.'

'Moody bitch,' I say then before I can stop myself.

'You can't talk, you're the moodiest person I know.'

I laugh, just to annoy her.

She glares at me and sticks her head in the air.

'It's your fault, Leah.'

'What's my fault? That you're a bitch?'

'You shouldn't say things and then stop. Friends don't do that to each other. What were you going to say about my dad?'

'Oh, here we go again. I'm sorry I mentioned it at all. I didn't know you'd go all psycho on me.'

I don't answer and we walk again in silence until we reach the school gates. I know she'll just march in and ignore me for the whole day and maybe for the whole week and I hate when she does that. And the only way to stop her is to fight back.

'I know anyway,' I say and I walk faster, through the gates and towards our classroom. The bell hasn't gone yet and the yard is thronged with screaming children.

She runs up to me and grabs my arm. 'Know what?'

'See, you don't like it when somebody does it to you. I know the secret, that's all.'

'So tell it.'

'There's no need to. Both of us know.'

'So if you know then tell it.'

I look straight into her face. 'Your mother and my dad.'

'What?'

I smile knowingly and start to walk again. She grabs my arm, the sore one, but I don't even flinch.

'What are you talking about?'

'They slept together – see, it's no secret.'

'You liar, you're mad.'

'Ask her. Ask your mother if it's true.'

She's crying now, really crying, and I think maybe this isn't the secret after all.

'You're lying.'

'Isn't that what your dad told you?' My voice is louder than I mean and a group of girls from our class look over at us. 'Isn't it?' I add in a loud whisper.

She shakes her head and wipes away tears with her coat-sleeve. 'No. He told me that your Dad is sick, like mentally and that, and he had to go to the nut hospital last year for six weeks and it runs in his family.'

'Why didn't you just tell me that last night?'

She shrugs. 'I wanted to but then you might think like you could have inherited it and . . .'

'Don't be stupid.' But in my head I know she's right. They never told me about Uncle Kieran. They never told me where Daddy went last year. No that's a lie. Mam said he had to go to London for work.

'Is it true about my mother?'

I shake my head.

'Don't lie again. It's true, isn't it?'

'No, I just . . . I made it up,' I lie.

She doesn't believe me.

'I hate you,' she says and marches off into the classroom.

She doesn't talk to me for the whole day and first I feel really bad. I told her something horrible that mightn't even be true. I mean Daddy could have made it all up for all I know and now she's gone for ever. I eat lunch by myself and she hangs out with another group of girls that we don't like and it's like the longest day of my life.

I go looking for Ben but his teacher says he didn't come to school. I try not to think about this. Then I find Leah to apologise yet again and she just lets me stand there at the edge of the group and they all ignore me. But I won't let myself cry even though I really want to. I hate her guts and my face is bright red just standing there like a fool and I call her cunt cunt cunt over and over in my head.

When the bell goes I see Darren walking out in front of me and I go up to him, all brazen, and I know she can see me and it feels good, like when I cut myself, but even better than that, and he says I'll walk a little bit of the way home with you and I'm like delighted because he lives just down the road from Leah – like the other direction completely.

He walks me the whole way nearly and then we stand at the corner of my road, behind the big oak tree, and I'm like mortified but thrilled and then he kisses me, right on the lips and it tastes of Taytos.

'Did you like that?' he says, grinning at me.

I nod even though it's disgusting. And then he kisses me again and pushes my mouth open with his tongue and I want to throw up but I don't want him to know.

'You're lovely, Jane,' he says then. 'You're cooler than Leah, do you know that?'

I'm delighted with this and when he bends down again I open my mouth a bit more and he really puts his tongue in and it's horrible. I try not to gag and then I feel his hand groping at my skirt, trying to force his hand between my legs. I bite down on his tongue as hard as I can and he screams and I run, leaving my schoolbag at his feet.

I race down the street and into my house and then I realise the key is in my bag so I run around the back and hide in the shed. I take in huge gulps of air and say bastard over and over.

Fucking bastard. I wait a full hour before going back for my bag. Mam arrives home then with Ben.

'What's wrong, Jane, you look very pale. Are you sick?'

'I've a really bad headache.'

'Poor Jane. Ben isn't well either, I had to collect him from your father's this morning.' She rolls her eyes and shakes her head at the mention of Daddy. I ignore her and follow Ben into the living room. He's playing the PlayStation. I sit next to him on the sofa.

'You OK?'

He nods his head but doesn't look at me, just keeps bombing things in the game.

'What happened last night?'

He shrugs. His hands flick across the controls like they're part of it.

'Ben, what happened? He phoned me and he was like mad, weird mad, not angry mad and you must have been scared.'

Another shrug.

I turn on the telly and find an episode of *Drake & Josh* that I've never seen before. It's the coolest programme and I discovered it first and told Leah about it and now we're both addicted. As I watch I text her to tell her it's on. I know she knows already but I miss her.

'We have to go with him tomorrow until Christmas Eve.'

I turn down the sound. 'What?'

Ben doesn't take his eyes from the game. 'Mammy is going away and we're staying with him.'

'No way. He was so mad with her last night, she'd never . . .'

'He wasn't mad with her this morning. He was really nice.' Ben looks at me wearily, and then he gets bombed and he swears at the screen. 'Fucking bastard.'

'Ben, Mam will hear.'

He just keeps playing.

She tells me in the kitchen. Her voice is bright and shiny and she smiles at me a lot as she talks.

'So Gordon said why don't you come? And I said I can't, it's Christmas and the kids – you two,' she beams at me and takes plates from the cupboard and begins to lay the table, 'and he said it's just a couple of days really, Evelyn, and you can do all your shopping. It's New York for heaven's sake!' She stops setting the table and looks at me. 'You are OK about this, Jane, aren't you?'

'Do I have a choice?' It's out before I can stop it.

Her mouth goes into a hard line just like Daddy's and she looks at me and walks over to the drawer to get cutlery. She doesn't speak for a while, just bangs things around.

'Your aunt is coming to babysit – I'm going to my work Christmas party tonight, that's if it's all right with you, Jane. I am allowed to go, aren't I?'

Ben creeps into the kitchen and takes one look and then creeps right back out again. I try to think of something to say to make it better but part of me really doesn't want to.

She ladles pasta on to plates splashing the cooker as she does so. 'I mean I can have a life surely? It's not all over because I made one lousy mistake. I married your father and I think I've paid the price for that, don't you?'

Her voice is getting higher and I turn to leave but she stands straight in front of me.

'Jane, listen. I'm going to New York for a few days, I'll be back the day before Christmas Eve and then we'll have a lovely Christmas together and then you'll be off skiing with the Collinses.'

I nod my head.

'What is the matter, for God's sake?'

I shrug and look away. I can smell her perfume.

'Come on, Janie. Your dad was thrilled this morning that you two are spending time with him before Christmas. He's making great plans.'

Another shrug from me.

'He wants you to put up a little tree in the flat and he's taking you ice skating. It'll be fun.'

I look at a tiny crack in the cream wall behind her head. I keep staring and try to make the crack bigger with just my mind.

'Don't you want me to have any life? Is that it?'

A tear escapes, even though I'm pinching my arm to stop myself from crying. The crack on the wall seems a tiny bit bigger.

'Come here, can I have a hug from my favourite girl?'

She puts her arms around me and she smells lovely and I hug her back tight and I think maybe it will be all right. Maybe Daddy isn't in the rope place at all.

My aunt Sarah comes to babysit in a whirl of shopping bags and chat and I think about saying something to her about Daddy. But she has Mam's happy voice too, all excited for Mam that she's met a guy like Gordon and isn't it great for her.

'My kitten died, Sarah,' I say instead.

She hugs me close, pressing me against her chest. 'Poor Janie. I know, pet, I know.' Then she holds my face in her hands. 'You're so pretty, do you know that?'

I go scarlet but I'm delighted too and I think for a second I might tell her about Darren Tierney and his Tayto mouth.

'And I have a surprise for you.' She giggles like Leah and winks at me.

'What is it?' I ask.

'What do you want the most for Christmas? What do you want Santa to bring you?' She winks again when she says Santa and nods over at Ben, who's glued to a repeat of *Father Ted*. Ben hasn't believed in Santa since he was six but he pretends he does.

I think about the question. I want Leah back. I want Daddy to be happy and normal again. I want Mam, the old Mam. I smile at Sarah.

'An iPod?'

She shakes her head. 'No, you're cold, ice cold.'

'Ashton Kutcher?'

Sarah laughs. 'No, I'm getting him, all wrapped up. Try again.'

'I give up.'

'OK. I'll give you a clue but you're not to tell your mother that I told you.'

'I won't. I promise.'

'Soft.'

'So it's not Ashton. That's not a great clue, Sarah.'

She giggles again. 'OK. Soft and stripy.'

'Pyjamas,' I say but I know it's a new kitten.

She looks at me, examines my face. 'What's wrong, Jane?'

'Nothing. Everything.'

'Come on, tell your favourite auntie.' She smiles at me and chucks me under the chin like you do to a small kid.

'I don't want to go to Daddy's tomorrow.'

'That's it?'

'Leah and I had a huge fight . . .'

'I see. That's the problem isn't it? I remember when I was your age, a fight with my best friend was like the worst disaster ever.'

I nod and tears are slipping down my face. She wipes them

191

with her hand. 'Listen, Jane, it'll all blow over. In a couple of days you and Leah won't even remember what the fight was about – I promise you that.'

'And Daddy is . . . Daddy is . . .' I can't think of the right word to tell her. I won't say mad because I don't want it to be true. And if I say it out loud and to lots of people then it'll be true.

'Jane, your mother has had a really hard time and now she has a chance at a little happiness – you won't ruin that for her, will you?'

I shake my head.

'Good girl. Your dad is delighted to have you for a few days and I'm coming for dinner on Christmas Day and Nana is coming too. It's going to be so much fun.'

'OK.'

'Just an OK? Come on, Janie, think of soft stripes. It's going to be a great Christmas.' She kisses the top of my head. 'Come on, your nails are terrible, they're so chipped. I'll do them for you.'

She goes to get her giant make-up bag from the car. I examine my nails.

'You don't want another one and you should tell her,' Ben says.

'Another what?'

'You know. A kitten.'

'How do you know I don't?'

He doesn't answer but he's right, Ben is. I don't want another kitten. Then I'll have to love it and worry about it and it'll die too.

Sarah comes in with her bag and she starts to do my nails. She doesn't talk, she's too busy cleaning and filing and trimming. She stops suddenly, just as she's about to put on the first coat called Movie Star. It has lovely shiny bits in it.

'I have it, Jane! I know what to do. I bought this extra gift today in Boots – you know the three for the price of two offer – and it's all wrapped up and all and it's gorgeous. We'll give that to Leah.'

'What is it?'

'It's a nail kit exactly like this one – it's got the little hand bath and loads of OPI colours – the really good polish and it's the best. She'd love it.'

'She would. But it's your gift, Sarah, I couldn't . . .'

'Of course you could. Three for two, remember.'

'I won't see her. School is over and we're going to Daddy's and she won't answer my texts . . .'

'I'll drop it in to their house. I know where they live. All you have to do is write a really nice card and everything will be fine. There's nothing like a good present to make someone change their mind.' She winks again and starts carefully applying polish to my nails.

And I think she's right. I'll say in the card that we need to talk. I mean, it's hard for her too with Jack and all of that and I forget that sometimes. That her brother is dead. I always think that she's better off than me with two parents and a lovely house and camper vans and ski holidays and a kitten that's way luckier than mine was. Jack wasn't so lucky.

'Thanks, Sarah,' I say, smiling at her.

'It's nothing. Don't even mention it. Now keep your hand still or I'll paint your fingers.'

The tree is too big for the small flat. Daddy says it isn't, that you can't beat a big tree, and Ben and I just stare at it when we come into the room. It's kind of scrawny, with thin long branches and very few needles. Our tree at home is round and fat and every branch has loads of needles, you can't even put on the decorations it's that thick with needles.

'It's a bit skinny – a bit of a Posh Spice,' Daddy says, and bursts out laughing at his joke. 'Come on, kids, let's get this show on the road. We'll put up all the decorations and then we'll go Christmas shopping and then ice skating – the whole works. Here, hang those garlands over the pictures.' He hands me a box of silver stringy tinsel. I still have my coat on and our overnight bags are in the middle of the room but Daddy doesn't notice. He pushes a box of shiny, red globes into Ben's hands. Ben starts hanging the balls on to the thin branches.

'Take off your coat first, Ben, and put your bag in the bedroom,' I say, putting the box of tinsel down on the couch. There are no pictures on the walls to hang it from.

'We're going to have the best time, the best Christmas ever,' Daddy says, hugging Ben tightly as he tries to pick up his bag.

In the small bedroom I sit on the damp-smelling bed and check my phone for a message from Leah. I know it's too soon for Sarah to have delivered the gift but I'm hoping maybe Leah sent a text anyway. She didn't.

I sit there listening to Daddy talking non-stop, cackling with laughter every ten seconds, and I know in my heart I'm right about him. Why didn't Mam notice at the front door? I watched her face to see if she did and she was all smiles and kisses for us and see you Fridays. I knew then that her head was full of New York, her head was on that plane already, sitting next to Gordon, having fun and being happy.

'Jane, are you hungry?' he calls from the kitchen.

'Coming,' I say but I feel so tired. I really want to lie down on the bed and sleep for a whole week.

Dinner is boiled eggs, pot noodles and beans. Daddy doesn't even sit down, he eats while walking up and down the kitchen, holding his plate in both his hands. After dinner we go back to decorating the tree and I plead a headache and go to bed early. I fall asleep straight away and then I'm awake and something is beeping and first I think I'm dreaming and then I realise it's my phone and I scramble for it in the dark. The room stinks and I find the phone and it's only a message from Mam – she's on New York time. The smell is piss. Ben has wet the bed again and I go out to search for clean sheets. Daddy is lying on the floor of the living room with his hands by his side. He has no clothes on, even though it's freezing.

'Daddy? Are you all right?' I ask nervously, turning my eyes away from his naked body.

He doesn't answer.

'Are you OK? You must be frozen there.'

No answer and my heart thumps so loud in my chest I think it's going to explode and my ears fill with the pumping noise and I know I have to touch him to see if he's alive. I take a deep breath and reach out my hand and touch his arm. He's so cold, ice cold, and I think of Lucky, and her stiff, striped body and then he suddenly grabs my hand and pulls me down on top of his nakedness.

'Do you love me?' he asks. 'Do you love me? Yes or no, do you love me?'

'I love you, Daddy, you're hurting my arm, I love you.' I can smell him, sweat and soap and noodles and he holds me so tight I can't breathe. He's crying, I can hear his sobs and he strokes my hair and relaxes his grip on me.

'I love you. I love Ben. You know that, don't you Janie, you know that.'

'I do, of course I do.'

'So no matter what happens on Friday, you know that, right?'

'Like what, Daddy?' I ask. 'What's happening on Friday?' I'm afraid to move off his body but he rolls me off and looks at me, his tears shining in the path of light from the street.

He smiles. 'When we have to say goodbye, hon. When your mother comes back.'

I smile back at him, relieved and worried all at the same time.

Twelve

Alison

'There's no milk,' Leah says, venom dripping from every word. I shake myself awake. It's afternoon, I know by the soundless pictures of an afternoon show on the TV.

'Isn't there?' I say and get up slowly from the couch. My legs are stiff and unfeeling and I wobble a little. 'Where were you?' I ask.

Leah looks at me like I'm something the cat dragged in. 'What do you care?'

I shrug. 'Where's Peter?'

'How should I know, I'm not his mother,' she says, her hand on her hip and a look of pure hatred on her face.

'I just . . . I just . . .' Her eyes bore into me, the hate almost tangible, channelling its way towards me. It bowls me over when it reaches me. Leaves me speechless. Another one of my children full of hate. I hear Jack in my head saying talk to her, so I do it, not because I want to, but because of him. To please him.

'Leah, what's up? You were so angry yesterday when you

came home from school and you're even worse today. What's wrong, honey?'

And then her eyes well up with tears and she's not a monster, she's my baby all over again. *A baby sister for Jack.* These words dance in my head, words once written on a long pink card with a gingham bow on the front.

I go to her and put my arms around her thin, narrow shoulders and pull her resistant body towards mine. Her hair smells of apples. She pushes herself back and looks me straight in the eyes.

'Don't touch me. I can't bear it if you touch me.'

'Leah, please, what's wrong?' I move forward again and she moves away. 'Don't. Just don't come near me.'

'Leah, whatever it is I'm here for you, you know that, don't you?'

She wipes her eyes with her hand. 'No, I don't, and you're never here for me, for us, for any of us.'

'Leah, come on, let's sit down here and we can talk.' My heart is pounding so loud that I can barely hear myself talk and the air is dry and I can't breathe it in.

'I hate you,' she says, still wiping tears away. 'I hate your guts.'

'Please don't . . .'

'You're a whore, sleeping around on Dad, you're just a whore and I hate you. I hate you so much I wish you were dead,' she says and the tears flow down her face unchecked now.

'I don't know what you're talking about Leah, that's not true . . .'

'Yes it is, you liar, yes it is. Jane told me about you and . . . oh God, I can't even bear to say it . . . her father . . .'

'Leah, listen to me . . .'

'How gross is that? You disgust me and I hate you, we all

hate you and Jack hated you the most,' she says and flies out the door banging it so hard that tiny pieces of plaster come off and land on the shiny wooden floor. I gulp air and run upstairs after her and knock on her door. I try the handle knowing even before I do that it'll be locked.

'Leah, that's not true,' I say, pressing my face against the glossy, cold surface of the door. 'It doesn't matter what Jane said, it's not true.' I close my eyes and see Jane's face looking at me in the sitting room. Her eyes full of knowing.

I tap gently on the door. 'Leah, please. Talk to me.' But I know it's pointless.

The doorbell rings as I come downstairs and I melt into the wall, hoping my shape can't be seen through the leaded glass of the sidelights. The bell goes again, three persistent rings this time. Leah doesn't come out of her room and I'm frozen to the wall, waiting for the bell ringer to go. I can't make out the person's shape without moving and risking being caught but I can hear shuffling and then a final ring of the doorbell and the sound of something plopping through the letterbox. I wait a full minute until I hear the car pulling away before I go down the stairs. There's a note on a folded pink Post-it and I know immediately it's from Rachel. I read it absent-mindedly as I wander into the cold kitchen.

Left millions of messages. Where the heck are you? Will see you tomorrow night for Chriskindle. Richard is coming too. Ring me. X Rachel.

Rachel. Richard. Chriskindle. It means nothing. Words on a Post-it.

When Brian comes it's dark and I'm sitting in the kitchen

and the lights are off and it's so cold. Peter's with him and his happy little face makes me smile.

'Petey, my baby boy,' I say, and get up and grab him in a bear hug. 'I love you Pete, do you know that?' I kiss the top of his head over and over. Then I pull away and look into his eyes. 'You have the bluest eyes. Clear, blue eyes. Blue is my favourite colour.' I kiss his face and then hug him to me all over again.

'Hey Petey, go watch TV while I talk to Mam,' says Brian, prying us apart. Peter glances over his shoulder before disappearing through the door.

'Ali, what's up, are you on something?' Brian says, examining my eyes like a Specsavers employee.

'Can't I hug my son?'

'Yeah, no problem, as long as you don't do it like a psycho – the poor guy was terrified.'

'No, he wasn't.'

'Yes, he was. You couldn't see his face. Ali, what's going on?' He walks to the fridge and takes out a beer. 'Do you want one?'

He looks at me, that look just like Peter's and I think how sexy he is, standing there next to the fridge with the beer bottle to his lips. I go over and lean my head on his chest. 'Yeah, I want one,' I say laughing, and circling my hands around his waist. I can hear his heart beating.

'Hey, hang on a minute. What in the name of fuck are you on?'

I laugh again and drop my hands to his arse, kneading it gently and pushing it towards me.

'Ah ha, no way. I want to know what's going on.' He takes both my hands and holds them in his.

'I just want to talk, to be near you,' I say because it's the truth. I look at him, into those eyes so like Peter's. I lean forward and kiss him on the mouth. He tastes of pizza. Pizza and beer. He pulls back and I kiss him again, this time pushing my body into his and I can feel him responding, familiar yet new.

'Ali, stop this for fuck's sake. You're acting like a madwoman.'

I shake off his handhold and open the fridge door. 'OK, be like that, I'll just have a beer instead. How's that?' I open the beer and take a long slug. It tastes like vomit.

'What's going on?'

I take another slug. 'Leah.'

'What about Leah? Where is she?'

'In her room. She won't talk to me. She says I was sleeping around. She says I'm a whore.'

'Oh fuck,' he says and goes storming off. I hear his footsteps on the stairs, running now. I slug back the beer and take another one from the fridge. I can hear voices and the distant sound of the TV. The beer starts to taste good. I go into the study and switch on the computer, slugging back beer as I wait for it to boot up. I click on Jack's Bebo page and my heart races as I see three new comments this time. The first is Colinator.

Hi Bud, just checking in. Made the Bowen Cup team Man! How good am I?

The next is from Munstermad.

Christmas won't be the same without you. Remember last year we went to see Santa in the Crescent and he wouldn't let us sit on his lap?

I'm surprised by this. After Jack died Munstermad had been the most prolific comment-leaver and then a few months ago he'd just stopped, completely out of the blue. I was mad with him at the time. I felt he was just another fickle friend like the many that had left messages in the first few weeks after Jack went. *I'll never forget you. Love you for ever. Friends for life. Will comment you every day for the rest of my life.*

And they did forget him. They moved on with their lives, settled down to do their Junior Certs, drank beer for the first time, surfed in the summer. Got themselves girlfriends and boyfriends. All except a couple of hard-core real friends. The last comment is from the queen of hard-core friends, Hugsy.

I keep thinking about your story – you know – the one I loved about St Colman in the Burren and Jack – guess what? The moral of the story at the end is all wrong. It should be your favourite phrase of all time – shit happens!!!!! That's the moral of the story – see – I told you I was clever!!!! xxxxx.

Tears stream down my face. He'd told her our story. Jack had told her. I wipe my eyes with the sleeve of my jumper, remembering the first time I'd told him. Leah and Peter have measles so Brian stays at home with them and I take a ten-year-old Jack off for the day. We end up at Eagle's Rock in the Burren, a place my dad brought me to when I was a kid. A magical place that I'd always wanted to go back to.

We climb through thick hazel scrub to reach St Colman's Well. Jack is enchanted straight away – before he even hears the story. I sit him opposite me on a small, flat rock, exactly where I'd sat years before with my father.

His face is eager and anticipating, he loves a good story.

'Do you know why this place is so special?'

He shakes his head. The trees rustle around us and the atmosphere is charged. Like the ghosts of those that lived here are listening too.

'This place is called Keelhilla and a long time ago, hundreds and hundreds of years ago, St Colman McDuagh was sent here by St Enda to do penance for seven years . . .'

'Why? What did he do that he had to do penance?'

'It's not so much what St Colman did – it's more what St Enda got up to and Colman got to pay the price. Enda was a terrible man for the ladies in his day and spent the latter part of his life trying to pay back God for his playboy ways.'

'What's a playboy?' says Jack.

'A man who likes lots of girls. Anyway, St Colman got sent here, right here to this exact place, just him and his simple servant.'

Jack nods frantically, afraid I'll stop talking.

'Look around you, there's nothing here to eat, just berries, nuts, fruit, nothing at all in winter. So the pair were constantly starving.'

'And?' says Jack, his eyes round.

'One Easter Sunday the pair were sitting here on this very rock . . .' I pat the rock beside me.

Jack laughs.

'The simple servant says that's he's starving, that it's the hungriest he's ever been and he'd give anything, even his life, to have his snout stuck in a big feed of pig's head and cabbage . . .'

Jack claps. 'Brilliant.'

'So what do you know? At that very moment King Guaire, up the road a bit in Kinvara, was sitting down to his dinner of . . . you guessed it . . . pig's head and cabbage!'

'Surprise surprise,' says Jack, a huge grin on his face.

'And then all of a sudden the plates left the table, and flew out the window carrying all the food. King Guaire and his followers chased the plates on horseback and kept after them until they got to Keelhilla . . .'

'Right here, to this very spot?'

I nod solemnly at Jack. 'They found St Colman and the simpleton laying into the pig's head, cabbage and wine. The poor simpleton was so hungry that he ate the plate and all and was choked on the spot . . .'

'Which spot?' says Jack, looking around the clearing.

'That one right there,' I say pointing to an area beside him. Jack shivers.

'Anyway they waked him that night and buried him decent the next day right over there. That's his grave. And to this day you can still see the tracks of King Guaire's horses all along the rocks of the Burren. It's now called Bothar na Mias – the Road of the Dishes.'

I smile at Jack.

'Then what happened?'

'Look up there, Jack, up there in the rock face – see the mouth of the cave – that's where he slept. Imagine that.'

Jack's eyes are almost black in the half-light of the clearing.

'The king took a liking to St Colman and told him to keep walking and when his belt fell off a church would be built on that spot . . .'

'Cool.'

'So poor old Colman started off on foot, followed by Guaire and his men on horseback. They travelled all day and the belt stayed where it was.'

'They were just outside Gort when Colman got short taken – he was bustin' for a pee in other words. So while he was relieving himself behind a furze bush . . .'

'What's a furze bush?'

'I don't know exactly – anyway didn't the belt fall to the ground. So on that very spot King Guaire built a grand big cathedral and a round tower and he made Colman a bishop for life and called the place Kilmacduagh.'

Jack beams.

'The guy that built the round tower was a Connemara man who was always drunk and so the tower is leaning to one side like the tower in Pisa. The moral of the story is be careful what you wish for.'

I open my eyes and shake myself away from that Jack memory, in that weird, special place. I go out to the kitchen and open another beer. And I laugh then. Loud and hard, tears running down my face. And I'm thinking Hugsy's right. The moral of the story is shit happens. Great big balls of it. And I'm also thinking what a clever girl she is.

My head pounds and when I stumble out of bed the room spins. I feel my way to the bathroom, trying to open my eyes. All the pain is there, in my eyeballs and sockets, blinding me. In the bathroom I splash water on my face, and find paracetamol in the press. I take the tablets with warm tap water and slide down on the floor, leaning against the toilet. The tiles are cold against my skin.

The pain eases after a while and I get up gingerly and climb back into bed. Brian has taken to sleeping in the spare bedroom and I miss him now, the warmth and nearness of him. I climb out of bed again and sneak across the softly lit landing to his room. I open the door quietly and slip in beside his sleeping form. I fit my body into his and feel his erection after the usual half a minute. I press myself into him desperate now for some sort of intimacy. His hands find my breasts under my T-shirt and I groan quietly. He wakes suddenly and pulls his hands away, sitting up in bed. I pretend to be asleep. I can feel him looking at me.

'Ali, are you awake?'

I say nothing.

'Alison, please don't do this to me again. It really freaks me, do you know that?'

I turn around and look up into his face. I can barely see it in the dark room but I can tell he's angry by his voice. 'You wanted this, all the time you wanted to return to normal, you know . . . holidays, sex . . .'

'Normal, Ali? You think this is normal? I'm moving out after Christmas, do you know that, Ali? Do you understand the reality of that? We're way beyond fucked up, normal is a distant memory.'

His voice rises a little. I want to cry but no tears will come. My throat hurts from dehydration.

'Ah for fuck's sake, I'm a bigger fool, even talking to you like you understand.' He jumps out of bed, his erection silhouetted in the tiny path of light from under the door. 'You don't even know it's Christmas, do you? Or that tomorrow is Thursday? I've had enough. A fucking saint couldn't put up with this. It's like living with an alien.'

'Brian, I do want to talk.'

He looks down at me. 'No, you don't, Ali. You'd have to be here to be able to do that.'

He leaves and then I hear the soft drone of the TV downstairs and I think it's the loneliest sound in the world. A TV on in the small hours of the morning. Sleep doesn't come any more after that. I lie in bed cataloguing every sound, a countdown to morning. The odd car, a dog barking, refuse collection. The postman singing along to his iPod. I get up and wander into Jack's room. I open the blinds and sit on the bed.

206

The room is cold. Brian must have turned off the radiator. I sit there on the bed and then I remember something. His phone. Jack's phone. I root in his bedside locker and pushing the charger into a nearby socket I switch it on. I go searching for the house phone and find it on the window of Leah's room. I bring it back into Jack's room and ring his number. My body tingles as I wait. The phone rings and rings and then goes into the message minder and then I hear it. His voice.

Hi, Jack here. I'm not here – which is pretty obvious now – leave a message. Or don't. It's up to you.

I drop the phone and stare out the window at the red morning sky and wish it was a year ago. Something moves behind a tree near the gate of the house and then emerges and, as if he knows I'm in the room, he stares up at Jack's window. Stares so hard I imagine he's making eye contact with me. Frankie. Poor Frankie with his closed eye and battered face. And then I have an idea. I run downstairs and find a black bin bag and run back upstairs and start to fill the bag with some of Jack's clothes. Not his favourite things, they're for me, but older stuff and when the bag is full I run down the stairs and out into the cold, crisp morning, dragging the bag behind me.

'Frankie? Frankie, are you still here?' I call. I shiver with cold, realising that I only have pyjamas on. Frankie comes out from behind the tree. Close up his face is a mass of bruises, purple and yellow in the watery winter sunlight.

'Oh Frankie, you poor boy.'

I reach out to touch him but he pulls away, searching the street to see if anyone is watching.

'It's OK, Frankie. It's OK. Look what I have for you. Here, take it.'

He takes the heavy bag and looks at me with his swollen eyes, his face like a nightmare Jack face from one of my dreams. He walks away down the street half-dragging the bag after him. I shiver again and go back inside the silent house. I stand in the hallway still shaking with cold. And then I have another idea. Something that must be done. Today if possible. And there's only one question – why didn't I do it all along?

Thirteen

Jane

Ben's crying again and that's not going to help. All it does is make Daddy madder and then he shouts and asks us do we love him because if we did then we wouldn't be crying and we'd be delighted instead to be here.

'Shut up, Ben,' I tell him. Daddy's in the kitchen making breakfast, he's singing along with a CD, singing so fast he's ahead in the song all the time so the words are all jumbly. 'Play your PlayStation and stop being such a baby.'

'I want Mam,' he says, snivelling like a two-year-old. I don't feel sorry for him at all, just mad at him because all the time I'm telling him what to do to keep Daddy from getting madder and he's doing the exact opposite.

I throw a cushion at him. 'She'll be back tomorrow, gay boy.'

I see the hurt on his face and he wipes his eyes with the sleeve of his sweatshirt as Daddy comes into the room. He stands in front of the couch, facing the two of us. I glare at Ben because he's snivelling again.

Daddy crosses his arms and narrows his eyes, his mouth a hard line. 'What's the matter?'

'Nothing, Ben is getting a cold . . .'

'Ben . . . look at me when I'm talking to you. What's the matter?'

Ben hangs his head and I want to stretch out my leg and kick him hard.

'I'm speaking to you. You could do me the courtesy of making eye contact.'

Ben keeps looking down, the snivels turning into sobs. The Scissor Sisters sing away by themselves in the kitchen.

'Answer me.'

It's a shout and I jump a small bit. So does Ben.

Ben looks at me when he speaks. 'I miss Mam. I want Mam.'

Daddy says nothing for what seems like ages. The Scissor Sisters stop singing and I can hear traffic outside the window.

'Do you know something?'

I look at Daddy when he speaks because he likes that. Likes you to make eye contact. He's smiling.

'I'd be better off if I didn't give a damn about you. If I waltzed off to New York whoring around, just days before Christmas. You'd like me more for it, wouldn't you?'

'We love you Daddy,' I say, nodding my head to make it truer.

'No – if I was a shitbag you'd love me, both of you. If I beat the crap out of you or treated you like dogs . . .'

'No, Daddy. We love you, don't we Ben?'

Ben nods his head and tears run down his face. He nods and nods like the little dog in Mrs Collins' car.

Daddy closes his eyes and takes a deep breath. 'You'll see

tomorrow who cares the most, you'll see her in her true light, that slut person. Imagine that – I married a slut. A prostitute.'

'Daddy, there's a smell of burning,' I say and jump up and run to the kitchen. The Scissor Sisters are roaring about taking Mama out all night, and the frying pan is full of smoke. I pull the pan off the cooker but it's red hot and it drops to the floor. The smoke alarm goes off.

'Shut up, just shut up,' I scream at the hi-fi. Blackened rashers and sausages and pudding are strewn across the lino and then I hear laughing and there's Daddy and Ben standing in the doorway laughing their heads off. Ben goes back into the living room and Daddy helps me to clean up, crying now, crying harder than Ben ever could.

'It's OK, Dad, it's grand,' I say as I pick up the hot, burnt food. 'We'll have cereal, or toast.'

But he doesn't even hear me he's crying so much.

We go to the market. Daddy says it'll be great because it'll be all Christmassy and in a way he's right. It's a really cold day with a blue sky and we can see our breath in front of us. The market is crowded but it's fun and even Ben is smiling now and Daddy is happy. He's saying Happy Christmas to everyone and waving at people and I forget everything for a while, I even forget to check my phone to see if Leah texted. I can't text her now because I've no credit and I asked Daddy for some and he gave me a huge lecture about how phones were evil and we should all live without them. I have my own money though so when I go home I can get some.

Daddy buys flowers and a really nice candle, a centrepiece he calls it, for the middle of the table on Christmas Day.

'Where are you going to have Christmas dinner, Dad?' I ask

wardrobe has rows of jumpers arranged according to colour and then skirts and trousers. Shoes have a whole wall to themselves. There's three pretty boxes right in at the back. Pink candy stripes. They contain sexy underwear. Not the expensive kind, more the Ann Summers kind. The last box has about four different vibrators and a pair of handcuffs. For some reason this makes me laugh because it just doesn't seem to fit with her at all.

I laugh and laugh until tears stream down my face and I take out one of the vibrators, a horrible purple thing that looks like jelly, and I switch it on and this makes me completely hysterical. The sight of the thing buzzing and spinning around.

The children's bedrooms are sweet. The girl's is pink with pale lilac embroidered bed linen. The boy's is blue with fluffy clouds muralled on the walls. He's still in a crib and sleeps with a dolphin teddy.

I go back downstairs and am feeling comfortable now, like I've made friends with the house. The pup has weed on the shiny kitchen floor and I go out to the utility room in search of a mop and there in front of me is the biggest clothes mountain I've ever seen. Two baskets overflow with ironing. Another basket full to the brim with dirty clothes. I roll up my sleeves and throw myself into sorting out the one room in the house that needs it.

I put on a wash, filling the machine first with a girlie wash of pinks and lemons. The fabric conditioner smells like almonds. There is a folded ironing board hanging on the wall and I take it down and set it up in the middle of the room. I find the iron on a shelf and plug it in. It sizzles a little as it heats up and the machine hums away in the background, the satisfying hum of someone or something else working for you.

I tackle the first basket of ironing, kids' clothes. Three tiny as we stop at a stall selling olives from big vats. They smell even worse than they look.

'I've had loads of offers, don't worry about me,' he says.

'Couldn't you come to our house?' I know once it's said that Mam would never have it. That Gordon would be coming over after dinner and her sisters and they all hate Daddy. But I'm glad I said it too.

He laughs that high, screechy laugh and it reminds me of the Scissor Sisters singing. 'She'd never agree to that. To us behaving like a normal family. Anyway we'll have our special dinner tomorrow. Just you, me and Ben. Before we go home.'

We move on to a stall selling pirate DVDs and Ben wants Dad to buy some. There's a girl my age with a basket of puppies and a handmade sign that says 'free to good homes'. She's standing by herself near the big archway that leads out on to the road. I go and stroke the puppies.

'They're so cute,' I say. 'How old are they?'

'Six weeks.'

I know by her voice that she wants to cry.

'They are like the cutest . . .' I stroke them again, all soft, black fur and pink tongues. First I think there's two but then I see a really tiny one buried under the others.

'Do you want one?' she asks.

'I . . . I . . . no.'

I look at her and notice that her eyes are red from crying.

'Ruby, she's my dog, she loved them you know and they made me take them away from her this morning.'

'That's so lousy.'

'And all I can hear in my head now is Ruby howling as we left and . . .'

She takes a deep breath and squeezes back tears.

'It'll be OK,' I say. 'She'll get over it.'

The girl looks at me, her eyes wet again and she shakes her head. 'You should have seen her look at me, like I betrayed her and . . .'

'Jane,' Daddy says as he approaches, 'is that where you got to? Come on, let's get this show on the road.'

Daddy doesn't even see that the girl is upset and as I follow him I realise that he didn't see the girl at all, even though she was right there in front of him.

'Let's all go and have coffee,' he says as we reach the final stall. 'There's a really nice place over there and you're still right in the middle of the hustle and bustle. This is great, isn't it? Absolutely great atmosphere . . .'

Daddy rattles on and on and it's like so annoying and so boring. We make our way towards the café and then suddenly, without any warning at all, Mr Collins is right in front of us. Leah and Peter are with him. I feel my face going bright red, and then redder and redder as Leah glares at Daddy. I barely hear the dads saying hello and I look over Peter's head at a pigeon on the tiled roof of the market building so that I don't have to look at her.

And then I hear Daddy, the fool, saying come on and have coffee with us on this lovely morning, and I'm really red now, so red that my face is hot and I hate Daddy for being such a fool, and then Mr Collins asks Daddy did he get a job yet and I'm staring at the pigeon now, watching him as he spreads his grey wings and leaps high into the air and just flies away off, just because he feels like it, and Daddy is kind of going ballistic and oh my God he's shouting so I cover my ears and close my eyes really tight and I hear only a jumble of words and then it's quiet so I take my hands away from my ears.

'Mind your own business – more in your line to look after your own family – like your wife, for instance . . .' and it's

Daddy's voice and my face is wet and I can't bear to look at Leah so I run. I run through the crowded market, pushing against people and stalls and cages with chickens in them and I run and run through the archway, bumping against a buggy and then knocking past crates of carrots and then I'm outside and kind of lost. I sit on a wall and try and breathe but air won't go into my lungs – like as if it won't fit and I pinch my arm – the sore one, so hard that it makes me shout out loud. And then I pinch again, the hardest ever, and the air fits in my lungs now and I want to be sick. I put my head between my knees like Mam taught me years ago and when I look up again he's there in front of me. Ben is beside him, his face white.

'What did you do that for?'

'I . . . I . . . I felt sick and . . .'

'No, you didn't, Jane. Please don't lie. You ran away like a little coward when that man started to belittle me.'

I look at him. At his angry face and the glinting earring. I want to say it out, the stuff that I kill Ben for, the stuff that makes him worse. My arm throbs like it has a little heart all of its own, it beats like a heart. I say nothing.

'Asking me if I'd found a job – such utter cheek. Who does he think he is? He's a nothing – that's all, a nothing and a nobody.'

I nod. 'Yes, Dad, you're right.'

'Are you being sarcastic, Jane?'

I shake my head.

'I'll tell you something, Jane. You will never stay in that house, ever again. Over my dead body – they're mad, both of them.'

I nod again.

'You ran away from us – your own family, your father. How can you think so little of your own flesh and blood? Do we mean so little to you that you have to run away – ashamed of us?'

'I'm sorry, Daddy.'

'We're better than them, Jane. Don't you know that?'

'I do.'

'You do? Then why did you do it?' He's shouting and a couple stop to look at us. I smile at them and they walk on. The man looks back and says something to his wife.

Ben looks terrified so I smile at him and wink.

And on the way home in the car I sit in the back, not in the front with Daddy, and I know he doesn't like it but I don't care and then I reach out my hand and search for Ben's and I hold it tight, really tight, like the tighter I hold the more he'll know that I'll mind him and that it'll be all right in the end. And Ben stops looking out the window and turns and smiles at me. I wink at him again and this time he winks back.

Fourteen

Alison

I run upstairs quickly and shower. My head hurts now and bits of last night and the Bebo page and bottles of beer come back to me in tiny snippets. The water on my head helps and I lather myself in sweet-smelling soap and my stomach tingles with excitement. When I come out I dry myself carefully and root out my favourite moisturiser, some ridiculously expensive one that Brian bought in a rush because he forgot my birthday last year. I'd put it away for special occasions but there hadn't been any until now.

It smells delicious, like something you could eat for dessert, and it's soft and cold on my skin. Then I apply some make-up and try to remember the last time I'd put some on. I know exactly what I'll wear. An olive-green skirt and matching jacket with brown leather boots and a cream sweater. The skirt is loose but otherwise it looks fine. I go downstairs and make coffee in the cold kitchen. Leah's kitten miaows at my heels and clings to my boots. I bend down and pick her up and see how cute she is. I haven't seen her for days.

'Where have you been hiding, Kitty?' I ask her now and she licks my hand. I put her down and she follows me into the sitting room. Brian is asleep on the couch, one arm thrown over the edge, almost touching the ground. His hair is tousled and a row of beer bottles are lined up on the coffee table beside him. The kitten makes a dash for his outstretched hand, jabbing her sharp claws into him. He wakes with a yelp and curses at the kitten. 'Stupid bitch.'

'Who, me?' I say.

He looks up at me, his eyes crinkling, his hand running through his hair. 'What are you doing up?'

'I'm . . . I'm going to do some shopping . . . some Christmas shopping. Do you want coffee?'

He looks at me strangely. 'Shopping?'

'Yes. I thought it was about time . . . you know . . .'

'Really?'

I nod. 'Coffee?'

'Please. And two Nurofen.'

He follows me to the kitchen and watches as I pour coffee into cups.

'You look . . . different, Ali . . . lovely actually.'

I hand him a cup and smile at him. 'What are your plans for the day?'

'I'm bringing the kids to the market – it's the Christmas one, and then we're going shopping and then some food – you should come – the kids would like that.'

'I couldn't Brian. I . . . the crowds . . . I'd be a misery . . .'

'No, you wouldn't, Ali. It'd be great for them – do you know how hard it is for them? We could go to Luigi Malones for dinner, the lads love that place and we'd be home in time for Chriskindle and it'd . . .'

217

He stops and lifts his cup to his lips and sips loudly – a habit of his that used to drive me mad.

'I spoke to Leah. I had a long talk with her and I explained as best I could and she's OK so don't let that stop you coming . . .'

'No. I'll go shopping by myself – you go with the kids.' I turn and start to clean the sink, scrubbing it really hard with a scouring pad. 'The crowds, you know . . .'

Brian touches my shoulder with his hand and when I turn around he takes it away quickly, like my shoulder is hot to the touch.

'I . . . we can talk Ali, if that's what you want. You said that you wanted to last night.'

I turn back and start scrubbing all over again.

'We can do that if that's what you want. Is that what you want?'

I scrub away at the now shiny sink and I want to tell Brian that all I wanted last night was sex. Pure, raw sex that could freeze everything, numb it without a hangover. Have that physical intimacy just by itself.

'And everything will have to be on the table. Everything. Including Jack.'

For some insane reason I hate him saying Jack's name. It makes me so angry and I want to kick him and punch him and bite him and tell him that all the talking, all of it is useless.

'Anyway, I'll get the lads up. They'd sleep all day if you let them.'

He leaves just in time. Because if he'd stayed one second longer I might have killed him.

Leah doesn't look at me. She sits there, spooning cereal into her mouth, the kitten beside her, miaowing up into her face.

She looks so grown up today, her hair in a kind of scrunched-up bun, her skin so perfect and young. I look at her and Peter beside her and it's like as if I'm seeing them after a long holiday. They look older, not my children, more Brian's children. I can't wait for them to leave.

And as soon as they do, I miss them. The noise and bustle and life of them. I try to clear my head, try to think of what I should bring. I run upstairs to his room and I barely look around as I open his wardrobe door. I reach in for the hurley with the grass stains on it.

The doorbell rings and I hide in the bathroom willing it to stop. My palms are sweaty and the ringing goes on and on. Richard or Rachel. Definitely. Although they're coming tonight for something. Chriskindle. The doorbell starts its incessant ringing again and for a mad moment I think its Mam. She's sick of the Alzheimer's and the nursing home with the peacocks and she's come looking for Jack, for her favourite grandchild. And then it finally stops and after a minute I leave the bathroom and walk silently downstairs. I'm in the hall when it starts again, making me jump a little.

'Hi, hellooo,' I hear a woman call. She's seen me through the glass and I don't recognise the voice so it's OK. I open the door and a pretty young woman who looks vaguely familiar is standing there holding a beautifully wrapped gift.

'Hi, I'm Sarah Cassidy – Jane's aunt.'

I struggle to place her and she smiles brightly. Jane's aunt.

'We met a couple of times when I picked Jane up?'

'Oh, right. How are you?' I say, vaguely remembering her.

'I'm terrific. Listen, I think Jane and Leah had a little tiff – you know how they are at that age – hormones have a lot to answer for.' She giggles so I do too.

'Well, anyway, I'm in a terrible rush, we're off to Adare

Manor on an overnight for our work party and Jane is staying with her dad because Evelyn is in New York and well . . .' she pauses and I smile at her.

She holds out the gift. 'This is from Jane and it's for Leah, for Christmas.'

I take the gift and realise that I don't know if we have anything for Jane.

'Em . . . thanks . . . Leah is in town shopping with her dad but I'll give it to her.'

'Thanks a mill. You might get her to ring Jane. She misses her.'

'No problem.'

She beams at me and waves her fingers and walks away. Then she turns back and smiles again. 'Christmas must be hard for you. I'm sorry.' And then she's gone and only her perfume is there and her words go round in my head and I think at least she had the guts to say it.

It's an incredible morning and as I climb into my car I'm tempted to go down to the river for a while. I know what it's like on mornings like these, the smell and sound of it massaging me inside. But I focus on the day and as I drive towards town I work out some sort of plan.

The traffic is chaotic and the radio churns out Christmassy music and I still can't believe that it really is Christmas. Three days before Christmas according to the radio. I laugh and think it's a bit late to start the Christmas countdown now. I park near the market and as I walk down the thronged street my chest tightens and I force air into my lungs. Christmas shoppers pass by in gaggles – chatting and laughing – full of bag-carrying purpose.

The crowded street reminds me of that nightmare weekend

in Rome – the weekend the Pope died and every Catholic in the world seemed to have congregated to wake him. The noise was a constant – traffic, throngs of people, queues everywhere, the insidious sound of praying and chanting all the time – like the backing track for everything that happened that weekend.

The crowds thin out as I reach the library building – there are no shops along this street – just deserted offices and a night-club with two huge marble lions at its entrance. My heart pumps harder and I get that lovely adrenalin rush that fills my head and my ears and floods my body and makes me feel so alive. And then I'm outside the doors and I try to push them open but they're locked tight. I push again as the adrenalin turns to anger. There's a bell on the door and I attack it furiously, holding it down with my thumb so that it rings on and on and on. I notice then through my rage that the Christmas holiday opening times are pinned to the inside of the door – I can read them through the glass. I'd forgotten the Christmas factor.

I kick the door hard and almost break my toe with the effort and then I storm off up the street and I'm trying to think what will I do now? Do I have a plan B? I jostle my way through the throngs of people, and the carol singers outside Brown Thomas, all happy and jolly, nuns with guitars and smiles and rattling boxes, Eastern Europeans shouting loudly in their own tongue, and people everywhere, jamming the shops, buying and buying and buying.

I end up outside her office and of course that's closed too. I peer in at the ghostly desks and chairs, at the glossy posters on the walls of new houses offering new lives. She's gone too, they're together for Christmas, John and Laura Culhane and their two lovely children and not a care in the world between them.

I walk desolately back down the street, taking to the road to avoid the crowds. Everything seems noisier now, like time is running out so we need to up the ante so that everything will be done or bought or seen. I think of the man that went to live in a ditch in England again and I wonder if he's still there and if so would it be possible to find him.

I pass the market area and just as I'm heading to my car I see a girl around Leah's age walking towards me. She's holding a cardboard box that says Fyffes on the side and her eyes are red-rimmed, probably from a bad diet. She gives me a tiny smile, a little hello. There's a small pup asleep in the box.

'He's lovely, can I pat him?' I ask

She nods. 'He's the last one, the runt, nobody wants him.'

'He's gorgeous.'

'I know, he's my favourite.'

'Are you bringing him home?'

She shakes her head. 'No, my dad'll kill me if I bring any back. I found homes for the other two but nobody wants this guy.'

I look at the tiny sleeping pup, his perfect little face wrapped in soft brown fur. 'I'll take him.'

'Really?'

I smile at her. 'Absolutely. I'll take him. We have a kitten but they'll get used to each other. I'll take him, definitely.'

'You have to feed him every two hours because he's the weakest, will you do that?'

'I promise.'

She hands the box to me and the pup senses something and opens his eyes and mews like a kitten.

'That's why people didn't want him today, he just sounds so weak . . . kind of sick.'

I take the box and he skates around inside, crying now.

'He'll be grand, won't you, buster?'

'His name is Ashton.'

'Oh right, like Ashton Kutcher, I bet.'

'How did you know that?'

'I have a daughter your age.'

She beams at me, a lovely smile of trust and innocence and child. 'Thanks.'

'No problem. And thank you. What's your name?'

'Natalie.'

'Thank you, Natalie. Ashton will be fine.'

She smiles again and watches as I place the box on the passenger seat. I wave at her as I climb into the car and pull off.

I head in the direction of home and the pup dozes off again in his little cardboard bed and I think of Jack and the constant begging for a dog. It was the year I got cream carpets.

What did he want for Christmas last year, my Jack? Leah wanted a dance mat, a two-person one so that she and Jane could practice – and Brian asked her what they'd be practising for – the dance mat world championships? And Peter. A PlayStation 2 – that one's easy. What did Jack want? What would a fifteen-year-old boy want? And where is it, the thing he wanted, the thing he hardly got a chance to use or wear or watch? I know it wasn't a skateboard – that phase was the previous Christmas, and the Christmas before that it was a stereo and an acoustic guitar. For the life of me, I can't remember.

I end up outside their house without even realising it. They live on the other side of the city, right across the bridge. Like Mam's Alzheimer's I can't even remember crossing a bridge but I must have because here I am, me and Ashton, parked outside their house, a lovely period semi with ivy on the walls and a huge bay window. I know this well. I sat here many times and watched the happy family coming and going.

Him building a grey melty snowman out of slush, the little children squealing beside him in shiny red wellies. Her planting summer bedding, her hair tied up in a pony tail like a young girl, her body trim and fit in a sky-blue tracksuit. Both of them fitting a roof-box to the car and then packing it for a summer holiday, and putting an Ireland sticker on the back window beside a red, white and blue one that said Hello France.

And then once when they were gone on the holiday the Guards came and slowed down as they passed me and I drove away and I hadn't come back since. And I knew why too. I knew that if I did come back then I'd have to go inside.

Fifteen

Jane

'I'll make us something to eat. What do you want Ben?'

It's the afternoon and I'm so bored and I wish I could go off with Leah, into town like we always do at Christmas. And we take a really small amount of money, maybe twenty euros and you have to like buy everybody presents out of it. We go to shops like Guineys and the Two Euro shop and it's so tacky and so much fun.

Last year was the best because everybody said I bought the best present. It was for Leah and it was a shiny bag that was the shape of a shoe, a real shoe with a stiletto heel. And I got Jack a sheep that pooed sweets and I got Peter and Ben mugs that had Star Wars on them. It was old Star Wars but they didn't care, they loved them anyway. And then we'd go and have lunch and we'd have tons of bags and stuff and then I'd stay in Leah's – I always stay loads when it's holidays.

'Can I have Koka noodles?' Ben is playing the PlayStation, his back to me. There's that clicking noise as his hands fly over the controls. Daddy's in bed.

''Course you can. Do you want anything with it? I think there's burgers in the freezer.'

'Yeah, a burger.'

I go into the kitchen and it's so cold my teeth chatter and I wonder if I could light a fire – I mean I've seen Mam and Daddy do it loads and I decide if he doesn't get up then I'll light one. I make the noodles and fry up the burgers and they smell great, or else I'm just really hungry, and then I put them out on plates and when I look up Daddy's there. Standing in the doorway just looking at me. Not saying a word, just staring at me.

'Hi, Dad, do you want something to eat? Here, have mine and I'll cook another one. It's just like burgers and stuff . . .'

I get another plate and then I put on two more burgers and he's still standing there watching me. I bring Ben's food out to him and I almost have to nudge Daddy out of the way as I pass and it's the same when I try to come back in. The burgers are smoking so I turn down the gas.

'We're burning everything today. There must be something in the air,' I say, laughing, and my voice sounds tinny and high.

'Do you want some tea?' I ask him because I really want to hear his voice. The fast, mad talking is better than this. The talking and playing the music really loud and the walking up and down the tiny flat.

He looks at me but it's like he can't really see me, like I'm see-through, like tracing paper.

'Here, have some tea. We'll light a fire in a while, Dad. It's so cold.'

Tears run down his face and I want to belt him. In my head I'm saying I just asked if you wanted some tea, there's no need to bawl your eyes out over it. But I turn back to the burgers and push them around the frying pan instead.

I'm really pleased with the fire. Daddy didn't help me, not even when the first lot of firelighters just went out, I mean how dumb is that for firelighters? And then I threw on another load, way more than the first time, and I placed the briquettes around them instead of right on top and the fire just took off from there. Even Ben says it's a great fire and it's such a pity it'll all burn out before anyone else can see it. We laugh at this, the two of us rolling around the couch laughing, and then Daddy comes in with his phone and hands it to me without saying anything at all.

I think first of course that it's Leah but how dumb is that after all the stuff today. It's Mam and she's so happy and excited and she talks in a rush, telling me all the stuff she bought for me. Nike trainers and Tommy Hilfiger tops and they were for nothing. And she talks about Ground Zero and Manhattan and the Statue of Liberty, and he stands there all the time, watching me.

Then she says how are you Janie, how are things and I say they're fine, Mam, just great and then she asks to speak to Ben. And Ben has the hang of things now too. He knows not to say anything, to just put up with it and then Mam will be back tomorrow and it'll all be grand. So Ben says he's fine and that we're having a nice time and we went to the market today and tomorrow we're going ice skating.

Daddy watches and he looks so pale that I think maybe he's sick, coming down with flu or something. He has this weird look, and it's like the rope look but he wasn't quiet then, he was flying around with the rope in his hand, a rope the exact colour of the sky and . . . I shake my head to make it go away, and it does, the picture shatters and falls away in bits of colour, mostly blue.

He goes back to bed then and we sit and Ben plays his

computer game and I read a magazine, it's an old *Sugar* that I found under my bed and I check my phone loads of times but no texts. Nothing. Daddy's phone is on the table and I go over and pick it up and Ben looks up from his game. I bring the phone into the kitchen and punch in Leah's number but I can't make myself ring it. Not after today and the mortification of it. And anyway she probably hates my guts now even more and she'll never be my friend again. And then I ring Nana and while the phone is ringing I think that I might tell her that Daddy's not himself and that I'm worried and maybe she could just like call and stuff. She could make it all OK – just have a chat with him maybe. I'm waiting ages and I'm about to hang up when I hear her voice.

'Hello, who's speaking?'

'It's Jane, Nana, Mam is gone . . .'

'Hello, who's there?'

'Nana, it's me – Jane.'

'Hello, is that you, Sarah? I can't hear you, is it you?'

I raise my voice. 'Nana, it's me, Jane.'

'Who is it?'

'It's me, Jane.' I'm almost shouting now and then I know he's behind me, I can just feel him staring and I turn around and sure enough there he is. He has no clothes on, even though it's freezing. He walks over to me and takes the phone from my hand and just hangs up in the middle of Nana saying speak louder I can't hear you.

Sixteen

Alison

There's nobody home. Both cars are gone. I put the pup inside my jacket and button it up so that he can't fall out. And then I take Jack's hurley from the back seat and I lock the car. I walk towards the house, swinging the hurley, and it feels like I'm in a movie and this is definitely the next scene.

The gravel drive is exactly like ours, small, grey, crunchy stones. There are trees and shrubs around the edge of the garden so that when you're in there it feels really private. The door has a fanlight and some stained glass along the sidelights. I ring the doorbell knowing already that there's nobody home.

Around the back of the house there's a trampoline that I hadn't seen before, not those giant ugly ones, just a little one for the small children. The garden is lovely and backs on to protected marshland and then the river. You can see the river clearly from their neat wooden deck, a silver snake of water in the fading wintry light.

There's a wooden swing chair near a huge oak tree and I sit in that and swing for a minute and the pup doesn't even budge he's so content and I think maybe being that close to me and hearing my heartbeat reminds him of his mother.

Then I go back to the front of the house and in the back of my mind a tiny voice says don't do this, it's mad and they could come home at any minute and a louder voice says do it, just do it, like that Nike ad. I know where the key is. I've watched the cleaner come and go many times. And I know also that there's no alarm and I'm pleased that I've stored up all this helpful information. The pup yelps as I bend down to take the key from under a blue ceramic pot and there it is, shiny in the dim light. That lovely adrenalin begins to strut its stuff in my head first and then my body and even my fingers tingle as I put the key in the lock.

There's a smell in the hallway. Not a bad smell, just something distinct and personal. Their smell. I walk into the kitchen. It's sleek and modern and so tidy. There are French doors to the garden and on one wall there's a collage of photographs.

Leaving the hurley on the spotless glass table I find a bowl in a press where everything is colour and size coordinated and I open the blue Smeg fridge in search of milk. The food in the fridge is like an ad for healthy eating. Fresh vegetables bearing tell-tale organic signs – brown marks and small in size. Then a row of probiotic drinks and yogurts, a jug of freshly squeezed juice, lots of containers with contents so disgusting looking they must be healthy.

I pour some milk into the bowl and then I put the pup on the floor beside it. He groggily stands up and then just collapses again. I kneel down beside him and dip my finger into the bowl and put it in his mouth. After the second time he realises this is food and he waits eagerly for the milky finger to return again and again. Then he curls up right there on the floor and goes off to sleep, his belly satisfied.

The collage is a history of their children, from the first photo in the metal maternity hospital cots right up to now. I can tell that the last photo was added recently – it's a photograph of the two blonde children, the girl smiling, the little boy roaring so much that his face is bright red – they're sitting on Santa's lap. The date is overhead – Parkway Christmas: 2005. Santa looks like somebody who'd rather be anywhere else except in his grotto. It's actually a great photo though – the reluctant Santa, the beaming girl, the screaming boy.

The living room is in show-house condition. Polished floors, period fireplace, beautiful bay window. In the bay there's the most perfect Christmas tree, real of course but in a pot so that she can put it back in her garden when Christmas is over. The gifts underneath are so beautiful that I think first that they're mock – just for show. I pick one up. A perfect symmetrical square. The wrapping is beige, handmade with a russet net bow and dried flowers. Exquisite. The tiny card reads *to Hannah from Mammy and Daddy*. Mammy. It reminds me of Jane and I know that Jane's mother is Protestant and that's probably where the Mammy thing came from. Are these people Protestant?

Suddenly there's a loud ringing and I drop the present and for a split second I think it's the doorbell but it's not – it's the phone because there it is on the coffee table ringing and ringing. It stops as suddenly as it started and I relax again and creep out to the hall and up the thickly carpeted stairs. Their bedroom is huge and I think it must have been two rooms made into one. There's an ensuite and a walk-in wardrobe. The

little dresses. A soft lambswool cardigan in the palest blue, bright Winnie the Pooh pyjamas. A little pair of cute combats. A miniature Munster strip.

I pile the ironed clothes in neat bundles of his and hers and am surprised when I realise that the basket is empty. The other basket has their clothes – his shirts and T-shirts, her blouses, and lots of gym clothes, his and hers tracksuits, tops, shorts, socks. Her underwear is delicate and lacy, matching bras and panties in pale colours, nothing like the trashy stuff in the candy-striped boxes. His are muted man colours – blacks and greys and navys. I iron each piece of underwear carefully and when the doorbell rings loudly and insistently I let out a scream.

I hear talking and creep out of the utility room, peeping out the hall towards the door. There's a crowd of silhouettes outside and then they burst into song. The twelve days of Christmas. On a mad whim I open the door and there they are as perfect as a Christmas card, with woolly hats and smiling faces and they sound so loud, the voices carrying in the quiet evening street. I smile at them and just as I think they're about to finish they launch into another carol, 'Silent Night' this time and I know then that I must give some money so I go looking for my bag and pay them off. They wave goodbye as they leave and I stand at the door waving back, as if I'm the woman of the house.

The house feels eerily silent now after the loudness of the carol singers. I pile the freshly ironed clothes into a basket and bring them upstairs. I put away the children's clothes first and am amazed at how organised their wardrobes are – there's a place for everything, underwear, vests, jumpers, pants, dresses.

I go back down and fill my basket again, and climb the stairs to their bedroom. I notice as I go in that there's a plasma TV screen on the wall in front of the bed. I put the basket down on the floor and pick up the remote and switch the TV on. It flickers to life and fills the room with Julie Andrews singing her heart out – *The Sound of Music*. I lie on the bed and watch the von Trapps, saying their lines in my head. I wonder if Leah's watching this, it's her favourite and mine too except that both of us know it off by heart. The bed is comfortable, soft pillows and a duck feather and down quilt with lovely, crisp cotton sheets. I kick off my shoes and climb under the quilt, propping up my head with pillows so that I can see the TV.

'Leah was your favourite. The only girl, pretty . . .'

We're in Lahinch again but it's Christmas here too. We're sitting on the prom wall and just down from us the surfers are changing into their wetsuits. Behind us, a tinny version of 'Do They Know It's Christmas' is playing on a PA system outside Seaworld and it sounds surreal in this wintry seaside location.

'I never knew you visited Nana. You never said.'

'You never asked. And anyway I like peacocks.'

'What did you buy her?'

'Who? Nana? Soap and soft rolls – that's what she always asked for. And she'd make me hide the rolls for later – you know – like they were starving her in there and then she'd take the soap out of the packet and keep stroking it and talking to it.'

'She always had favourites – I tried not to have favourites. It's wrong.'

He's wearing flip-flops and he lets them drop to the ground, bringing his feet up on the wall and then standing up.

'That's only pretending though, isn't it? Trying not to have favourites when really you do. Nana has the right idea. Call it like it is.'

I watch as the surfers move down the steps towards the sea, carrying their boards. They do it in pairs, one at each end of the board, their steps synchronised as they march in unison across the sand.

'Nana says you always made her feel bad.'

'What's that supposed to mean?' I look at Jack, the grey Atlantic behind him, the tinny music wafting through the icy wind.

'I know what she meant.'

I say nothing, almost afraid of the answer.

'It's like she couldn't ever get a handle on you – she could with the others but not you.'

The minute he says it I know it's right. I smile at him. 'Like you and me?'

He nods but he's not smiling, his eyes dead-looking and soulless. I reach out my hand to touch his face but he steps back, steps away from me.

'When it's like that, there's no pleasing somebody, sure there isn't?'

'That's not true, Jack . . . you would have understood once you were older . . .'

'For fuck's sake, Mam, get with the programme. That's not going to happen so we're left with what did happen. We could never please each other – not in a million years.'

'I miss you so much. I'd give anything to have you back.'

'One of the others?'

'Jack, that's childish . . .'

'I'm fifteen. It's allowed. You were glad it was me. If you had to pick one then I was the one.'

'No. Never.' I reach out again but he turns away from me and when he turns back his face is battered, just like Frankie's. There's blood coming out of his ear, scarlet blood dripping down a grey-white face. His eyes have blood in them like *crimson tears. He melts then, right there in front of me. He just melts away. His flip-flops are still on the ground and I bend down and pick them up, holding them tightly to my chest like they are him.*

He's standing over me when I wake in his bed, one of his pillows clutched into my chest. I can hear an ad on the TV for Budweiser beer, the Christmas one with the carriage and the jingle bells. I cover my head with the duvet.

'Who are you? What the fuck are you doing in my home?' he says, pulling the duvet away from me.

'The ironing,' I say, jumping out of the bed. My heart is pumping and my brain refuses to work properly. Where are my shoes? I search the floor for them, toppling the basket of ironed clothes. I hear the harmonies of the von Trapps singing 'Do-Re-Mi' drowning out his words.

Seventeen

Jane

'Turn it over, gay boy.'

Ben ignores me as 'Do-Re-Mi' blasts from the flickering telly. I hate the stupid *Sound of Music* and I know *Dirty Dancing*'s started on TV3 but Ben's being a little brat and Daddy said I was to let him watch it and that I could change the channel when he came back. But that was like ages ago, at least an hour. I check my phone again for messages but there are none.

I make us some cereal and then I force him to watch *Dirty Dancing*, and then an *X Factor* Christmas special. I send Daddy a text from my phone to ring me but there's no reply. I'm getting scared but I don't want Ben to know and I try to think of a plan in my head if Daddy doesn't come back soon. Maybe just go to bed and wait until Mammy comes home tomorrow? There's singing and shouting outside and Ben looks over nervously. I turn up the volume on the telly. The noise in the street gets louder and then it's right outside the front door and my heart thumps in my chest but I smile at Ben.

237

'Just drunk people messing,' I tell him, trying to convince myself as well.

There's the rattle of keys as someone tries to unlock the door. I jump up as the door opens and the voices are in the hallway. I hear Daddy's voice. Two men and a woman come into the living room, carrying plastic bags. They smile at us, glassy drunk smiles and their clothes are stained and dirty. Then Daddy comes in and I know the second I see him that this is worse than the rope. Way worse. His eyes are wide open and they don't blink and his voice is high-pitched and screechy. He stretches out his arms for silence and stands in the middle of the tiny room.

'My children – Jane and Ben – seed of my loins, my heirs!'

The woman starts giggling and takes cans of beer from one of the plastic bags and hands them around.

'Let's drink a toast to heirs,' she says, and laughs wildly. One of the men staggers and his beer spills on the lino. Ben has crept over next to me and I seek out his damp hand and hold it tight.

Daddy takes a can of beer and slugs it back. Then he holds the can in the air. 'To heirs and to life – wonderful, terrible life.'

'Life,' say the others.

Daddy lifts the can to his lips again. 'I should have been a pair of ragged claws, scuttling across the floors of silent seas.'

The woman claps her hands, spilling beer onto the floor. 'Shakespeare. I did him in school.'

The two men laugh. 'You did more than him, Lorraine,' says the smaller man.

They all laugh at this.

One of them, the taller man, sits down on the couch beside us and I can smell cigarettes and beer and old sweat. He grins at me, a weird, drunk grin. His teeth are yellow. Daddy sits down too and takes out a silver foil from his jacket pocket and puts it on the small coffee table. Then he takes out cigarettes and another little green packet that says Rizla on the side. The woman and the other man are leaning against the wall kissing noisily. Daddy starts breaking up a cigarette into a thin piece of paper and I know that he's rolling a joint. I saw it in a movie once. The woman goes into the kitchen and then the Scissor Sisters are blaring and Daddy is laughing and the other man next to me on the couch is grinning and I want to die. Ben grips my hand so tight it hurts.

'Let's go to bed,' I whisper and he nods and we get up and Daddy doesn't even notice. It's freezing in the bedroom and Ben climbs into bed without getting undressed. His face is snow-white and he looks ill.

'Are you OK?'

'My head hurts,' he says, his eyes full of tears.

'It's all right, Ben, it's OK. I'll get you some aspirin, how's that?'

'Can I come with you?'

'No. Wait here, I won't be a second.'

They're all busy drinking now in the living room and I walk past into the kitchen and search for some tablets and then go to the sink and pour a glass of water for Ben. The door closes behind me and before I can turn around the man with the teeth is pressing himself into my back so hard that I can't even turn around.

'Little sweetheart, aren't you love?' he whispers, pushing his hips into my bottom. I try to wriggle out of his grasp and I'm crying now, hot tears on my face, and his breathing is getting faster and the Scissor Sisters are singing.

'Teasing me you little minx?' he says, and tries to grab my chest. I elbow him as hard as I can and he staggers and I run for it, still clutching the tablets. He grabs me by the hair just when I'm nearly away from him. He pulls my face towards him and sticks his tongue into my mouth exactly like Darren Tierney but he doesn't taste like Taytos, he tastes like vomit, and then he staggers back, his eyes glassy and I run like hell.

Back in the bedroom Ben is sitting up in the bed, his face a picture of terror.

'What happened?' he says, as I try to catch my breath.

'Nothing. They're just silly drunk people, that's all. Here, take the tablets, Ben.'

'I can't. I've no water.'

'Just swallow them without water.' I lock the bedroom door with the bolt, switch off the light and climb into bed in my clothes. But I can't sleep with the noise. And then I hear Ben crying to himself. Little whimpers like a tiny hurt animal.

'Do you want to come into my bed?' I ask, and immediately he's in beside me, his body rigid next to mine.

And when I wake up again it's morning and I think last night didn't happen at all and then I feel Ben's body curled into me. The sheets feel damp and I know it's pee from the smell. I creep out into the living room. It smells horrible, like a pub, but at least they're not still here. Cans and bottles and cigarette butts are all over the table and even the floor. I knock on Daddy's door.

'Daddy?'

No answer.

'Are you in there?'

No answer.

I open the door slowly and peek in but the room is empty. The kitchen is empty too. There's a green basin on the kitchen table and I go to look inside, half-dreading what might be in there. It's full of water and at the bottom are mobile phones. Mine is there, and two others I don't recognise. I look out the kitchen window to the laneway at the back of the flat where Daddy usually parks his car. It's not there. I look back down at the basin of drowned mobile phones and I know something terrible is going to happen.

Eighteen

Alison

'I know you from somewhere, don't I?'

He says this to me just before he makes a call on his mobile. He's standing in front of the doorway blocking my exit. I sit on the bed looking up at him. The TV on the wall wishes us a happy Christmas from all at Harvey Norman's.

I don't answer. I just watch his face – it's like a calculator totting up all the figures.

'You're his mother, aren't you? You're Jack's mother?'

The familiar way that he says Jack's name shocks me at first. Jack – like he knows him casually from the neighbourhood or school or football.

'You're Jack's mother.' I see his face clearing now, all the sums added up and the right answer finally arrived at.

I get up and straighten the bedclothes – a lovely soft cream and beige quilt on paler cream sheets. I pick up the freshly ironed clothes strewn now all over the floor and begin to fold them all over again, their delicate almondy smell filling the room.

'Jesus!' he says. 'Fucking hell.' He's pacing up and down, running his hands through his hair. 'Jesus. Fuck me.'

When the clothes are arranged in a neat bundle on the bed I open the door to leave. 'Goodbye,' I say as I walk out into the bright landing and down the stairs.

'Hey, hey. Come back please. Why did you come? Why did you come here?' He grabs my arm and I almost stumble on the bottom step of the stairs. I push his hand away and try to open the front door. He grabs my arm again, harder this time.

'Tell me what you want from me. Tell me.'

I turn around to face him, and look straight into his luminous blue eyes. His grip on my arm tightens.

'You owe me an explanation,' he says. 'You owe me that.'

I can feel a knot of anger in my chest, a tight, hard knot that's filling my chest cavity and now my heart and up along my throat into my head and then back down to my free arm, and then I punch him, I punch so hard straight into the mouth that he reels backwards, eyes wide open in shock or pain or both. Blood erupts from his lip in a rivulet of bright red and drips on to his starched white shirt.

'I definitely owe you that,' I say and then I realise that that's the first thing I've ever said to him. Despite all my imaginary conversations with him that's the first thing.

'Jesus Christ, you're mad,' he says, wiping blood from his mouth.

And then I feel the knot inside me again and this time it's unstoppable like a tornado and I throw myself at him, beating him repeatedly over the head and chest, and then my lungs start to close and I can't get air into them, it just won't go in, and I feel my head floating and the air squeezing out of my chest, and his face over me, looking at me, and my hand hurts so badly now, throbbing with pain.

When I open my eyes I'm lying on the couch in his living room. He has a glass of water at my lips and I sip it and it tastes cold and good. He's crying and tears and blood have gathered in a pool at the corner of his mouth.

'I think about it . . . I think about it all the time you know. Not a day goes by, not a minute, not even a second where I don't see his face, his . . . Jesus Christ . . .'

He shakes his head and takes a drink of the water. 'I keep thinking did I miss something? You know, was there anything else I could have done? Why did I go that way that day? I never go home that way. There was a huge traffic jam at Sarsfield Bridge and that's the reason . . . How dumb is that? That's such a stupid reason to die . . . so stupid.'

He wipes his eyes with his suit sleeve. 'I held him you know. I held his hand and then his eyes . . . he closed his eyes and squeezed my hand. He squeezed my hand and later that helped me . . . isn't that strange? Gave me some comfort – you know – like he didn't blame me or something . . .'

A car pulls up in the driveway but he doesn't even hear. 'I wanted to go with him but they wouldn't let me. I didn't want him to be alone in the ambulance, to die by himself in that ambulance . . . but they wouldn't let me . . .'

I can hear the front door opening and a child's sing-song voice. 'Daddy, Daddy, look at my Santa hat . . .' A small blonde girl bursts into the room and freezes when she sees me and then her Daddy's bloodied face. Her mother comes in then, wearing the same red suit she wore the day I watched her at the house, and carrying a sleeping baby in her arms. She looks at me and then at her husband. 'John, what in the name of God is going on? Why are you . . . what happened your face?'

He doesn't answer her. He just drops his head into his hands.

'Who are you?' she says. The little girl knows something is wrong and hides behind her mother's legs.

'I'm Alison Collins.'

'Alison Collins?'

'The boy's mother,' he says.

'Jack's mother,' I say.

Her face hardens immediately and she walks out of the room, the small girl following, clutching her skirt. We sit in silence.

She comes back in, without the children.

'I rang Henry Street. They're on their way.'

'Why did you do that?' he says, standing up. 'We're just talking, it's fine.'

'No, it isn't, John. We have nothing to say to her. It was an accident, plain and simple. And I'm sorry her son is dead but he walked – no – he ran straight out in front of you and you didn't have a chance and you've been cleared of all charges, don't forget that.'

'Laura, please. We're just talking. She lost her child, for God's sake.'

'Death by misadventure – that's what the verdict was. The Gardaí said you couldn't have done anything else. They said you were blameless, John. You don't have to . . .'

'I don't have to but I want to.'

He smiles at me then. 'Would you like some tea?'

I smile back. 'I'd like that.'

'Come on. We'll go into the kitchen,' he says. I follow him.

The little girl is playing on the floor with the puppy. He puts on the kettle and picks up the hurley on the table. 'What were you going to do with this?'

I shrug. 'I've no idea.'

He strokes the boss of the hurley and swings it like he's taking a puck of a sliotar. 'Was he any good?'

'Good enough. He loved it – he was on the first team.'

'That's unusual for a city lad.'

The girl comes over with the puppy in her arms. 'Daddy, is he mine? Did Santa bring him for me?'

'No, Hannah, he belongs to the lady but you can play with him for a little while – how's that?'

'OK, Daddy, but I love him and he loves me.'

'I know, sweetie. And when you're bigger you can get one too. I promise – OK?' He bends down and kisses the top of her blonde head. The kettle boils and he makes the tea.

'Do you take sugar?'

I nod. 'One please.'

He stirs the sugar in.

'Milk?'

I nod again.

He hands me the mug and I sip the hot liquid, leaning against the worktop. The doorbell rings and I can hear voices in the hall.

'I'm sorry,' he says. 'I'm so sorry.'

I take another sip of tea and look at him, right into his face, with the sad eyes and busted lip.

'I know you are.'

He smiles at me, dried blood congealing on his mouth.

'You look like a vampire that just had dinner.'

He grins and his eyes crinkle at the corners exactly like Brian's. 'How's your hand?'

'Sore. Really sore.'

'Maybe you should have it X-rayed – you have some left hook.'

The voices in the hallway draw nearer and the woman comes into the kitchen followed by two guards. One of them is Sergeant Tom Healy.

'Alison,' he says, nodding his head at me.

'Could you please remove this person from our home? We could have her arrested you know – breaking and entering, harassment, assault. I'd like her gone right now.' She stands there with her hand on her hip, her blonde hair beginning to show signs of disarray.

Her husband shakes his head at the gardaí. 'There's no question of charges, none at all.' He goes and gently takes the pup from his daughter, picks up the hurley from the table and gives them to me. My hand is really stiff now, and it's agony to bend my fingers around the hurley. Tom Healy takes it for me.

'I'll bring you home, Alison,' Tom says.

'I'll drive myself,' I say, following him and the other young garda to the front door.

'No, you won't. I'll bring you home and Garda Burke will follow in your car.'

The husband stands at the door as we walk out into the dry crisp night.

'I'm sorry,' he says again.

I turn back to face him, the pup nestled once again inside my jacket, his tiny heartbeat thumping rhythmically against mine.

'Shit happens,' I say.

'Shit happens,' he repeats.

Nineteen

Jane

'Daddy, stop. Please stop Daddy, Ben is sick and we should take him to the doctor and . . .'

Daddy is nailing down the window in the living room – banging nails and wood together so hard that tiny flaky pieces of the ceiling are falling down like rain made from dust. Suddenly he stops and looks at me and I'm sorry now that I said anything. He puts his hands to his head like it's exploding.

'Shut up. Shutupshutupshutupshutupshutup,' he screams, making me jump. Then he closes his eyes and opens them really wide and stares at me.

'Be quiet,' he says, his voice no louder than a whisper. 'We have a lot to do before they come. A lot to do.'

I want to ask him who he means, does he mean Mammy and what do we have to do but now I'm scared. He turns back to his hammering and I go to check on Ben in the bedroom. He's sleeping but his forehead still feels hot. I go to the kitchen to get a cloth and some cold water and as I fill up a pot I hear a noise – a mobile phone beeping. It's coming from the top of the fridge and I find the small stool and reach up. There's a blue bag that says Body Shop on the front and the noise is coming from that. I look at the door before I take it down. The phone has stopped beeping now and I open the bag and reach in for it but instead of the phone I pull out something hard and cold. A gun. A small, silver gun that looks like a child's toy. I drop it on the floor in a panic and then I'm sure he's heard and he's going to come running in. I stand still as a statue but the hammering doesn't stop. I pick the gun up. It's heavier than it looks but it feels safe, like it's just metal and won't really hurt you. I put it back in the bag and take out the phone. My hand shakes as I look at it. Who should I ring? I go through people in my head – Nana – she can't help us; Mammy is in New York or else on a plane home, and anyway I don't have their phone numbers – not in my head, only in my own phone and that's all wet – and then I think there's one number in the world I know off by heart. I punch in the numbers and they're wrong and I have to start all over again. There's a pounding noise in my head and my hands are shaking so badly that it's making the screen on the phone all blurry and then it rings, once, twice, three times and there's no answer and in my head I'm chanting please please answer the phone and then I hear him coming and I'm frozen there like a statue and the phone has rung out. But he doesn't come in, he's outside talking to Ben. I can hear the low murmur of voices. I press the redial button, my heart pounding in my chest. It seems to take ages for the first ring. It starts to ring and I can still hear the low voices or maybe it's the telly . . .

'What are you doing?'

Daddy's standing in the doorway, his face icy, like I'm a stranger and not his daughter. My stomach flips over and warm, wet pee runs down my leg.

'Give it to me,' he says, walking towards me. I can hear a voice answer on the phone but I'm scared to say anything.

He grabs the phone and presses the button to hang up.

'Bitch.'

I keep my head down, looking at a tiny cornflake stuck to the lino near the leg of the kitchen table, pinching my arm behind my back all the time. This makes me feel smaller, nearly invisible and I pinch so hard I'm crying. Suddenly the phone beeps and Daddy reads the message but I only look up once and then drop my head again.

'Fucking bitch. Dirty filthy fucking cunt. Slutbag, fucking shitbag.' He says all of this quietly and it makes it even scarier and now I need to pee a lot and the pinching isn't working anymore.

'I'm sorry, Daddy.'

'Fucking slut, I'll teach the slut a lesson she'll never forget. I'll show her for once and for all that she's not the only ball breaker around.' He laughs then, like a drunk person laughs.

'I'm sorry, I didn't mean it,' I say, sneaking a look at his face.

'That fucking bitch misses her fucking flight home – that's how much she cares about her children – fucking swanning around New fucking York with her fucking boyfriend – bitch.'

He takes the phone and smashes it against the wall and more wee runs down my leg and I want to be sick. He goes and gets the broken bits of phone and puts them in the basin of water with the others and then he picks up the bag and takes out the gun.

He smiles at me. 'This was my father's gun. Did I ever tell you that?'

I wish he'd just put the gun away.

He looks at the gun, a small smile on his lips.

'So, Jane?' he says, stroking the gun like it's a small animal in his hands.

'Yes, Daddy?'

'Your mother's flight has been delayed or cancelled or something.'

His voice sounds grand now, like the old Daddy, the normal one.

'When is she coming so – later tonight?'

He smiles at me. 'She's always late, she'll be late for her own funeral.' He laughs then, the mad laugh, and points the gun at the kitchen window and pretends to shoot, making bullet noises. 'She's not coming tonight, but we won't miss her one little bit. Our plans don't have to change at all.'

'I have to sponge Ben's forehead, Daddy. He's sick.'

He turns and points the gun at me and then winks. 'I'll help you.'

He sticks the gun inside the top of the waistband of his jeans, the top of it sticking out. Then he picks up the blue bag and empties out a handful of small harmless-looking bullets and puts them in his pocket. Then he gets a bowl and fills it with water and squeezes out the dishcloth.

'Right! Let's do this,' he says, marching out the door. I follow him into the bedroom. It smells of wee and sweat and petrol from Daddy.

Ben opens his eyes and I can see the panic in them when he sees Daddy with the gun stuck down his pants. I smile at Ben and squeeze out the cloth and start sponging his face. His hair is wet with sweat and his eyes are huge and round as he looks up at Daddy and me.

'You'll feel better after this, Ben, and then we'll make you some soup, won't we Daddy? And before you know it you'll be up and running around again . . .'

'I want Mammy.' Ben's eyes are fixed on the gun. 'I want Mammy,' he says again.

'I bet you're starting to feel better already, aren't you?' I say as I sponge his bare chest. His body looks so small and white and I can feel the heat from it as I sponge and sponge.

'I want my Mammy, want her, want her, want her . . .' Ben is talking to the gun all the time and his eyes spill over with tears. Daddy just stands there, holding the bowl of water, smiling at Ben, but not really seeing him.

'Daddy, go put on the soup,' I say.

He stares at me like I'm talking to him in Japanese but he leaves the room. I climb into bed with Ben and hold him. He's crying and the hammering is starting all over again in the sitting room.

'It's OK, Ben, it's OK. I'll mind you and then Mam will be back and it'll be Christmas and everything'll be fine. I promise you, Ben.'

I stroke the top of his damp head and try to think of what to do. Ben's crying stops and when I look down he's asleep and he doesn't seem to be hot anymore. I lie there trying to think of a plan for us while Daddy hammers away. Hammers and hammers and hammers.

Twenty

Alison

They're all standing in the driveway as the squad car pulls up. I see their faces in a blur of familiar features. Rachel, Richard, Donal holding a baby carrier. My baby, Petey. Leah, God she's so pale. And Brian and his worried, drawn face.

'Are you OK to go in, Alison?' asks Tom. He opens the dash in front of me and takes out a pack of Kleenex. 'Here, love, dry your eyes a bit before you get out. That's the girl.'

I take a tissue and wipe my eyes. I hadn't noticed the tears and I wipe at them furiously but they just keep coming until the tissue disintegrates. He pulls out another one and hands it to me as Brian opens the passenger door. Brian has deep lines around his mouth that I never noticed before. New lines. I touch them with my fingers and he holds my arm then as I get out of the car.

'I'm sorry,' I say. The tears are pouring down my face now and I lay my head on Brian's chest. He puts his arms around me and it's the best feeling in the world and then I really cry, my

253

body shaking with the effort. And then something else is crying too and I remember.

I try to pull away from Brian but he tightens his grip.

'You'll squeeze Ashton Kutcher to death,' I say, through tears and snot. I open my jacket and show him the tiny mewing pup and Leah and Peter see him and start squealing with excitement. And then, surreally, Frankie and his mother are in the driveway. She's holding the bag of clothes I'd given him earlier that morning.

'Jesus, what's happening now?' says Richard.

The mother walks up to me and plonks the bag of clothes down in front of me.

'Frankie has no need for these,' she says.

Frankie has his head down, afraid to look at me.

'I'm sorry, I thought he might be . . .'

'You thought too much,' she says. 'Come on, Frank, let's go home.' She takes Frankie by the arm and walks back down the drive, their feet crunching on the gravel.

Brian leads me into the house and sits me down on the couch in the study.

'I met him, Brian,' I say, then blow my nose in the soggy tissue.

'I know. Tom rang me from the station. He told me he'd bring you home and that I was to wait here.'

I nod. He's sitting beside me, his head in his hands.

'I'm sorry, Brian.'

I can hear people leaving outside, muffled voices, the crunch of cars in the driveway. There's a TV on somewhere in the house. A track from *Dirty Dancing* – 'Time of My Life'.

Brian gets up and leaves and I close my eyes and lean back into the couch, suddenly exhausted. He arrives back with a bottle of wine and two glasses. He pours a glass each and hands me one.

'It's your favourite – Cloudy Bay.'

'Jesus – what did you do? Rob a bank?'

He grins and I notice the new lines again, etched into his face for ever. 'A present from a client who has more money than sense.'

'God. Celtic tiger times – it used to be a tin of USA – Foxes if they were really pushing the boat out.'

He sips the wine. 'It's lovely though – have a taste.'

The cold liquid makes me shudder but it's really good. I watch as Brian takes another sip. He smiles at me again and I smile back. It's infectious.

'A dog, Ali?'

'I know. It's a long story. It was for Frankie but I don't think that's a good idea now. They love him though, don't they?'

'They're in the kitchen feeding him and playing with him. It's like the perfect present for those two.'

I take a gulp of the wine this time and I can feel its icy goodness as it warms my stomach. The tears have stopped.

'I know I shouldn't have done it, Brian, shouldn't have gone there but I had to.'

He runs a hand through his wiry, greying hair. 'I understand why.'

'Really?'

He looks me straight in the eye. 'Yeah. Absolutely. I wasn't even surprised when the sergeant rang me.'

'I thought you'd be mad, that you'd think I really was insane, you know, like you said last night.'

'No. It has a logic of sorts – a kind of Ali logic.'

'I liked him, Brian – can you imagine that? I liked him.'

I close my eyes as tears sneak out again. 'All the times I followed him, planned what I'd say – no, planned what I'd do to him and then I liked him.'

'Followed him? Christ, Ali, followed him? Now that is insane.'

'You look at someone, read their name in a police report, connect the two and then you invent – your perception of things is skewed and you invent stuff . . . he made me tea and he was . . . nice, a good person. You always know a good person.'

Brian hands me a new tissue. 'Here, wipe your nose.'

I obey him. 'Shit happens.'

Brian nods. 'You can say that again.'

I lean my head against Brian's shoulder, hungry for his comforting heat and smell. He strokes my hair with his free hand. 'That was some shopping trip you went on, Ali. Fucking hell, and me here with the Chriskindle lark.'

'I forgot about that.'

'Too right you did. You should have seen Richard's face when I matter of factly announced that you were arriving home via squad car. And then the grand finale, our friends the Travellers. Richard's still reeling.'

I laugh and so does Brian, and then both of us are laughing and laughing so hard and I'm crying again, but laughing too, and spilling my expensive wine all over the floor.

'Jesus, I'll think twice before I ask you to go to Dunnes again,' he says, and the laughing starts up again.

'And the stalking and breaking and entering – Jesus, Ali, they must be sick of you in Henry Street.'

I stop laughing and so does he and then we're all over each other, tearing at each other's clothes and Brian jumps up, naked, from the couch and locks the door and then he's on top of me, in me and his mouth searches for mine and it's the sweetest thing in the world and my legs grip his body and push him further inside me and when I come I shout, trying to muffle it but not able to.

Afterward, we lie there, his jacket thrown over us, and for the first time in a long time I don't feel alone.

'The morning it happened . . .'

'Don't, Ali, you don't have to . . .'

'Jack and I had a huge fight. He gave his brand-new iPod to Sean Fahy. Brand new – his Christmas present – and he gives it to Sean – a loan supposedly – like all the other stuff he loans . . . loaned to people . . .'

'Ali, stop it. Not now.'

'And then he gets up in foul humour and he knows I have loads on so he . . . he dawdles on purpose because he knows I'll lose it with him and the iPod is the last straw . . .'

Brian sits up and begins to pull on his clothes. 'Are you hungry? I'll make us something to eat – the lads had dinner in town but . . .'

'There's a song on the radio – and I just for the life of me can't think of the name and Jack comes in banging doors and growling at the other two and do you know what he does then?'

Brian's head is bent and he's sitting there in stripy boxers and one sock.

'He wangles a loan of Leah's iPod – her little Nano! Fuck's sake, Brian – he's given away his own and then has the cheek to borrow his sister's and she gives it to him in the hope of keeping the peace between him and me and then I just lose it . . .'

'Ali, you don't have to do this, really, you don't have to . . .'

'We're standing in the kitchen. It's raining outside. I can hear it spitting against the window. That song is on the radio and Jack is staring me down, half-smiling at me, challenging me. In his face I see hatred, undisguised contempt and his voice saying "calm down, look at the state of you" and the look in those eyes . . .'

I stop and take a breath, and feel wet tears again on my face. Permanent tears today.

'So I slap him, Brian. I slap him hard and loud and with the full force of my hand and Leah is crying and Petey is . . . he's just standing there with this look of disbelief and then I see Jack's eyes water and I'm glad . . .'

Brian holds his head with both his hands. 'Fuck it, stop.'

'He leaves the kitchen and Leah is crying softly and I go and hug her and tell her it's all right . . . and the song is over and I remember what it is. "Wichita Lineman", Glen Campbell.'

Brian is still holding his head, like he's trying to keep something in there.

'Nobody speaks the whole way to school. Jack sits in the back, looking out the window. There's a red mark on his cheek and I'm glad about that.'

Brian is crying.

'We don't say goodbye to each other. Jack and me. I kiss the other two and say goodbye to them . . .'

'Ah, Christ, stop it, please stop it . . .'

'And then I speak to Jack, no, it's not speaking, it's more spitting words at him, and I tell him don't come home without your iPod, don't bother coming home if you don't get it back . . .'

I stop and close my eyes and see Jack's eyes that morning and remember thinking they were so full of hate. But it was hurt. Simple childish hurt. I open my eyes.

'And there's this one moment as he's walking away from the car, when he turns around and looks at me and I think then that he's being defiant to the last but he isn't, he's just being fifteen.'

I laugh suddenly and Brian looks up at me, his eyes full of pain. 'Do you know what he does then? Guess what he does?'

'I don't know, Ali.'

'He takes out Leah's nano and puts the earphones on and off he goes into school. That's so Jack, isn't it?'

I sit up and start pulling on my clothes.

'And for the rest of that day I hear that song in my head – "I am a lineman for the county" – like it cheated its way into my brain that morning and just keeps playing over and over – you know – like a CD on repeat.'

I take a large gulp of wine and close my eyes. 'I knew the minute I picked up the phone that it was Jack – that something had happened to him, and nobody would tell me anything . . . and do you know something Brian? I deserved it. I deserved never to see him again.'

'No, you didn't. It was an accident, you didn't cause it.'

'Yes I did.'

'No, you didn't Ali, you're not God.'

'He was killed running after Sean Fahy. The boy that he'd loaned his iPod to.' I smile at Brian. 'You see I did cause it all.'

Twenty-One

Jane

We're locked in and Ben keeps asking when Mam is coming and why the doors are locked and why Daddy is hammering all the windows down and most of all what time is Mam coming and I know I can't tell him the truth. And I can't think of a plan either. Daddy won't answer me when I ask him what he's doing. He doesn't hear me, I know that now. And I have to keep everything OK for Ben. He's lying on the couch watching telly, so pale and frightened and babyish, and I want Mammy so badly that when I think of her face tears come and my chest hurts.

Daddy comes into the sitting room. He walks right past us and heads for the door, locking it behind him. Ben looks at me with huge scared eyes and I run into the kitchen looking for, I don't know what I'm looking for, a phone, a plan, something that'll help us.

And then I see Daddy through the nailed-down kitchen window, he's leaning into the boot of the car in the back alleyway, taking a big white container out of the boot. I have to do something but I can't think of what to do.

I try the window but it's nailed down tight and he glances up at me, like he knows what I'm doing even though I'm sure he can't hear me from out there. I go into the sitting room and try all the windows in there and Ben just stares at me, doesn't even ask now what's going on. It's the same in the bedrooms, all nailed down tight.

And then I have an idea. I look around for something small and rock hard, Jesus, there must be something in this whole flat that's small and hard and able to break glass . . . and then I hear the rattle of his keys and he's standing behind me in the room, I can feel him now, the mad thing going on inside him. I run to the bathroom and close the door and lean against it. He's right outside, I can feel him again.

'Come out, now,' he says, his voice low and steady and not Daddy's.

'I'm coming, I'm just going to the loo.'

I close my eyes and decide to do it again. It worked before but this is different, but it's all I can think of.

I go to the cupboard above the sink and take out a pack of his blades. A new pack with the wrapper still on. My heart is pounding in my chest as I slide a shiny blade out of its crisp white paper, like a chewing gum wrapper. I try to decide – arm or leg? Face? Arm. I roll up my sleeve just as he starts to bang on the door. I slice my arm as deeply as I can bear, not like I usually do because this time I need lots of blood. I feel the lovely rush of pain as the blood begins to run down my arm, covering the tracks of all the other cuts, all the small half-healed ones. My head spins but I don't feel helpless anymore, I feel strong. I open my eyes and there's blood on my new white Nike Airs. He bangs at the door and I go and open it.

'Daddy, look,' I say and lift my arm right up in front of him. The blood drips on to the lino and the pain is almost unbearable now.

He looks at my arm and then at me. He lifts his hand and looks at it for a second and then slaps me across the face, the sound so loud it's like an explosion. I fall against the door and then Ben is there in front of me, crying but with no sound so Daddy won't hear. Daddy walks away and I get a towel in the bathroom and wrap my arm in it and catch sight of my face in the mirror with his handprint on my cheek like someone painted it on.

'Is Daddy going to hurt us?' Ben asks.

Twenty-Two

Alison

I should have allowed Brian to bring him home. I should have done that at the very least.

I wake with a jump. Weak winter sun streams through the open blinds. I sit up and rub my eyes and then Brian is there in front of me. 'Breakfast,' he says, placing a cup of coffee in my hands.

'I'm sorry, Brian. I can't change it now but I should have left you do it.'

'Do what?'

'You wanted to bring him home. You wanted to bring him home for one last night. Stay up all night with him, have a chat, sleep in his own bed . . .'

'Oh Ali, don't go there . . .'

'He was gone for me as soon as he closed his eyes in the middle of the Ennis Road. And even in the morgue when the nurse pulled down the sheet and I looked at his white, dead face and you were sobbing in the corner, Brian, and the nurse was so still, tears on her face too, but Jack was gone. All that was left was the container he was in – do you know what I mean?'

Brian is sitting on the bed, his head in his hands. 'Look, Ali . . .'

'And I put out my hand and his face was ice cold. His lovely face, half-boy half-man, his eyes closed tight for ever and I kissed his dead mouth. Your mouth. But he was gone. I should have thought of you . . .'

'I stayed with him anyway, Ali.'

I look at Brian, tears running silently down his face. He's smiling.

'I stayed in the morgue with him, held his hand, joked with him. I stayed anyway. I stayed all night.'

'I'm glad.'

I pick up the warm cup of coffee. It smells incredible. I take a sip and we sit in silence for a few minutes.

'I deleted his Bebo page.' He looks at me, waiting for a reaction. 'I found it open again on the computer the other night and I deleted it. It was time. For everyone. It was time, Ali.'

I nod.

'It's not about forgetting him.'

'I know that.'

The silence resumes. He reaches out and strokes my hand.

'What time is it?'

'You slept until midday, Ali. Like a baby.'

He grins and he looks so like Jack. I put the cup on the bedside table and pull him towards me and we have the same urgent sex that we'd had the night before – intense and three minutes long.

'Jesus, that must be a record,' he says, as he rolls off me, his breath still ragged.

'We've a lot of catching up to do,' I say and kiss his arm.

'Tell me about it,' he says and kisses me long and hard.

Somebody coughs from the doorway. We both guiltily sit up. Peter is standing there, the little pup in one arm and the kitten in the other.

'Leah is crying,' he says, 'she got a prank call on her phone and now she's bawling.'

Twenty-Three

Jane

'We're going to have a great Christmas, just the three of us.' Daddy grins and winks at us. 'A great Christmas, one to remember,' he says, and then he laughs that mad, scary, high-pitched laugh. The gun is cocked in the band of his trousers and now he takes it out and strokes it like it's my kitten, Lucky.

'But we're having Christmas with Mammy, aren't we, Jane? Mammy is coming for us, isn't she, Jane, isn't she? Isn't she?'

I don't answer Ben because Daddy looks so crazy. I try to glare at Ben so he'll shut up but he's too scared.

'Please, Daddy, I want Mammy to come and take us home for Christmas and if we stay here Mammy'll be sad and and. . .'

'Shut up,' Daddy says, his voice so low and tight it's worse than screaming.

Ben starts to cry and Daddy stiffens, he looks like he's going to explode and I just want Ben to stop, I want it all to stop and my arm throbs like it's talking to me and I know now that Mammy isn't coming.

'Shut up shut up, shutupshutupshutupshutupSHUTUP-

SHUTUPSHUTUPSHUTUP,' Dad screams then and Ben runs behind my back.

'It's OK, Dad, Ben's just tired,' I say and smile at him, smile right into his mad stranger eyes. He closes them and rubs his temples. The smell of petrol is very strong and I know it's coming from the white container. It's out in the hallway now; I saw it earlier when Daddy went out there.

'I'll make some lunch,' I say and before he says anything I'm out in the kitchen looking for things to cook. Ben is behind me, still crying. I glance at the door to see where Daddy is and hear him in the bathroom, peeing.

'Stop crying, you baby, and just act normal, and don't say anything about Mammy, not a word,' I whisper but he keeps sniffling as I butter bread and cut slices of cheddar.

'I'm scared, Janey, and I want to go home.'

He buries his head in my chest and I rub his hair. 'It'll be fine, Ben, Daddy's not well, that's all. Mam'll be here soon and then we can go home.'

He looks up at me, big fat tears running down his face. 'It's like that time isn't it?' he whispers.

'Sssh, it'll be fine, you'll see.'

'It's like the time when he tried to hang himself with the rope and Mammy was screaming and then you cut your arm and the blood was everywhere and I didn't talk to anyone for a full week.'

Daddy's standing there in front of us then, so still and silent. He's looking at us like he's deciding what to do. The telly in the sitting room is singing 'White Christmas'.

Twenty-Four

Alison

I know the number instantly. The minute I see it on the screen of Leah's phone.

'Tell me again what you heard, Leah,' Brian says.

'Just a man's voice, really angry, saying "give it to me", and then the phone went dead and it was like really scary, that's all.' Her face is pinched and white and it makes her eyes look darker than usual.

'And why do you think it was Jane on the phone?' Brian says.

Leah shrugs her narrow little shoulders. 'Just stuff. The voice sounded like her dad and we met him in the market yesterday and she was like really freaked out and stuff and I just got a feeling, Mam, do you know what I mean?'

I smile. ''Course I do. Woman's intuition.'

She nods like she knows what it means.

I remember then the package that Jane's aunt had left in the day before and I have an idea. I find the present under the tree in the living room and bring it into the kitchen.

'Jane's aunt left this in for you yesterday and I forgot all about it. It's from Jane – here open it.'

Leah looks at the present in her hands like it'll bite her. 'I can't.'

'Why not?' I ask.

'Because I don't deserve it.'

'Why not?' I ask. Brian and Pete have gone off into the living room to watch televison. I can hear Bing Crosby singing 'White Christmas'.

'Because I've been a really bad friend, Mam.'

'I don't believe that.'

Her eyes spill over with tears and she looks like the little baby I remember breastfeeding, looking into those pools of eyes for hours on end.

'I was mean to her and she texted and asked if we were cool and I didn't write back and then yesterday she was so upset over her dad, he's like bonkers, Mam, I mean seriously bonkers, and I could have followed her and Dad said I should but I didn't and now . . .'

'Open the present, Leah, and then I have this great idea. We'll go and buy Jane something really nice and drop it off at her place – no – her dad's place – I think her aunt said they were staying there – what do you think?'

She smiles at me, a big Jack grin, and my heart does a flip at the double familiarity of it. 'I'd like that.'

She tears off the gorgeous silver wrapping and inside is a lovely nail kit.

'Oh my God, this is like the coolest thing, oh my God, we'll never find anything to get her that's half as good, oh my God!' She opens the coral-coloured kit and rummages through the myriad nail polishes and files.

'Look Mam, there's even a nail bath. This is so class.'

'It's lovely.'

She smiles at me. 'Can we go now?'

I nod. 'I think we should get dressed first though.'

'Funny, Mam, funny. I'll be quick – can we go to Luigi Malones after, just you and me?'

'I'd love that Leah.' And I realise as I'm saying it that it's true.

'And can Jane come too, if she's allowed?'

Twenty-Five

Jane and Alison

'What a fucking cocksucker of a wife I got.'

Daddy's saying this in a low, mean voice and he's pacing up and down the floor and I'm so scared that my hands are shaking. I know I have to calm him down but I don't know how.

'Let's go out and get fish and chips,' I say, trying not to sound scared. Ben is sitting on the couch, pretending to watch TV. He has the sound turned down really low.

Dad's leaning in the doorway, watching me. I smile at him. 'We always do that at Christmas – get a takeaway and then watch the Christmas movies and light a big fire and . . . you'd like that, Daddy, wouldn't you?'

The front doorbell rings suddenly and it's the loudest sound in the world. Daddy jumps and his face is scared, just like Ben's. He grabs me by my arm, the sore one, and I let out a cry.

'Shut up,' he says and pulls me into the living room, pushing me down on the couch next to Ben. The doorbell rings again and it sounds louder this time and I think that it's the best sound in the world.

He stands near the door to the hallway of the flat, pointing the gun at us. Ben starts crying and Daddy comes over and puts his hand over his mouth. Poor Ben looks terrified. He's pointing the gun at just me now.

The doorbell rings and rings and rings and then I can hear voices, low and urgent, and then a huge knock on the door and a voice, it's Mrs Collins.

'Jane? Dermot? Are you home? Anybody there?'

I look at Daddy, and his eyes dart around the room and then back at me. The gun shakes in his hand. I think about screaming but I'm too scared.

Then there's a loud rap on the window. The blinds are closed but I can hear their voices now. Mrs Collins and Leah, talking together, Leah saying there's nobody there and Mrs Collins saying that she saw Daddy's car in the alleyway behind and then a loud rapping again on the window and Daddy pushing the gun right into my hair. I shut my eyes waiting for the loud explosion but I don't hear that, instead I hear the telly, turned up full blast. I open my eyes and see that Ben has the remote in his hand. Ben thought of a plan.

'Fucking bastard,' says Daddy, trying to grab the remote from Ben and then Mrs Collins rapping on the window again saying open the door please, open the door or I'll go get somebody who can.

Daddy puts the gun inside the waistband of his jeans and goes to open the door. The telly is still blaring, it's a Shirley Temple film but I can't remember which one, and then Leah and Mrs Collins are in the living room and Daddy is pretending everything is grand except he sounds mad and Mrs Collins just looks at us and then Daddy locks the door and takes the gun out and Mrs Collins hasn't seen it yet but Leah has and Mrs Collins is sitting beside us now, stroking Ben's hair and feeling his forehead and asking me if I'm OK and Leah is standing near the door and there's tears in her eyes.

'Phones,' says Daddy. Leah gives him her phone and then Mrs Collins turns around and . . .

*

'Dermot, what in the name of God is going on?' He's standing next to Leah, pointing a gun at me. 'What in the name of God is going on?' Ben leans into me and Jane is crying.

'Give me your phone,' he says, standing in front of me now, and aiming the gun right at me.

'Dermot, look, calm down, we can talk about this on our own. Let's go get a coffee and the kids can watch a movie or something . . .'

'Give me your fucking phone,' he says.

I root in my bag and find the phone and hand it to him. He walks backwards out of the room, still pointing the gun at us.

I follow him into the tiny, dark kitchen and watch as he throws the phones into a basin of water.

'Dermot, please don't do this – the children are frightened . . .'

'Shut the fuck up and get back into the room with the others,' he says, his eyes wild in his head, darting all over the place.

I obey him. Leah and Jane are sitting on the couch holding hands, both of them crying and whispering to each other.

'Sit down,' he says and I obey again, sitting on a small, hard stool. He stands over us, waving the gun like it's a flag.

'I'm glad you came,' he says, 'because you told me what to do so I'm glad you're here to see me finally do the right thing.'

He smiles at me and winks and he pretends to aim the gun at his own head. I hold my breath.

'Jesus Christ, don't,' I shout. The children cover their eyes. He laughs like a madman.

'Only joking,' he says and cackles loudly again.

My stomach is churning and then I feel the thing in my chest start up and I know I must stop it and I gulp air into my lungs, dry, stale air that smells of petrol and somehow I manage to not faint.

'Let's talk about it,' I say. My voice is high-pitched.

'What would you like to discuss? How you helped me to come to a decision – how about that?' he says.

'Dermot, look, I don't know what you mean by that, but couldn't we . . .'

'So you dish out know-all advice and then can't even remember giving it? Fucking typical woman – a shower of fucking sluts is all you lot are . . .'

'Dermot, listen to me . . .'

He laughs, a screechy laugh that make the kids cover their eyes again.

'Listen to you? I fucking well did listen to you – *if you did love your children you'd fight for them* – so here we are now, I am fighting for them and I'll tell you something – no slut will ever get her hands on them again. Not as long as I'm alive – I fucking swear that.'

'Dermot, this isn't what I meant, not this . . .'

'What did you mean, so? Did you mean that I could see them every other weekend and live in this shithole and work to support two households and then die?'

'Please . . .'

'Ah, for fuck's sake, I'd rather die now – what's the fucking point of this?'

He punches the wall beside him, making his knuckles bleed but he doesn't even feel it. Then he holds the gun to his head again.

'OK, guys, on the count of three – one – two . . .'

*

'Daddy, don't, please don't,' I shout, jumping up and running towards him. He looks down at me, still holding the gun to his head, and his eyes fill up with tears and for a second it's Daddy in there, the old Daddy, and I bury my head in his chest but he doesn't smell like him, just petrol, and he puts a hand on my head and I think maybe it's OK and then he pushes me away from him and I go back to Leah. She holds my hand so tight.

'Stay here with me,' she whispers.

'I'm glad you're here even though it's scary. I'm so glad you came,' I say.

She squeezes my hand even tighter.

*

'You don't love them, not one bit,' I say, changing my tack. The softly softly approach didn't work.

He looks at me, tears in his eyes, blood dripping from his hand.

'If you loved them then you wouldn't hurt them like this.'

Tears spill down his cheeks, the chiselled cheeks that I once admired – that seems like so long ago now.

'You'd do whatever you feel you need to do, but you'd spare them. That'd be loving them – loving them properly like a parent should – protecting them, not placing them in danger.'

He closes his eyes tight, as if he's trying to shut out the words.

'You'd reassure, instead of scaring them. You'd put them first, their feelings, their needs, their world.'

'Shut up,' he says, his eyes still welded shut.

'You'd take the pain for them, if you could. You'd die for them.'

'Shut up, shut the fuck up.'

I glance over at the kids and Leah, my beautiful brave girl

275

smiles at me and I smile back and I want this to be over and I want to get back to being alive.

'You're right,' he says, looking straight at me. 'You're absolutely right as usual. I want you to do something for me.'

'Anything.'

'I want you to take this gun, and I want you to place it in the basin in the kitchen, and make it safe. Do you think you could do that?' He smiles at me, and it's the old Dermot, the one with the boyish face.

'No problem.' I put out my hand for the gun.

He hesitates for a second and then hands it to me. For such a small thing it feels heavy in my hand. I force myself to walk slowly towards the kitchen and through the door and over to the basin. As I place the gun beside the collection of mobile phones I hear scuffling and shouting in the living room and as I run Leah is screaming Mam, Mam, please, Mam, help them. I run into the living room and Leah's standing there, her face snow-white.

'He took them, Mom, and he's locked the door, it won't open, he's going to hurt them I just know he is . . .' Leah starts wailing and the panic thing starts in my chest again and I gulp down air.

'Fuck this, fuck it, fuck it,' I say out loud, trying to think straight.

I try the door into the hallway but it won't budge. I run back into the kitchen, Leah following me, crying hysterically now. I run towards the window. Fuck it, nailed down tight. I look around in desperation for something to break the glass and pick up a frying pan. I climb into the old ceramic sink and batter the glass with all my force. Tears and snot run down my face and I realise I'm screaming too, not words, just nonsense.

I look towards the alleyway through the kitchen window.

Nothing. Then I spot them coming around the corner. He's holding their arms really tight, pushing them into the car. There's a white container at his feet. Now he's locking them in and he's walking around towards the boot. I raise the pan above my head and smash and smash against the window until there's a satisfying crunch of glass. I grab a towel and push the remaining glass out and climb out to the alleyway. He's getting back into the car and there's an almighty smell of petrol and . . .

*

'Hold my hand, Ben, hold it tight,' I say as Daddy locks us into back seat of the car.

'What . . . what's . . . he . . . what's he doing, Janey?' Ben sobs.

I hold his head into my chest, and won't let him look. Daddy is pouring petrol over the car. Petrol from a big, white container and it swishes over the windows like when you're in a carwash and the foamy water comes on.

'It's smelly, Jane, what's he . . . what's he going to do to us . . . I want Mammy . . . I want my Mammy,' he sobs into my chest. I pull him in closer to me and whisper into his soft, matted hair. 'I'll take care of you, Ben. You just stay like that, close into me like that, and you'll be grand, I promise.' And then Daddy's climbing into the car and he turns back and looks at us and I say what Mrs Collins said. I say it straight at him and I don't look away at all.

'You don't love us. Mammy loves us but you don't give a fuck about us. I hate you and Ben hates you and you hate us.'

*

The noise is horrific. And the brightness of it. And the heat. The fucking heat. I can feel the heat and I'm still not halfway down the alley and I can't believe the bastard has done it.

'Fucking bastard,' I scream as the car is devoured in huge, billowing flames. 'Fucking bastard, fucker, fucker, fucker.'

I stand there beside the burning car, the heat scorching my face. My whole body is shaking as I try to get nearer but the heat drives me back. The air smells acrid, and black smoke billows from the burning car.

And then I hear it. A tiny, muffled cry. Where is it coming from? Leah is behind me now, crying and screaming at the same time and I want to comfort her but I can hear a tiny little sob and it's not Leah. It seems to be coming from the car. Not from the car, surely not the car. I snake around the car, pinning myself to the alley wall to avoid the flames and then I see them. Both of them sitting in the middle of the laneway. Jane has Ben in front of her, his head buried in her chest.

'Oh Jesus, how could he?' I whisper as I make my way towards them. Ben wriggles out of his sister's vice-like grip and runs into my arms. A crowd of people have started to gather and I can hear sirens in the distance. Jane is staring at the burning car – I can see the flames reflected and dancing in her eyes.

'Jane, honey . . .'

She keeps staring and even when I stand right in front of her, even when somebody takes Ben and I kneel down and put my face right in front of hers. Even then I can still see the flames dancing in her eyes. Like they're going to be there for ever.

Twenty-Six

Alison

'Tell us the exact itinerary or I'm not going.' I drop the cool box on to the kitchen floor and cross my arms in mock anger. Brian laughs and shakes his head.

'Nope. No way. It's a magical mystery tour, Ali.' He winks at Leah and Peter and puts his fingers to his lips. 'Not a word from you two or you'll both be sleeping on the side of the road, do you hear me?'

They look at each other and then at their father.

'Not a word,' says Leah.

'Dad, I've like a great idea, let's blindfold her, that'd be class. Let's blindfold her until we get to France.'

'Peter!' Brian and Leah shout together.

Peter puts his hand over his mouth. 'I'm sorry, Dad.'

Brian leans across the island where the three of them are seated and ruffles Pete's hair. 'It's all right, Pete. She'd have guessed anyway as soon as we hit Rosslare. Now go say goodbye to the animals before I take them over to Richard's.'

They jump down from their stools and head for the garden.

'God help the animals – staying in Richard's for a month,' I say as I pick up the cool box and put it on the worktop.

'God help Richard, more like – I didn't break the news to him yet that Ashton chews everything in sight and that Sandy follows him peeing on the chewed-up stuff for good measure.'

'Jesus, he'll put them in the pound when we're gone.'

Brian smiles and climbs down from the stool. 'No he won't – they'll be fine.' He puts his arms around my waist and kisses my neck as I fill the cool box with food from the fridge.

'How are you?' he asks, still nuzzling my neck.

I shrug. 'OK, I think.'

'OK about going?'

I turn to face him. I reach and trace the lines on his face, the new ones that I'm just getting used to. 'Just about.'

He nods, his head cocked to one side like a question. 'Just about will do fine.'

He kisses me lightly, barely touching my mouth, and walks out to the garden, whistling to himself.

A shiver passes through my body, even though it's a warm June day outside. A cold shiver deep inside me, like something bad trying to get out. My chest constricts slightly and I breathe my way out of it. One. Two. Three. One. Two. Three.

I go to the open French doors and watch them as they chase Ashton – now a half-grown pup and the ugliest dog in the world. And also the biggest.

Brian rugby tackles Peter to the ground, and Leah trips over them and then there's a huge tangle of dog and cat and children and man. My chest constricts again, seeking the wound, the empty place, the space left when something is amputated. I close my eyes. Open them. And then I say it out loud.

'Just about will do fine.'

Twenty-Seven

Ben

Mammy says Janey's getting better and I really want to believe her but it's so hard. But at least Jane doesn't hide in the wardrobe anymore. That was weird. She did it for weeks and sometimes I'd just climb in and cuddle up with her or Nana would spend hours trying to talk her out.

And it's very hard to get her to talk. I thought when she came back from the hospital that we could be friends and talk and stuff – she used to like talking – but sometimes she doesn't speak for like days and then the only sound in the house is Nana's radio and that does a lot of talking, trust me, and sometimes Nana talks back to it. She fights with the people talking on it like they can hear her.

Except for the radio I like Nana living with us now. She cooks these great dinners and she even makes desserts but she doesn't call them desserts, she calls them sweets and I think that's a really funny thing to call them. Sweets. Every time she says it I think there's going to be a big plate of pick 'n' mix on the table for me but instead there's apple tart and custard or cake with swirly colours or jelly and ice cream.

I love football. It's way better than karate and I wish I'd discovered it ages ago and I'm really good at it although I'd never say that to any of the lads on my team. Peter Collins is the captain and he says I'm the best centre forward in Limerick, but when he says it I just say no, I'm not, you fool and I laugh but I'm dead delighted that he thinks I am. He's so sound, Pete is. I love going to stay in his house and it's grand cos his mom knows what happened, she knows all of it so I don't have to pretend anything or watch what I'm saying. And there's no whispering behind my back.

Like my first day in school after it happened. It was better when some of the boys just asked out straight what happened instead of the whispering or the pretending that it never happened at all even though it was on Sky News. I can't help being chuffed about that and I know I shouldn't but the doctor guy that talked to me said I could feel and say anything I wanted and that I was to write it all down.

At the start I wrote everything down. It was like talking to Jane but talking to an eighty-eight-page copybook instead. I could say all the stuff then. I wrote twenty-eight-and-a-half pages on the smell. Petrol and the sweet smell of something burning and the smell of Jane, forcing my head into her chest. See, I can still write it down and I don't cry or nothing. Copybooks are great and now I only write in it once a week or when something happens that I don't like. This week it's Pete leaving for a month. Imagine that – a whole month. He might forget about me when he comes back. A month is like for ever.

Mammy says we'll go on a holiday too. Spain if Jane is well enough, otherwise Kilkee. Peter asked me to go with them and part of me wanted to but I was glad when Mammy said no, that it was way too long and that she never lets us go anywhere without her anymore.

Jane cries at night and it scares me. She cries and walks around and cries some more and she doesn't know who I am. She saw the doctors too and for way longer than me but she's finding it harder to get better. Maybe it's because she's a girl. But there's one doctor, Doctor Bob, and she likes him the best and she'll talk to him and Mammy says he's the best and that Jane's really getting better now.

But I can't see it. I mean she said thanks yesterday and Mammy and Nana looked at each other like she'd recited the whole of *Harry Potter and the Philosopher's Stone*. I try to talk to her but she does this really freaky staring thing with her eyes, I mean really freaky, so yesterday I said to her about the copybook. She stared at me. So I bought her one – a big fat one-hundred-and-twenty-page one and three biros too and I gave them to her and told her write it all down. Anything at all that comes into your head. Even the stuff that doesn't make sense, horrible black stuff that you can't say out loud. All of it. She just stared at the copybook like it was something from another planet.

Anyway I'm going to Samba Soccer Camp and next season I'm going to be brilliant. There's a Brazilian coach who once made the reserves for Brazil – that's like making the first team for anyone else – and he knows Ronaldinho – so I'm going to get all his secrets from him. Class.

The other thing that's great is reading. I read everything, even the newspaper when I don't have a book. I can read anything at all and in my Drumcondras I got the highest in the whole school even though I'm only nine. That's why I'm so good at writing. And I had another great idea about writing in the copies. When I'm a famous footballer then they'll be worth like millions upon millions and Mammy won't have to work anymore and Jane might get better. We could bring her to Los Angeles. That's where all the top doctors live. And we'd have to bring Doctor Bob too – just in case the others aren't as good as him at talking to her.

I really want Jane to be better. But I want it tomorrow because we're getting a dog – a pup called Stevie. I got to name him – I asked Jane what she thought but she didn't say anything. Anyway he's called Stevie after Steven Gerrard, the Liverpool captain. He's my favourite player after Ronaldinho but I couldn't call the pup Ronaldinho – it's too hard to call a dog – like this – Here Ronaldinho, come here Ronaldinho – it takes like way too long so Stevie's better. I can't wait for tomorrow and I know Jane'll love it and the doctor said it'd be good for her. But I still wish she was better and we could have great fun together with the pup and bring him for walks in the park and wash him and play fetch with him.

Peter has a dog with a really bad name. Ashton after Ashton Kutcher. Pete and me know it's a really gay name for a dog but he's lovely. He's all huge and floppy and he makes Jane smile. Sometimes we bring her to the Collins' house and she sits in the garden and Leah holds her hand and Ashton goes bonkers around the place. Mrs Collins says he really is Ashton cos he loves an audience. But Ashton can make Jane smile. And sometimes when he's really loony she nearly laughs.

I've got to go now. I'm going to make a space in the garden for the dog kennel – Mam's bringing it home from work. And then I'm going to practise taking penalties – I'm really good at penalties but Peter says you have to keep practising so you're sharp as a razor.

One last thing. There's black stuff in my head today to do with Daddy. Not the fire – I didn't see any of it because Jane held me so tight against her I could barely even breathe – I just smelt it. And it's not even all the stuff with the gun that happened before it. It's not that all. It's that I really, really miss him. I miss my daddy.

BOOK CLUB NOTES

1. *The Cut of Love* deals with a number of themes including family breakdown, self-harm and the death of a child. The story is told from two viewpoints – one a 12-year-old girl's and the other a middle-aged woman's. Does this work?

2. Alison is intolerant and dismissive of Brian's therapy sessions in trying to come to terms with his grief (p135). Has she come to terms with hers? Compare the way each parent has dealt with their grief.

3. Why does Alison begin the ill-fated affair with Dermot Harris?

4. In the early stages of the novel Dermot Harris appears to be a harassed separated father determined to remain central to his children's lives despite the changed circumstances. At the close of the novel he is psychotic. What pushes him over the edge?

5. Does Dermot deserve any sympathy/empathy?

6. One of the themes in the book is how adults take responsibility for their actions. How does this unfold in the book? Is it fair to say that at times Jane comes across as more adult in her behaviour than her mother Evelyn? How is this expressed in their actions?

7. How does Jane's self-harm escalate through the course of

the story? What are the inciting incidents that make her self-harm?

8. Is Jane's self-harm a believable reaction to her situation?

9. Jane's mother Evelyn is blind to Dermot's spiraling psychosis. Why?

10. A theme throughout the novel is grief. How does each character deal with their grief?

11. Alison neglects her living children in favour of the ghost of her dead son. She begins an affair with Dermot regardless of how this might affect her relationship with her husband. She interferes in Frankie's life while ignoring the plight of her own children. Is it fair to say that her behaviour is selfish or are there other motives at work?

12. Is Ben's voice a fitting one to close the story?

13. Marital breakdown, while extremely common, is not often explored from the child's perspective. Does Jane give a believable insight into how it feels for a child caught in the crossfire?

14. If you could meet any character from this book and ask him or her one question, which would it be and what would you ask? Why?

Acknowledgments

The scary thing about acknowledgements is that you're almost certain to forget somebody. But here goes anyway. A big shout out for Mary Coll – my first reader and invaluable advisor. Also Rena, Ellie and Kay for always making the time to read my work and listen to me moaning (not simultaneously). Dee, my indispensable rugby pal, and Donna, Maire, Breda, Angela, and the Liscannor crew. PJ O'Donnell and Helen for the writing venue off season. Monica and Trisha, two more stalwarts in my life. John Ryan, the third stalwart, and cuz Helen. Munsterfans.com for the entertaining breaks from writing. Munster for that All Blacks match I was honoured to be present at. A huge thank you to my editor and publisher Ciara Considine, and all at Hachette Ireland. It's great to be back! And finally my agent Faith O'Grady, who has always believed in my writing. Even when I didn't.